VIRAL

ANDREW PEACOCK

VIRAL

ANDREW PEACOCK

Published in Canada by Engen Books, St. John's, NL.

Library and Archives Canada Cataloguing in Publication

Title: Viral / Andrew Peacock.
Names: Peacock, Andrew (Veterinarian), author.
Identifiers: Canadiana (print) 20200284851 | Canadiana (ebook) 20200284878 | ISBN 9781989473603
  (softcover) | ISBN 9781989473610 (PDF)
Classification: LCC PS8631.E215 V57 2020 | DDC C813/.6—dc23

Copyright © 2020 Andrew Peacock

NO PART OF THIS BOOK MAY BE REPRODUCED OR TRANSMITTED IN ANY FORM OR BY ANY MEANS, ELECTRONIC OR MECHANICAL, INCLUDING PHOTOCOPYING AND RECORDING, OR BY ANY INFORMATION STORAGE OR RETRIEVAL SYSTEM WITHOUT WRITTEN PERMISSION FROM THE AUTHOR, EXCEPT FOR BRIEF PASSAGES QUOTED IN A REVIEW.

This book is a work of fiction. Names, characters, places and incidents are products of the author's imagination or are used fictitiously. Any resemblance to actual events or locales or persons living or dead is entirely coincidental.

Distributed by:
Engen Books
www.engenbooks.com
submissions@engenbooks.com

First mass market paperback printing: August 2020

Cover Image: Kaleigh Middelkoop

Advance praise for
VIRAL

"An unnerving portrayal of a collapsing society.
There is no staying safe in Andrew Peacock's Viral."
Glenn Deir,
CBC host and the author of
The Money Shot and *Sick Joke*

"This novel presents a vivid and timely prophecy of a pandemic worse even than Covid -19. The novel explores the fragility of our society in an intensive, fearsome way and yet leaves us deeply relieved that our current pandemic is not so bad after all. This book is a must-read; painful in its forceful depiction of society, yet somehow leaving us feeling better because it depicts a scenario even worse than that which we are facing in 2020."
Dr. William Pryse-Phillips,
W.E.M., M.D., MRCP, FRCPC, FRCP,
Professor of Medicine and Neurology

"Few people can pull together the elements required to create a gripping, terrifying, realistic pandemic. Peacock's novel Viral is as contagious as the outbreak in his story."
Paul Carberry,
bestselling author of
Zombies on the Rock: Outbreak

For Casper,
a ray of light and joy in pandemic times

"By hook or by crook this peril too shall be something that we remember."

— Homer, The Odyssey

CHAPTER 1
WELCOME TO THE MONKEY HOUSE

Where he came from it never got as hot as this. Sweat plastered John's shirt to his torso, but he dismissed the discomfort and prepared himself for action.

The young statistician in a tight white T-shirt and shorts leaned back and served. It took every bit of his concentration to watch the ball rather than the fascinating curve of her hips.

The serve wasn't hard and it was easy for him to set the ball up cleanly for the geologist next to him. She jumped and spiked the ball back over the net, but not with enough force to give the other team any trouble. Their return moved the play deep into John's end, and the thickset man, who did some mysterious work on measurement standards, popped the ball up high and so far sideways that it was beyond the boundaries of the court. John made a wild dash, dove into the grass and managed to put the ball back in play. The girl he had just set up lobbed it over the net, high and slow enough that a muscular guy on the other team smashed it down into an empty space for the final game point.

John didn't worry much about losing. This was just

a healthy and friendly way to spend his lunch hour. He was far more concerned with impressing girls than scoring with the ball.

He looked at his watch and seeing it was a quarter to one waved goodbye to the other players and headed off for the research building. Because he worked in a biosecure facility, he was required to shower every time he came in or out. The advantage was that he was able to comfortably engage in sweaty sports half-way through the day, but it meant his lunch hours were shortened to allow for his time under the nozzles.

John had moved from his home on the island of Newfoundland eight years earlier and was now studying veterinary medicine at the University of Guelph. He was thrilled to have a summer job at the Tunney's Pasture animal research building in Ottawa. During his time with an experienced veterinarian, he was expected to develop an understanding of--and perhaps even love for--lab animal medicine. Although John had no intention of ever permanently being involved in this kind of work, it was an enjoyable way to spend a summer.

The animal research building screamed of sterility. The two heavy metal doors to the outside had small windows lined with strands of metal. Inside, there were no posters or notices on the walls and the floors were spotless.

He took the elevator to the second floor and came out to a small hallway with doors to men's and women's showers. He'd been through the procedure so many times that there was no thought involved in undressing and stepping under the cold water. These showers were refreshing, but he could feel that his skin was suffering from the constant washing.

He dried off and pulled on the clean underwear, socks and OR suit that were neatly folded in his locker. John finished dressing by putting on running shoes that had never been worn outside of the building.

It was just a short walk from the showers to his workspace. He didn't have his own office but shared quarters with Olga and Beth.

Olga was an older, heavyset woman who was the senior lab technician in the building. She had done her training in Germany and continually went on about the lax standards of Canadian biosecurity compared with what she had experienced in the institutes at home.

On his first day on the job, Olga had complained that John's hair was too long for someone who intended to work in a secure facility. Olga's own hairstyle was a serious affair that looked more suited to a young boy.

As he walked in, she looked up from a folded sheet of paper that she held in her hands.

"Hello, John. I'm so glad you decided to join us for the afternoon. I have been spending my lunch hour going over the libretto for a marvelous piece of opera that I will be attending this Saturday. Do you like Wagner?"

She pronounced the composer's name as he would have said it himself and pushed out the first syllable harshly.

"Don't know much about Wagner, Olga. The most I could tell you is that some of the stuff he wrote involves big women with Viking hats and a lot of it can be pretty long."

"You Canadians have no appreciation for high culture.

Wagner is perhaps the greatest composer that this world has known. It's a shame today's youth don't have the attention span to understand challenging works."

John knew that his comment about Viking hats had been as far as he could tease Olga and he wisely changed the subject.

"So, you must be looking forward to your two weeks in Europe."

"It will indeed be a relief. I intend to take in enough opera and lieder to spare me through another few months working here. I hope you two will keep everything clean and proper. Can I can trust you to water my plants while I'm away?"

For all of Olga's insistence on strict biosecurity measures, John couldn't understand how she managed to have two plants in pots full of regular dirty dirt in her office. Their quarters were classed as level three biosecure and he was sure that plants and soil from the outside didn't meet those standards.

Beth turned from her microscope and reassured Olga that her plants would be taken care of.

There were a lot of things about Beth that John hadn't figured out. From his conversations with her, it seemed that she had nothing beyond high school education. He never heard exactly what her job description was, but she was skilled in microscopy and understood all of the blood analyzing machines they worked with.

The one thing he was certain of was that Beth was a stunner. She had a winning smile, a spectacular figure and thick blonde hair that curled down below her shoulders. Although she couldn't have been more than a year or two older than him, she treated John like a little boy.

In the months he'd been working there, he had learned nothing about Beth's interests or home life. Despite his invitations, she never came outside for their noon break. She never read or listened to music, and, as far as he could tell, all she did for the hour off was to eat her delicate lunches.

The afternoon promised to be interesting. Earlier that morning, Dr. Jamieson had told them that they would be collecting blood samples from all of the green monkeys in room 347.

John had a love/hate relationship with the monkey work. He found the animals endlessly fascinating, but he had some trouble seeing that keeping these intelligent beings caged up was worth the scientific knowledge that came from the research done on them.

When John had free time, he would go into the monkey rooms and just look at the animals. It amazed him how the monkeys seemed just as interested in him as he was in them. At the beginning of the summer, it was obvious that they recognized him as a stranger and cowered in the backs of their cages when he came into their rooms. As time went on, they became bolder and would eventually come up to the bars of their enclosures to stare at him.

It amused him to watch the monkeys for a while. Sometimes, he'd open the door as if he was leaving and then sneak around the side of a cage where they couldn't see him. When he would step back into the centre of the room, the monkeys would let out a collective "oh" that seemed to express surprise and perhaps some amusement. John always believed that this game gave the monkeys some respite from their boring existences.

Because there were three new greens in 347 that had just come out of quarantine, Dr. Jamieson wanted blood work done on all the animals in the room. The newcomers had tested negative for every disease they had been checked for, but the vet was always cautious and worried about false negative results.

Fifteen years earlier, one of the vets who had worked in the facility died from a monkey bite. Although the biting animal had been seronegative for every test that had been done, an autopsy of the victim showed he had died of simian Herpes B disease.

John and Beth filled a cart with all the equipment they would need for blood collection and took the elevator to the third floor. Derrick was patiently waiting for them in room 347. He was the all-round assistant in the facility. He hadn't even finished high school, but he was the best pig wrangler, chicken holder, and monkey catcher John had ever come across.

The monkeys realized that something was up when three people came into their room. The fact that one of them was carrying a clipboard was an indication that they would be caught and taken out of their homes. The cages were a poor replacement for the trees back home in Senegal, but they did offer a degree of security.

Every time the humans pulled them from the cages, something unpleasant happened.

Everyone had their roles in processing the monkeys. Derrick would catch, John would draw blood samples and Beth would keep records. Jamieson was at another of his endless string of meetings on biosecurity standards.

Derrick swatted John across the shoulder with his heavy leather welding gloves.

"Why don't you try grabbing a couple of these fellas? You've watched me do this enough times that you shouldn't have any trouble."

Since he started his summer job, John had hoped he would some day get the chance to actually handle a monkey. Derrick's suggestion excited him and scared him at the same time. He wondered if he really had the nerve to reach into the cages.

It seemed that he watched himself from above as he put on the gloves and moved to the nearest cage bank. The first monkey was a small female. She was well under a half-metre in height and likely weighed less than four kilograms.

As he stood in front of the cage, the female let out a high-pitched squeak and moved up to the bars to stare. She was a beautiful animal with a long grey face ringed with golden fur. John had come to appreciate the different facial expressions that the monkeys were capable of. This one had a puzzled look that suggested she was wondering what John was planning to do and why he seemed so nervous.

Derrick said, "Let's get on with it", and undid the complex closure mechanism on the front of the cage. He positioned himself directly in front of the opening as he pulled the door back.

"You gotta stand right here or the little buggers'll jump right out past you."

As soon as the door started moving, the little monkey turned and squeezed into the back left corner of the cage.

This timid animal had no intention of making a break for the freedom of the rest of the room.

Derrick moved to allow access to the opening and John reached inside. The monkey didn't move as he gently wrapped his gloved fingers around her upper forearms. He pulled her out into the room and felt pressure around his own biceps. Looking down, he could see that the monkey had reached up with its feet and now it was a question of who was holding whom.

"Nice work, you're a natural monkey catcher. Now you have to hand her over to me because there's no way I'm taking the samples from this animal. I don't mind being around monkeys, but the sight of blood makes me faint."

"But, Derrick, I've got on the only set of gloves we have. Maybe I should just put her back in the cage."

"Nah, you've done all the hard work. I can hold onto her without gloves while you get the samples you need. Here, just move your hands down towards her wrists a little."

No one in the room was really sure who's fault it was, but somehow in the transfer from John to Derrick, the little female green monkey got free. The stainless-steel cage banks didn't quite reach the ceiling and with a quick leap, the animal was cowering on top of her enclosure.

The rest of the monkeys in the room went wild with excitement; the hooting and screaming was deafening. The noise panicked the escaped animal, and she started moving along the tops of the cages. The banks lined all of the walls of the room with gaps where the two doors were situated.

The space above the cages was enough for the monkey to build up some speed and she started a clockwise course around the room. At the gap by each door she would leap from the cage and grab onto the door closer to swing over to the top of the next bank of cages. John and Beth cowered back to back in the centre of the room. They both knew how fast these animals were, and how potentially deadly they could be if they ever bit someone.

Derrick put his hands on his hips and slowly spun around following the monkey's orbit.

"Shit. The boss is going to be upset when he finds out about this. Maybe it would be best if he doesn't hear anything. What do you think?"

Beth and John were so tight against each other's backs that it seemed they might end up permanently joined. It never occurred to John that there was any pleasantness to being so close together. Both of them silently nodded.

"Well, I guess I'm going to have to fix this."

John and Beth were horrified to see Derrick leave the room just as the monkey was at the farthest point from his door. Their first reaction was that he had abandoned them to the dangers of the hurtling primate. They remained frozen in place for what seemed like an hour before Derrick came back in carrying a broom.

"Alright ya little bugger, let's see what you think of this."

Derrick placed the broom over his shoulder and standing in front of the door, faced the direction of the monkey's travel. When the animal leapt into the door space Derrick swung for the bleachers. His timing was a little off and he only brushed the golden end of the monkey's tail.

The second time around, Derrick's technique had improved greatly. His timing and placement resulted in the broom catching the monkey square in the middle of her abdomen just as she reached out for the door closer.

The animal tumbled backwards and slammed heavily into the side of the cage she had just jumped from. There was a loud hollow crack from her head hitting solid metal. The other monkeys in the room let out a collective cry of horror and went silent.

"Oh shit, I think I've killed her. This is going to be big trouble. How about if we just stick her back in the cage and say we found her like this when we came into the room?"

John knew that there would be a careful postmortem done on any animal that died in the facility and that head trauma would be obvious to any trained observer.

He didn't answer but remained riveted to his spot in the centre of the room.

Beth moved over beside Derrick and the two of them knelt down over the prostrate animal.

"The poor little girl. She was just scared. You shouldn't have hit her so hard with the broom."

As she spoke, the monkey let out a little moan and circled it's head like someone in a martial arts movie getting ready for a big fight. Beth and Derrick moved in closer.

It was obvious to John that the monkey was recovering, and he was just about to warn his colleagues to get away when the animal's eyes sprang open. The humans in the room all panicked. John froze, and Beth and Derrick both opened their mouths and gasped. At the same moment, the monkey sneezed.

Derrick regained enough composure to turn his captive over and take hold of her arms. The monkey was dazed but apparently not seriously hurt. John threaded a double-edged needle onto a blood collection sleeve and picked a purple and red-topped tube from the cart. He'd had enough excitement with this monkey and wanted her finished with and back in her cage.

The rest of the captures and blood collections went without incident. Even with the excitement of the escape, John didn't miss one vein.

As John and Beth packed the last tubes into cardboard containers on the cart and checked the numbers on the samples against the form in the clipboard, Derrick stood behind them.

"So, do you think there is any need to tell anyone about our little adventure this afternoon? I don't think any of us will look too good if this gets out."

John looked in on the little female and decided that she was back to normal. She hissed when he came close to the cage, but he reasoned that this was an appropriate response to humans who had just assaulted her with a broom.

John and Beth agreed that there had been no harm done and it was better for everyone involved if nothing was said.

Back in the office, John and Beth spun down the samples in the red tubes to separate out the serum for virology testing and ran the blood from the purple tubes through the blood-analyzing machine. The only unusual finding in any of the results was that the three new monkeys had high lymphocyte counts.

Once they finished all of their blood work, it was time for another shower and a weekend off.

Monday morning, the sun was shining when John came in for work. He went through the showers thinking that the weekend hadn't been long enough. As the summer wore on, he found that one of his joys on holidays was the escape from constant washing. It was always possible to get too much of a good thing.

Although John was five minutes early for work, Olga was there before him. He had never been the first one in and he wondered what time she actually arrived in the mornings.

Despite her promptness at arrival, Olga never did any work until the clock indicated it was exactly 8:30. She was a dutiful worker, but would never give her employer a second of time they didn't pay her for. She waved her libretto at John.

"Wagner tonight and then off to the old country on Wednesday."

One thing John appreciated about his job was that there was no such thing as a routine day in the office. Every morning Dr. Jamieson would outline his activities and if the vet wasn't in, there would be a project already lined up for him. His work varied from interesting things like catching the monkeys to a dull day helping Derrick clean up after the miniature pigs.

Beth came in at 8:45 apologizing for her tardiness. She had been sick all weekend and had only decided at the last minute that she was well enough for work. The dull cast to her skin and darkness under her eyes suggested that she hadn't slept well.

John was concerned right away about Beth's deep rattling cough. She hacked continuously from far down inside her lungs.

Just before nine o'clock, Dr. Jamieson came in from his office down the hall and asked if Beth could help sort some files for a presentation he was preparing. John's task for the day was to help Derrick with some repairs on the fourth floor.

This part of the building was one level higher biosecurity than the rest and as a result, there would be at least another two showers that day. When anyone went to the fourth floor, they had to completely change clothing and shower in and out. Because of the high security level, outside workers weren't brought in for minor structural repairs.

John took the elevator up two floors and met Derrick in the showers. It was obvious right away that Derrick had the same cold that Beth was suffering from. John tried to keep a healthy distance away, but as they worked together on the sticking door, it was necessary to be in close proximity.

The repairs took the full morning and John sighed as he realized he would need two complete showers to get outside for lunch. He decided that he would forego the pleasures of the outdoors for one day and read up on the research project that was a requirement of his summer employment.

John showered out of the fourth floor and took the elevator down to the library. He picked out two articles on the 1989 Reston virus outbreak in crab-eating macaques in Virginia. This particular strain of the Ebola virus had proven non-pathogenic in humans but showed how easy it was for dangerous viruses to make their way to North America.

John's project was to review the history of Ebola and discuss possible means of transmission of the virus. Everything he read suggested Ebola was only passed through direct contact of infected individuals, but John wondered if it was possible for the disease to disperse through the air in aerosol droplets. Some of the cases he read about seemed to spread too quickly to be explained by direct contact.

John always brought his lunch in to the office in case rain kept him from getting outside. Today he would eat at his desk with references propped up in front of him. In the office, Olga was starting into a delicious looking thick sandwich that was made from bread that didn't come from an ordinary grocery store.

As he sat down, Olga told him that she had sent Beth home after she had come back from the vet's office.

"The silly girl was coughing all over me. I can't be sick before I return to Germany."

John loved the way that Olga pronounced "Chermany" and the emphasis that she always put on the word.

After lunch, Dr. Jamieson was free, and John and Derrick spent the rest of the day helping him attend to the green monkeys' teeth. The process involved the injection of a mild sedative into each animal, a thorough dental exam, and then cleaning with ultrasound equipment.

Because of the water droplets that were splashed up by the machine, all three of them wore surgical face masks and safety glasses during the procedure.

The next day neither Beth nor Derrick came in and both Olga and Dr. Jamieson had mild coughs. John asked if anyone knew how their missing co-workers were doing, but they hadn't been in contact with anyone at work.

Olga complained all morning about her cough and said she was going home soon to look after herself so she wouldn't miss her flight to Germany. Jamieson was in a foul mood and at noon told Olga she should go home.

Wednesday morning, Dr. Jamieson was obviously sicker, and Beth and Derrick were still missing. When the vet told John to spend the day working on his research paper, he was disappointed that he wouldn't get to go home early.

On Thursday, John showed up to an empty office. He was clean and ready to go, but had no direction for his day's work. He started with a quick tour of all of the animal rooms. If no one else was working, he wanted to make sure that all of the animals had been properly fed by the night staff.

Every animal he looked at was in good condition and there was ample water and food in every room. The only concern he had was that a number of the green monkeys in room 347 were coughing. None of them looked sick, but when he stopped and listened, there were quiet snicks all around the room.

John whistled and listened to the lonely echo as he walked in from the monkey room back to his office. When he opened the door, he was startled to find three figures in complete hazmat suits.

The apparent leader walked up to John and ordered him to sit at his desk. Through his face mask, John could make out that he was middle-aged and had a white moustache. It wasn't obvious even what sex the other two were.

While the man asked John if he had experienced any coughing or headaches, a second figure opened a plastic case filled with blood tubes and reached out for John's arm. He was too stunned to complain about the blood samples taken or the collection of throat swabs that followed.

When John finally regained enough composure to ask what was going on, the leader told him that he had received reports of a possible disease situation and that anyone working in the building might be at risk of infection.

The man was unwilling to give more information until John insisted that he might be able to provide some useful background if he had some idea of what was going on. The man reluctantly admitted that Derrick had died the previous night and that they had not been able to contact Beth or Olga. He finished with a strict insistence that none of this was to be told to anyone.

John understood the importance of a clear history and he carefully outlined the incident with the green monkey in room 347. It was fast becoming apparent to him that the little female's sneeze could be an important part of the story.

He also told them blood samples had been collected the same day and that there was serum in the fridge from the three new monkeys. John was ordered to give his contact information and to leave the building immediately. If he had any sign of coughing or sickness, he was to contact the number on the card that the man with the white moustache provided. Until he heard otherwise, he was to stay in the city and minimize his contact with other people.

CHAPTER 2
HERE COMES THE FLOOD

Mike Scarlett was never near the top of his class in medical school. He was bright, but he could never convince himself to study harder just to get high marks. During his school years, he chose summer jobs more for their promise of outdoor activity than any experience they offered in the everyday world of medicine. Even before his training began, he knew he would never be content to spend his life behind a desk in an office.

At the end of his first year, Mike entered the army's officer training program. He didn't care much about the financial incentives but was drawn by the promise of a life of adventure.

Upon graduating , he joined the Canadian Armed Forces Search And Rescue team and spent considerable time training in advanced skydiving and rock climbing. By the time he was five years out of medical school he had been involved in some of the most hair-raising rescues in the country.

Fifteen years into his career, a jump onto a rocky ledge surrounded by fire had fractured his leg badly and put him behind a desk for six months. He was forty years old when he returned to the SAR team and found his enthusiasm for physical heroics had gone.

Mike's reading while recovering got him interested in the field of foreign diseases and their pandemic potential. When he got back in the field, the younger members of his team started sheltering him from the more demanding and dangerous details of their work. Within three months, he decided that his SAR days were over.

He headed back for school and spent three years on a master's degree in foreign disease control. After graduation, he started working for the federal government's emergency response team.

From his studies, Mike understood that the world was overdue for a major disease outbreak. He believed that the planet had gotten off easy from the 1918 influenza pandemic--and that affair had killed more people than the First World War. He also felt that the next big disaster would come from domestic animals. Every time he was called out to look at large die-offs on chicken farms, he wondered if he was witnessing the start of the big one.

Although Mike's office was in Ottawa, much of his work involved flights to the far reaches of the country. Occasionally he was seconded to disease outbreaks around the world. Nothing he had worked on had spread to even hemispheric proportions, but he felt it was only a matter of time.

When Mike was called to a government lab facility in Ottawa, he was a little relieved that he would be able to come home to his apartment every night. The unsettled nature of his job and his own inability to sit still had resulted in him never marrying. He had a couple of girlfriends when he first started with the army, but they soon moved on when they realized how little he stayed in one place. He was a wealthy man at fifty because of his well-paying job and his lack of interest in material possessions.

The call to the animal facility was in response to the death of a thirty-two-year old male who had been working in the building. The patient had been brought into the hospital by his girlfriend after he had started bringing up blood. He had vomited once more in the packed waiting room and then thrown up again while he was being processed. The examining doctor reported that both times the vomitus was mostly frank blood.

Mike was disturbed that it had taken until the man's death the next morning for the hospital to report the incident. Surely those fools should have had alarm bells go off when a patient who worked with primates presented with such ominous signs.

Other than three incidents of bloody vomiting, the patient showed no signs beyond a mild headache and a cough. When the hospital staff put him to bed for the night, the man seemed convinced that the worst of his ordeal was over. A nurse found him dead during her six am rounds.

The phone call to Emergency Measures didn't come in until eight am. The hospital official who called explained that she didn't think anyone would be in until that time.

The call came into Mike's desk just as he settled in for a day of reviewing his report on the avian influenza outbreak he'd seen the week before in British Columbia.

He was taking no chances with this one. He first called the hospital with an order to close down the emergency ward and stop all visitations. His characterization of his suggestion as an order was a bit of a bluff. He knew that to get an actual order, someone far above his level would have to be involved. Mike felt deeply that this case needed immediate action and he would deal with any bureaucratic problems later.

He assembled a team to head off for the hospital. Mike wanted blood samples from the dead man on the first flight to the National Microbiology Laboratory in Winnipeg for Polymerase Chain Reaction testing. Ebola was high on his list of suspects, and, if he could get samples quickly to Winnipeg, there should be results within a couple of days. As well, he needed someone on the ground at the hospital to control who entered or left the building.

He would lead the team checking out the lab animal facility. This was where he felt the key to the problem would be. Mike found information on the building with a quick internet search and saw that the entire place was level three or four biosecure. His first task was to find a way to get inside the facility. Three phone calls got him in touch with the office of the assistant deputy minister of Health. The secretary who answered the phone understood the gravity of the situation and promised to have the building's concierge have the place open for a visit.

He and two technicians assembled sampling equipment and full sets of protective gear and set off for the lab animal building. They put on their suits in the van once they reached the parking lot. The concierge seemed unfazed by the three surreal looking visitors encased in white plastic.

It was ten am by this time and Mike realized that most

of the staff would already be inside. He told the man at the door to make sure that no one else entered until he gave instructions. Mike was always amazed at how readily people followed orders from someone in a full hazmat suit.

They walked through the shower room and by the signs painted on the wall that ordered everyone who passed to wash carefully. In the hall on the other side there was no sign of life. The first person they saw was a young man – Mike assumed he was a student – coming out of one of the animal holding rooms.

The kid was co-operative, but Mike sensed that he was holding something back.

He wasn't keen on telling the student about the death of his co-worker, but ultimately decided that this information would reinforce how serious the situation was and help guarantee that he got all of the history he needed.

His worst fears were realized when he heard that three days earlier a monkey had sneezed in the dead man's face. Even more worrisome was the fact that two other workers in the facility hadn't come in to work because of symptoms similar to the victim's.

The student didn't object when the technicians took a blood sample and then he helpfully provided information about the monkey at the centre of the story. The kid knew how the facility's database worked and they soon had full records of the animals in the room where the suspected contact had occurred.

Green monkeys had been housed there for over six years, but three of them had come in from Senegal within a month.

Although he didn't know much about the health of monkeys, Mike decided to take a look at the animals and see if he could recognize any problems. If the green monkey was the source of the outbreak – and he felt confident that calling this situation an outbreak was a reasonable conclusion – the student was likely already exposed to the virus. Still he didn't want anyone without full protection in the room.

When he stepped inside, the monkeys all moved to the backs of their cages. Not many unfamiliar humans came into their domain, and this swishing bulky white-coloured individual was unlike anything they had encountered.

Mike stood quietly in the centre of the room until the animals calmed down and carefully made their way to the fronts of their cages. They called out to each other with tentative hoots and soft cries. When the communication finished, he could make out coughing. The student had given him the location of the animal that had escaped from its cage, and this one seemed in a little more distress than the others. Beyond the coughs though, he couldn't discern other signs of sickness in any of the animals.

Mike was a little surprised when he came back to the office and the student asked whether he felt there was any chance that there was Ebola virus involved. The kid started into a history of Ebola outbreaks around the world and said that he personally worried that some day the virus would mutate to a state where it could be passed in aerosols. He had obviously done some serious reading.

There was still serum left from the samples that had been taken the day of the monkey escape and one of Mike's technicians gathered these up for shipment to Winnipeg.

For now, he decided his only action would be to limit access to the building as much as possible.

There was no need to euthanize any animals at this point. He still wasn't even sure that they were responsible for the death reported by the hospital.

It was suppertime before Mike returned to his office. The technicians had taken the blood samples from the student and the monkeys and driven them directly to the airport. One of them would fly to Winnipeg with the samples cased in multiple layers of sealed plastic and Styrofoam. The technician flying was conscientious, and Mike knew she wouldn't let the serum out of her sight until she reached the lab.

He had a list of everyone who had been in the lab animal facility over the past week and was able to contact most of them. He told them they should stay in the city until he got in touch with them again. Everyone seemed to understand the dangers of animal borne disease and promised to comply.

The vet from the facility was the only other person he could track down who had any symptoms. He called, but only was able to get his wife. She insisted that her husband had nothing but a mild cough and he seemed to be improving. He was feeling well enough that he was out playing cards with a group of his friends.

Mike was worried by the information that one worker from the lab who had been coughing had flown to Germany. He was able to verify that she had arrived in Munich but nothing else. The student from the research building wasn't sure what town she was visiting, but did know that she didn't have a cell phone.

There were also problems at the hospital. No one was able to say how many people had been in the emergency department waiting room and it was obvious that the number they could track down from looking at appointments was less than half of those present.

Mike was convinced that there was a link between the coughing monkeys and the death of the worker, but the senior bureaucrat he spoke with was adamant that no public statements or appeal for identification of people who had been in the waiting room would be made until there was more evidence that there was real danger.

The technician returning from the airport knew Mike well enough to bring in takeout Chinese food for his supper.

Mike didn't leave the office for the next two days. He spent most of his time reading and organizing phone calls to follow up on individuals who had possible contact with whatever it was they were dealing with.

At seven in the morning on the third day after the investigation started, the head microbiologist from the Winnipeg lab phoned with results from the Polymerase Chain Reaction testing. The dead man's blood was full of virus. They had run complete sequencing and found that the agent was a filovirus, not Ebola or Marburg but from the same family.

This virus seemed to be something completely new. It wasn't just a mutation of one of the other haemorrhagic viruses. Because of the organism's novelty, they had no idea about how it was transmitted, how deadly it was, or how long it would take for any signs of disease to develop.

As Mike hung up the phone, he realized that he was

at the centre of something horrendously huge. He had a small amount of evidence to work on, but from what he'd seen, symptoms of the disease could develop within twenty-four hours, kill within three days of contact, and it likely could be passed by coughing or sneezing.

Shortly after his call from the Winnipeg lab, he got news that a young female who had worked in the monkey building had been found dead in her apartment.

Her state of decomposition made it clear she had died several days previously. He phoned his superior back with news of the second death and virus identification. The man finally understood the enormity of the situation and agreed to issue a public warning and description of symptoms.

Mike's disgust as he hung up was only tempered by a fatalistic realization that no warning at any time would have made much difference in the course of this disease.

Mike didn't go home again that night and he couldn't sleep while he was at the office. Once it was too late to do any more calling, he went back to reading reports on previous Marburg and Ebola outbreaks.

Just after five o'clock the next morning, the Winnipeg lab called back with news that the same new virus had been found in the green monkeys and the student. Mike waited until seven before he phoned the kid from the monkey building who had given him the initial history. He was relieved to hear that all of his symptoms had disappeared and he was feeling fine.

Monday and Tuesday there were reports from four hospitals in Ottawa of deaths preceded by bloody vomiting.

On Wednesday morning, Mike woke with a vague raw feeling at the back of his throat. His education and experience made him a little paranoid every time he had any illness. Now there were real reasons for concern, but he consoled himself with the fact that he'd been in a completely sealed suit for all of the time that he'd been in places where the virus was known to be.

Late Wednesday night, news broke that a woman in Toronto had presented to a hospital with violent bloody vomiting and had died the same evening. Mike's throat was much worse and he started coughing Thursday afternoon.

Paramedic crews throughout the city soon began refusing to attend to calls that included any hint of vomiting and all hospitals were closed to visitors. Four major centres were designated to receive all patients who presented with suspicious symptoms.

CHAPTER 3
THE ISLAND

Dave Fletcher moved from Calgary to Newfoundland three years ago. He hadn't worked too hard at university. A small-time drug selling operation ensured that he had lots of friends, good parties, and low marks. His degree in English didn't qualify him for any interesting jobs, so when his cousin told him of a disc jockey position that was open, he moved to St. John's.

Dave was a natural at talk radio; he found the skills required were consistent with those he had developed selling pot. Slick talk, some exaggeration, and the ability to convince people that they wanted what you were pushing guaranteed success. Within six months of starting, he had the coveted afternoon show on one of the most popular stations on the island.

The trick to staying on top was to find subjects that would upset people and push them into a frenzy of whining and radio addiction. Dave didn't personally care much about some cabinet minister who had underhandedly got a good deal on a new deck for his cabin or was a little too friendly with a secretary, but controversies like these kept him a star.

The outbreak on the mainland was perfect. Days before the story hit the papers, Dave came across an internet video showing some unfortunate man vomiting blood in the waiting room of an Ottawa hospital. By coincidence, he'd watched *The Hot Zone* on Netflix the night before and recognized the similarity of symptoms in the two stories. He didn't even know that the victim had worked in a monkey facility when he opened the next day's show with a piece on how the world was just waiting for a major disease outbreak.

"It's Fletch here with you on this sunny Thursday afternoon. I was doing a little research last night and it's set my mind to thinking about some of the terrible diseases that the world has known. Way back, they had the plague in Europe and since that time we've had flus that have killed millions. We've all had the flu. I had a dinger of one just this winter. But you know, I never considered that it might kill me. We hear about Legionnaires' disease and viruses from mice, but no one ever considers how important they are. Here in Newfoundland we are lucky to live on an island. If big diseases start up, I can guarantee you, they won't be starting here. We live in a wonderful place away from all the horrors of the rest of the world. Why don't you give me a call right now and tell me about the sickest you've ever been. Maybe you'd like to say a bit about how poorly the hospital system has looked after you. My experience is that no one believes you when you're really sick. Our lines are open, and we have Marjory, a regular caller on the line to start."

The show wasn't one of Dave's best. The usual complainers called in, many of them with a nearly word for word repetition of a previous call about how sick and poorly looked after they were. But whether it was intentional or not, Dave's timing was impeccable.

Five days after his first disease broadcast, it was starting to become apparent that there was serious trouble in Ottawa. Dave took to the air again, reminding his audience that he had warned them of the trouble brewing. Before anyone thought the disease might spread as widely as it did, he brought up the possibility of shutting off the island.

As the dire reality of the outbreak became apparent, other talk show hosts took up the cause. There was a range in the wildness of their suggestions, but they all insisted that it was a simple matter for government to save the population from this mainland scourge by keeping all visitors out.

Indignation and rage spread as quickly on the island as the virus had on the mainland. It seemed that all anyone in the province could talk about was how and when quarantine could be instituted. The main argument was whether everyone should be excluded or if family working away should be allowed to come home.

When one of Dave's callers warned that shutting the province off could have unintended consequences like shortages of food, Dave only hesitated a beat before insisting that the risk was too great to worry about minor inconveniences.

Soon there were hundreds of people protesting outside of the airports in St. John's, Deer Lake, Gander, and Stephenville. In Deer Lake, about thirty residents got through the fences around the airport and stood arm in arm across the runways. The airport manager wasn't in the mood for a fight and immediately announced that the facility was closed to all incoming flights.

The other airports followed suit, and by noon the next day the government announced that no individuals would be allowed to enter the island by any means. The union for the ferry employees insisted that they wouldn't put their workers at risk of violence or disease. Once the first ferry runs were canceled, the government put out a notice that no boats from outside of the province would be allowed to come ashore.

The day after the announcements, Dave had a show on the challenges of maintaining a secure border. The planes and ferrys were easy to stop, but he wondered out loud how the province could keep out the thousands of mainlanders who would be at this moment gassing up their yachts for a desperate run to the safety of Newfoundland.

Boat owners phoned in promising to keep their eyes peeled for foreigners trying to sneak on to the island. The first man to call in suggested that it was a simple matter for every fisherman in the province to bring a shotgun out while they were on the water. He promised that no one was coming ashore in his corner of the island. Subsequent callers to Dave's show and the CBC's Fisherman's Broadcast spread the idea of a naval militia around the island.

In the first two weeks there were no attempts by any mainland vessels to land anywhere outside of the St. John's harbour. One fisherman in St. Bride's was shot by a colleague who had been drinking, but most agreed that the incident had nothing to do with the disease.

The St. John's Harbour Authority agreed to close the port to outside vessels the day after the airports were shut down. Commercial transport ships were allowed to leave with a warning that they would not be let back into St. John's. The owners of the ships were near unanimous in the opinion that they couldn't afford to have their expensive vessels tied up in a backwater harbour.

After a day of negotiations between the Harbour Authority and the fishermen's union, it was agreed that fishing boats could return from fishing if they signed assurances that they would not land anywhere off the island.

The naval frigate HMCS *St. John's* was on its way back across the Atlantic when news of the disease outbreak came through. The crew had been at sea for seventy-two days patrolling the horn of Africa and everyone on board was looking forward to a short visit to the ship's namesake port of St. John's and then some down time back home in Halifax.

Captain Len Pickford was surprised when his frigate was stopped at the St. John's narrows by a string of fishing vessels. A man in a longliner cupped his hands and yelled up to the bemused sailors lining the deck.

"I'm sorry, boys, but the port of St. John's is closed to visitors. You'd be best just pushing off before things get rough."

The Deck Officer shook his head and turned to a seaman by his side.

"Run up and get the old man. I'm not paid enough to get involved in this kind of crap."

Captain Pickford loved his ship and was respected by his men, but he was tired from his long deployment and had little patience for disruption when he was so close to home. He picked up a megaphone and made his way to the railing above the fishing boats.

"Good afternoon, sir, as you may have read on the side of our vessel, we are the HMCS *St. John's* of the Royal Canadian Navy, and we are scheduled to pay a short visit to your city."

"Buddy, I don't care if you are Santa's sleigh. No one is getting onto this island. There's a disease out there that's killing people like nobody's business, and you aren't getting into this harbour."

Pickford sighed as he looked at the shotgun cradled under the man's arm and the Bofers 57 mm machine gun mounted just a short distance from where he was standing. He rubbed his forehead and looked down at his shoes before answering. The pirates of Somalia were no match for the might of the *St. John's,* and these fools weren't even in the same league as the African brigands. In his own mind, the idea of skipping St. John's and just heading home had an appeal, but he had orders.

"Sir, please back away from the *St. John's*. We will be stationing ourselves outside of the narrows to await instructions. We don't want to sink you when we start moving."

No one on the fishing boats cheered as the frigate backed offshore. The most belligerent of the defenders knew that the smallest of efforts from the *St. John's* could sink them all.

The captain made his way back to his personal quarters and put in a private call to his commanding officer in Halifax.

"Admiral, this is Len Pickford on the *St. John's*. We've had a bit of an incident here in Newfoundland. We're scheduled to spend a little time here and a bunch of fisherman have blockaded the narrows. They claim that the island is closed and we're not welcome. Frankly my preference is to forget about them and head on home."

"Desperate times, Len. Things look to be falling apart here. I've already got half of my staff sick or dead and the rest are so scared that hardly anyone is coming in for work. People are panicking and there has been looting throughout the city. If I were you, I'd just stay put over in Newfoundland until this blows over. The news I've heard suggests that the disease hasn't made it to the island. You might be in the safest place in the country right now. The fishermen may be on to something. You just do what you think is right and I'll back you either way."

"Thanks, Admiral. We'll just stay put here offshore and wait for a couple of days and see how things work out."

Len hung up from his call and sat looking out the porthole of his quarters at the rocky shore of Newfoundland. He knew he couldn't stay there long. The ship's supplies were quickly running down and the crew was anxious to get back on friendly dry land.

Life at sea wasn't conducive to long happy marriages. Len met Maggie when they were both in training and had married to make it easy to get on the same ship. Len's career blossomed, but Maggie never moved beyond being a steward. She got out after she'd put her minimal time in and looked after their spectacular home in the south end of Halifax. They'd talked of having kids when they were young, but work always seemed to get in the way.

The romance was gone from their lives, but they had stayed comfortable together. They enjoyed his shore leave times, but were both relieved when he went back out to sea. They didn't talk often when he was sailing. At first it was to keep from worrying about each other, but as the years went by, he found fewer reasons to think about his wife at home.

Len hadn't called Maggie for over a week. The news indicated that the virus had spread across all of mainland Canada, but it never crossed his mind that his wife might be in danger. The admiral's information made him realize that he should have been in contact with Maggie as soon as he heard about the disease outbreak. He called three times that afternoon and didn't get an answer. He knew she never went anywhere without her cell phone.

After the third failed call he started trying to contact neighbours. He dialed four numbers before he got a response. The cranky spinster three houses down from his place picked up on the second ring.

"Hello, this is Len Pickford, and I've been trying to get a hold of my wife Maggie. Do you know where she is?"

"Oh, Mr. Pickford, didn't you hear? Hasn't anyone called you? She was one of the first to get sick. She's been gone for four days now. I hate to be the one to tell you bad news, but she's not the only one. "

She paused, and Len could make out a muffled cough as she turned from the phone.

"The only thing I can say, Mr. Pickford, is don't come back here. If you are someplace where everyone isn't dying, don't think about coming to Halifax."

Len put his phone down and slumped into his chair. Things had been better with Maggie in the past, but a big part of him still loved her. His life and the world were unraveling together.

He called up to the bridge with an order to stay in place just outside the harbour. After a pause, he told his Officer of the Watch to take control of the vessel; he would be in his cabin if needed.

The next morning, something had settled in the captain's mind. He knew that his future was on this island. He was certain that his problems and those of the planet weren't blowing over soon.

The first priority was to contact headquarters again and let Halifax know that the *St. John's* would be sailing into its namesake harbour and no one would be keeping them out. It didn't surprise him completely when there was no answer at Halifax command.

Pickford gathered the full crew on deck for a talk.

"I'm not sure how many of you have been in contact with your loved ones back home, wherever that may be. The information that I've been able to gather indicates that this virus has spread just about everywhere in the world. Halifax has been hit hard and it's not a safe place for us to go.

"There is no evidence of the disease in Newfoundland, and, for now, this will be the safest place for us to stay. We don't have enough supplies to wait out here on the ocean for weeks. We will be heading in through the narrows in approximately one hour. My hope is that we can enter the harbour without incident, but anyone who resists us will not be successful. I don't want to see any fishing boats sunk out there, but I do want all of the rail guns manned.

"Once we get on the wharf, we will have further discussions about our future. If there are any of you who want to go to the mainland and can figure out a way to get there without using this vessel, you will have my blessing to leave. I must warn you though that I think the best choice and perhaps the only sane choice is to stay with the ship. For now I want everyone to their stations."

An hour later, the *St. John's* entered the narrows. Len came to the railing and addressed the fisherman lined up in front of his ship.

"Good morning, gentlemen. Please don't interrupt me while I speak. The *St. John's* will presently be entering the St. John's harbour. If your boat is in front of us, we will go over top of you. If you fire at us with your shotguns or rifles, we will ignore you unless you do damage to our vessel or harm any of the crew. If that should happen, we will fire on your vessel with the guns you can see arrayed along our deck. We will not fire our most powerful weapons, as it would be a waste of ordinance. Good day gentlemen, choose your next move carefully."

Len handed his megaphone to the sailor standing beside him and headed for the bridge. There was no response from the small vessels around him.

Back at the bridge, the captain ordered the helmsman to head slowly but directly for the St. John's harbour port without a pilot and to dock at the open spot closest to the centre of the city. He asked for the top boarding team to be assembled and sent to his quarters immediately.

The fishing boats moved aside as the *St. John's* started for the wharf. The man who had spoken for the fishermen shrugged and called out to the man in the next boat over.

"I suppose it wouldn't do any harm for us to let the boys through. They've probably been out at sea where they wouldn't be picking up the disease anyway. Let's stay here and make sure no one else gets by."

Word of his opinion passed between the boats and everyone was quick to agree. None of them were interested in arguing with the machine guns of the *St. John's*.

Back in his quarters, the boarding team stood at attention in front of their captain. None of them had been in this room before and they all realized something unusual was afoot.

"At ease, gentlemen. We all know the port of St. John's. This is a great old city, and I think we can all agree that we're proud to have our ship named after this place. However, where we are headed now is truly into uncharted territory.

"I have been unable to contact anyone in Halifax or Ottawa, so we can assume our command and control is gone. This means that I will be making all of the decisions from this point on. Some of these will be difficult. We may have Canadian citizens in this port who will resist us, and we may have members of our own crew who have problems with our course.

"It appears that the viral outbreak we've all heard about is worse than any of us could imagine. The mainland of Canada is not safe for us to return to. No doubt there will be members of our crew who will feel that our vessel should return to Nova Scotia where their families are. We have difficult times ahead and we must maintain order on this ship and in this city. It will be important for me to have a strong core of men that I know I can depend on. I'm asking you gentlemen if you are prepared to be that core."

The boarding crew responded without hesitation and in unison.

"Yes, sir."

"Very good. I know what calibre of sailors you are and I knew I could count on you. Now, you will all report to the Deck Officer in the armory who will issue you with sidearms and assault rifles. From the time you return, two of you will remain with me night and day. The Deck Officer will command the rest."

"Yes, sir."

The boarding crew turned as one and hurried off to the armory.

***

It didn't take the world's news agencies long to realize the devastating nature of the disease from Canada. Early on, reporters named the agent "the Ottawa virus" and broadcasted dire warnings of the possibilities of widespread devastation.

In Newfoundland, television stations relayed footage showing the chaos developing around the world. The first reports were of deaths in hospitals and, as the disease spread, looting and riots erupted.

Because there were no outbreaks on the island, the response in Newfoundland was more subdued. Reporters asked hospital officials and workers daily if there were any cases that looked like they were from the dreaded Ottawa virus. Nothing was seen. After reports from around the world of the seeming breakdown of civilization, the island's news would return to results of local soccer games and accidents on the highway. The closing of the airports and denial of access to the island were initially the only evidence anything was wrong on the planet.

In the second week of the outbreak, reports from around the world gradually began falling off. Outlets in Toronto initially reported that they had nothing from their affiliates in Ottawa. Two days later there was nothing from Toronto.

Producers in St. John's tried calling stations around the country to see what was happening but soon realized that there was no one in any of the offices. The last off-island contact they had was with a secretary in Saskatoon who said that no one else who worked in the station was able to come in. She insisted that her colleagues were brave and devoted enough that they would be trying to get out the news if they were able. She had no idea herself how to work any of the broadcast equipment.

The Newfoundland television stations realized that there was no way to exaggerate the seriousness of the outbreak. Individual reporters tried to soften the reality of what was happening in the world, but the public was soon aware of the disaster that had occurred. Many of them emphasized that there was no evidence that Newfoundland was in any immediate danger. As long as no one from the outside world was allowed into the province, everything would be all right.

The measured response from media may have been a major factor in the lack of a panic from the public. There were people who insisted that they needed to get to the mainland to see their husbands or sons and daughters they'd lost contact with. Friends and neighbours convinced most of them that there was nothing useful they could do by leaving. The rest of the world was a dangerous place and it wasn't long before there was no one with a boat or plane that hadn't left already that was interested in going anywhere. There were rumours of fishermen on the northern peninsula offering rides to the north shore of Quebec for exorbitant prices, but there were no reliable reports that anyone had actually done this.

There were very few tourists who stayed in St. John's. Once it was obvious that a major disease was on the loose, almost everyone who was away from home hurried back to tend to their family, pets, or flowers.

The first signs that there might be supply problems in Newfoundland was the disappearance of potato chips. It was a common occurrence for stores in the province to run short on chips when major storms came up. The problem had always been limited to individual locations and the wholesalers had quickly resupplied them.

When word got out that chips were disappearing from the store shelves, people began buying up every stockpile within a short drive. No sooner were the stores resupplied than the chips disappeared again.

The potato chip situation brought enraged calls into the radio stations. Dave's on-air response was that this was a warning to the province that they shouldn't depend on outside manufacturers to provide such an important food staple. It was time for the province to have its own potato chip manufacturing facility. Not one caller suggested that there might soon be shortages of other types of food.

Four days after the blockade of the province was in full effect, there was a noticeable decrease in fresh vegetables in the grocery stores. Soon there was nothing available that wasn't grown in the province. The stores scrambled to get local producers to provide the traditional crops that had been grown locally for generations.

***

Dave Fletcher got a call on a Wednesday afternoon from an irate woman in St. John's wanting to know why a big grey ship bristling with guns had come into the harbour.

"I thought that we were closing off the province. But this big military boat gets in just because they have some kind of connection to the government."

"Well, Martha, I'm so glad you called in with this information for all of us. I had no idea that there was anyone coming into the harbour. Like you, I was under the impression that our boys were keeping everybody away. Sounds to me like someone is slipping up. I'd like to hear your comments on this development. We're all in this together, folks, and we all have to do our part."

"Fletch boy, this is Phonse calling from Upper Gullies. I say bring 'em on. I think having a Canadian Navy ship locked and loaded in our harbour is the best thing that could have happened. My worry is that some boat full of Arabians is gonna come in here and really mess things up. Put me down as in favour of bringing the Navy on board. They can call their friends up too and have them join 'em. The more guns we've got in the harbour the better."

The show went on with calls evenly split between the

first two opinions. It wasn't long before a chronic caller phoned in from the wharf with information that the vessel was called the *St. John's* and she had all kinds of heavy machine guns and missiles on board.

The information that the ship had the same name as the city seemed to tilt opinion in the direction of feeling that the arrival of the frigate was indeed a good thing.

The radio show stirred up enough interest that there was soon a small crowd of onlookers down at the wharf. Six of them had fashioned bristol board signs that they held above their heads. Two were welcoming the crew and four were against the intrusion. Of the four negative signs, one complained of the possibility of the crew members bringing Ottawa virus to the province and three protested the presence of missiles and guns in such a peaceful corner of the world.

The Royal Newfoundland Constabulary was called when a woman with a "No Missiles" sign started wrestling with a woman who had a son on another Canadian naval vessel. By the time the scuffle was settled, four of the six signs were in tatters.

On board the HMCS *St. John's*, Len Pickford watched the women fighting, sighed, and turned to the leader of the boarding team.

"You know it's a good thing we have such evident artillery on this ship. I think any gun nuts who are worried about closing off the province will be so excited by our armaments that they won't mind us here at all."

He turned to one of the men surrounding him.

"Crawford, you're from St. John's aren't you."

"No, sir, I'm from Mount Pearl."

It took everything the captain had to avoid rolling his eyes.

"That will have to do, son. I want someone with us who knows their way around the city. The first thing we need to do is to find some place that can provision us. Do you know where there is a big grocery wholesaler around here?"

The Mount Pearl native provided directions to two of the largest stocks of groceries in the province.

"Now, I need six of you to take a taxi out to the airport and rent three of the largest vans that you can find. Take your weapons with you and if anyone says they won't take government purchase orders, tell them that you will have to expropriate their vehicles. Once you have the vans I want you to drive to the grocery wholesalers that Crawford has told us about. He can lead the way so no one gets lost. Fill those vans to the roof with all the food you can carry and bring it all back to the ship. I've ordered a taxi big enough for all of you and it should be on the wharf any time. Now get going."

The protesters stopped arguing when the gangway was lowered from the *St. John's* and six heavily armed men stepped out on the wharf. A local television reporter pushed through the throng and had a microphone in the first sailor's face before anyone in the crowd gathered their wits enough to attack or welcome the men coming off the ship.

"As you can see behind me, a number of men have just come ashore from the St. John's. Excuse me sir, are you surprised that you are being allowed to enter the city when the whole province has been put under quarantine?"

"Sorry, I can't talk to you, buddy. I'm pretty sure that taxi over there is for me and I wouldn't want to miss my ride."

The sailors looked straight ahead as they moved to the van and got inside. The taxi was well down the road before the reporters or crowd could respond.

The boarding team got their vans without incident. The rental company was happy to have an open-ended hire to a government agency. They'd done rentals like this before and ended up with vehicles out for months at a time at regular fee schedules. Their only concern was that everyone knew how slow government worked and it would likely be a long time before they were actually paid.

There was just a little more trouble getting food. The manager of the wholesale centre initially insisted that he only sold to registered retailers. When the sailors repeated the captain's instructions that they would be forced to take the food if there was a lack of co-operation, the problem of registration disappeared. When the men backed their vans up to the loading dock and walked through the aisles inside they discovered that there were no fresh fruits and vegetables.

"We've been out of them for three days now. There's nothing coming in to the province and there's big competition for the stuff from the local farmers. I'm working on it, but we haven't managed to get anything in yet."

When the vans returned to the ship, the captain put a contingent of armed guards around the loading zone. No one in the assembled crowd tried to get past the guards, but there were shouts accusing the sailors of being disease carriers, war pigs, and food thieves. Once the vans were empty, the captain had the men return four more times to the wholesaler before they were satisfied that they had sufficient provisions for his crew.

The frigate carried 226 sailors and Pickford realized that feeding all of these people on an island that had no outside food arriving was soon going to be a problem. The two possible remedies were to increase the food or decrease the crew. He assembled everyone again and stood in front of them surrounded by the armed members of the boarding crew who weren't collecting provisions.

"Ladies and gentlemen, as you all know, we are now in the city of St. John's. This is no ordinary visit. We will be staying in this port for the foreseeable future and I cannot guarantee that you will be paid for your time here."

There was a muffled but audible groan from the crew.

"Of course it isn't fair for me to insist that you stay on board when you won't be paid. I have nothing to offer you beyond the safety of this vessel. You may be presently in the safest location in the world. We have the good fortune of being on what may be the only place on the planet that has not been affected by the Ottawa virus. Better still, we are on a ship that is both protecting and protected from the city.

"So you all have a choice to make. I will not be forcing anyone to stay on board the *St. John's*. If you want to try to make your way to family on the mainland, you are welcome to leave. I'm not sure how you will get there, but that's your business. If you decide life would be easier on the island of Newfoundland, you are welcome to go ashore. I am asking all of you to return to your quarters and spend some time thinking. If you want to leave, please gather your belongings and exit the ship by the time the sun goes down tonight. Before you go, you can visit the purser's office and he will issue payment for all of your time served to today. No one will think worse of you for leaving. Dismissed."

By late that evening there were just over one hundred crew left on the vessel. Pickford was pleased to note that it was the best and most trusted who had stayed.

There was only one woman with a "no missiles" sign standing in the dark by the gangway when over a hundred people came off carrying all of their belongings. Nearly half of them had relatives in the city. A young female sailor who came off with tears in her eyes was taken home by the protester.

CHAPTER 4
THINGS COME APART

It took nearly three weeks for John to admit that there was no future for him in Ottawa. His only friends in the city were gone and there was no chance he could return to work.

He had come down with a cough, but it passed after four days. A number of things suggested that he was either extremely lucky or had an exceptional resistance to the disease. His proximity to the initial outbreak and the similarity of his cough to what he'd seen in his colleagues convinced him that his symptoms were almost certainly from the same virus.

People around him were getting sick and without exception dying within a few days. His nosey landlords usually checked in on him every second day. They hadn't been around since he had been told to stay away from the animal care building. Everywhere he went, there were people coughing and there was a bad smell coming from one of the apartments somewhere above him. By the end of his first week at home there was no evidence of life from any of the fifteen units in his building.

The man with the white mustache had told him to stay

in the city and keep in contact. Another government employee had called him once asking if he had symptoms and then nothing.

Ottawa was fast becoming a ghost city. When he walked downtown, a half hour would pass before he saw anyone walking or driving. When a vehicle did come by, it would veer away from him and move off quickly.

John didn't have a car and his first thought was to take the bus or train somewhere. He'd been watching the television and knew that Toronto was fast becoming as bad as Ottawa. The news from the rest of Ontario made it clear that the disease was moving rapidly, but everything he heard suggested that Newfoundland was unaffected.

He found an abandoned bicycle near his apartment and started spending his days exploring the city. Neither the trains nor buses were moving and every section of Ottawa he explored was empty. In all of his time travelling he only found two dead people on the streets. He assumed that people hid away like dogs when they felt they were dying. For their part, the dogs he saw seemed to be doing well. He wondered how they were finding anything to eat or how many of them were trapped in houses by well meaning but deceased owners.

It didn't take him long to find a car with keys inside. This was his solution to getting out of the city and heading east and perhaps even home to Newfoundland. He had heard media reports that the island had closed itself off, but surely there was a way for a native son to get home.

The white Mazda 3 was a perfect little vehicle for his purposes. He drove it home the first day and parked in front of his apartment. There were resources in the city that he didn't want to leave just yet. He had survived this long and there was no need to panic. Before he left he would fill the car with groceries and provisions.

He initially worried about whether he had enough money for the food and gear he would need, but soon realized that if he could find any of these things, he probably wouldn't be paying for them. Money wasn't likely worth anything in disease-ravaged Ottawa.

The first grocery store that he drove up to was closed and surprisingly hadn't been looted. On his bike rides around the city he'd seen a number of stores with the windows smashed in. Most of the damage was to high-end retailers of things like computers and jewelry.

There was no one around when he pulled up to the front entrance of the grocery store. Out of habit he locked the doors of his car when he got out. He found a brick in the parking lot and stood looking around as he juggled it up and down. It took three throws before he could smash the glass. The second time the brick came back and landed hard on his toes.

Once the glass was broken it was a simple matter to reach inside and unlock the door. He found a shopping cart and started walking up and down the aisles. Everything in the store looked reasonably fresh. Some of the lettuce was wilted, but still edible. He filled his cart, put everything in the car, and drove back to the apartment.

It was pure delight to have fresh food again. He had bought groceries twice since the problems started, but it had been four days since he had been able to find an open store. As he ate his steak and asparagus supper, it occurred to him that he should be more careful about what kinds of provisions he collected for his trip east. He would need not only food, but also some way to prepare it. The next day he would visit an outdoor store.

When John started his new Mazda the next morning he noticed that there was only a quarter of a tank of gas left. The shortage of fuel made him realize that there were things beyond food that he would need for his trip east. He turned off the car, walked back up to his apartment and started a shopping list. In the back of his mind he had to admit that this was more like a looting list.

That thought sent him off on another tangent worrying about the morality of his plans. John had always tried to be a good person and had never had as much as a speeding ticket. He was one of those people who believed that even when laws didn't make sense they were necessary for the common good.

But the realities of this disease that the television people were calling the Ottawa virus changed everything. How could he steal something from someone who didn't exist? He was certain that the owners of the stores he would go into were all dead. Still, he wasn't happy with the idea of stealing things that weren't his. Somehow the notion of smashing store windows bothered him more than actually taking anything.

He decided that he would stay in Ottawa for another two days and enjoy all the fresh food he could find. The electricity was still on and water was still running. He would enjoy the comforts of machine-washed clothes, showers, and stove cooked meals for just a little longer.

His looting plan was to start with non-food items and then stuff the remaining space in the car with as much non-perishable food as would fit. For travel he decided that he needed a tire repair kit and air pump that ran off the car's electronics. He would take his laptop computer and try to find a solar charger in an electronics store.

For his day-to-day living, he would get a sleeping bag and a small tent. Candles and a solar-powered light would be helpful. He had an interest in camping and realized that there was no reason not to have the best compact cooking outfit and cook set he could find. It would be important to have equipment that used regular car gas. As well he would find something that he could use to efficiently siphon gas from other vehicles.

As John's list grew, he wondered if he would need anything for personal protection. His first thought was to get a firearm and some bullets. Although he had a personal aversion to guns, he realized that in his present situation a weapon might help feed him and keep him safe.

John spent three hours sitting and writing his list. When he finished he was emotionally exhausted. Thinking through all of these requirements drove home the desperate situation that he was in. The world was falling apart and little things like getting this list right could mean the difference between survival and death.

He had a long hot shower then sat in a chair reading a historical novel about the French adventurer d'Iberville. Life in Canada was hard in 1700, but it was easier than what he was facing in the present. As he read, John thought he should pay a visit to a bookstore and get material for what could turn out to be many lonely nights. In all of this misery he realized that he was given the chance to read the books he had always been afraid to start.

He went back to his list and wrote down *"War and Peace, Remembrance of Things Past, Ulysses, Infinite Jest"*. Just those four books could keep him occupied for many nights.

After an hour of reading, John went out for a walk around his neighbourhood. For the first time in days, he didn't look over his shoulder. He tried to burn images of this still beautiful city into his memory. Soon he would be gone and never return.

The next day John started his looting. His first stop was at a hardware store. The doors were already broken in. He was surprised to find that almost none of the camping equipment was touched, but all of the guns and ammunition were gone. The thought that the first priority of survivors was to arm themselves sent a chill through him. Even if there were only a few people left, surely they could work together to survive.

There was a crossbow in a glass case just away from the hunting department and John decided that this might work even better than a gun. It could be used for protection and procuring food and he could even fashion his own bolts if he ran out of ammunition.

Once his cart was loaded, he took one last walk through the store to see if anything else came to mind. The only other object he picked up was a hammer. This would be an efficient way to get into stores and houses.

After successful visits to an upscale outdoors store, an electronics establishment, and a bookstore, John returned to the grocery store he'd previously visited. Inside, it was apparent that no one had been there since he had come two days before. A part of him wished that the place had been cleaned out. At least that would mean there were other survivors.

He took all of his new possessions out of the car, arranged them on the pavement and then started filling every available space with canned food. The arrangement inside the car was critical. The crossbow and gas can should be close at hand and cooking and sleeping equipment that he would use every day shouldn't be buried under mountains of food.

John had another fine meal of lobster and fresh vegetables. As he cracked open the shell he wondered if he would ever get the chance to enjoy this delicacy fresh from the ocean as he had in his childhood. As he finished off a small container of ice cream, he wondered why he hadn't thought of finding some expensive wine. Perhaps his priorities in this new reality were changing.

The next morning, John walked around his apartment and sat in each of the chairs and the old sofa in his living room. Nothing was fancy, but he was sure that he would look back fondly on this as decadent comfort. He wasn't sure why he locked his door and put the key in his pocket. The maracas and name "Calypso" carved into the wooden sign outside his apartment belied the dismal situation he was leaving. He understood that there was no way he was coming back to Ottawa.

On the way through the city John drove by the parliament buildings and past the American embassy. All that display of power and pomp meant nothing now. He thought of all the concerns that the people who had occupied those buildings had and how trivial they were now.

He drove around the front of the national art gallery

and stopped to examine the giant spider that loomed in front. The piece was majestic, but took on a new sinister meaning for him that no one had likely thought of before. As he sat looking at the building, it crossed his mind to break in and take one priceless painting. A little Pollock or a Group of Seven landscape might look nice in his home if he ever settled down. It didn't take long to decide that food was more important.

John was amazed that he didn't see one living person on his drive through the city. This disease meant business; if anyone else had survived, they were too scared to come out into the open.

He drove out to the Queensway and had to shake his head at the surreal appearance of four lanes running through a major city with no traffic. He was surprised by the small number of abandoned vehicles he saw on the way out to highway 417.

As John drove through the countryside, he strained to see if there were people around the houses and barns. If anyone was still living, they were inside and hiding.

Just after he passed Casselman, he saw a cloud of dust in a farmer's field. He slowed down and could make out a tractor plowing just behind a barn. This was the first live person that John had seen in days. Ever the law-abiding citizen, he signaled before he turned in to the farm lane.

John looked over at his cross bow before deciding to walk out unarmed. As the tractor came close, John could make out a grizzled looking man with a patch over one eye behind the wheel. Until he waved his hands over his head, the man didn't show any sign that he intended to slow down or stop.

"Hello."

The farmer stopped his tractor and climbed down from his seat.

"Hello, stranger, it's a mighty hot day isn't it?"

"You're getting some plowing done are you?"

"Yes, sir, the fall is coming on and if I don't get this finished, I'll never get the winter wheat in."

John wondered how the two of them could be talking about plowing as the world fell apart around them.

"Troubled times, sir," John said. "I haven't seen anyone on the road since I left Ottawa."

"There are troubles, you're right there."

"Is your family all right?"

"The family is gone, the neighbours are gone. It's all up to me now. I have to do it all. It's been a pleasure talking with you, but I have to get this plowing done."

"Sir. There's no one left around here. There's no one to buy your grain. I'm heading east where things might be better. You're welcome to join me in the car if you'd like."

"That's awful neighbourly of you, son, but I have a barn full of sheep to look after and there are still crops to take in. Best of luck on your trip out east. I hope things work out the way you plan. This field won't plow itself."

John stepped forward and extended his arm. The farmer shook his hand and kinked his head before he turned back to his machine. John stood watching the tractor move away and looked down at his fingers. It had been a long time since he had touched another person.

CHAPTER 5
DOWN ON THE FARM

Joan Mercer grew up on a small farm in Bay Roberts on the Avalon Peninsula of Newfoundland. Her father grew vegetables and savory and had a horse, a half dozen cattle and a couple of pigs. The business kept him going, but he worked hard for every dollar that came in. Joan's mother had died when she was small and her younger brother never showed much interest in farming.

Joan was always at the top of her class and as a small child had enjoyed being around the animals. When she was fourteen, she brought her first boyfriend home and was disappointed to find he was more interested in her father's tractor than he was in her.

In order to impress the boy, she started asking questions about the machinery around the farm and found she had a knack for understanding how mechanical things worked. Soon she was taking engines apart and discovered she was more interested in inanimate objects than she was in boys.

When Joan finished high school she got an engineering scholarship to Dalhousie University. She felt a little lost on the mainland with classmates who were more worldly and laughed at her strange Newfoundland accent. Her first real friend was a roommate who accepted everything about her. The girl introduced her to a vegan diet and a sensitivity to the importance of sustainability.

The veganism didn't last through her first year, but a deep concern for the fate of the planet stayed with her. She graduated top of her class and took a job with a high-powered engineering firm in Halifax. It took less than six months for her to be disillusioned with the profit-at-any-cost attitude of her company. When the firm took a job designing an industrial complex that would ruin an entire wetland ecosystem, she decided that she would return home and work to develop a sustainable operation at the family farm.

Her brother had moved to the mainland, and, other than hired help, Joan's father was alone. He tolerated her constant talk of ecologically sensitive practices and ethical farming because he was so pleased to have his daughter home. It amused him when she bought two work horses and started spending her free time driving around looking for old horse-powered farming equipment.

By the time of the Ottawa virus, Joan had been home ten years. Her father had stepped away from the day-to-day running of the operation and spent a month every year in Arizona. The farm had thirty beef cattle, six pigs, a shed full of laying hens, and two magnificent Percheron workhorses. Her house was completely off-line. Solar panels and a windmill provided all of the electricity she needed.

Joan was quick to see the seriousness of the Ottawa disease outbreak. She decided to immediately spend all of her money on solar panels, seeds, and livestock. Provincial regulations limited her poultry operation to one hundred birds. She knew that regulators wouldn't see the importance of raising as many animals as she could feed, so she didn't even ask for permission to increase her flock size.

Her first step was to go to the bank and take out everything. She had a strong feeling that money would soon be worthless. She spent the rest of the day in St. John's visiting all of the retailers who sold equipment for alternative energy production. By evening, the back of her pickup truck was overflowing with solar panels, windmill parts, and heavy-duty batteries.

The rest of her spending required careful planning. In order to raise more animals she would need more buildings and enough feed to last her until she reached true self-sufficiency.

She picked out the best local contractor and arranged for him to put up two large buildings on her land. One would shelter her animals and the other would be a holding space for feed. Once she calculated how much money was left after putting up the buildings, she phoned the feed company and paid for enough animal provisions to fill her new storage facility. The company was happy to be prepaid for such a large order.

The new buildings were up within two weeks and they were soon filled with animals and feed. With all of her money spent, she put up the windmills and solar panels by herself. It was no problem for her to set up the battery array for her new system of energy production.

CHAPTER 6
HARD TIMES IN THE CITY

The day after Pickford's sailors collected their groceries, the city of St. John's heaved a collective sigh of relief. One hundred and thirty-seven visitors came down the gangplank and every one of them had a pocket full of cash. The restaurants and bars downtown were filled for the first time since the tourists had stopped coming.

The next day, callers to Fletch's afternoon show were in unusually buoyant moods. Several commented on how busy George Street had been the night before. Things were looking up and all was well in St. John's.

It took the last caller of the afternoon to break the spell of optimism.

"We've got Cal on the phone to finish off today's program. As you all know, he's a regular caller. What's on your mind today Cal?"

"Fletch, I think everyone has got it all wrong. They're all going on about how great it is to have these sailors in town. I'm not so sure about that."

"And what exactly aren't you sure about, Cal?"

"First off, did anyone notice that it's mostly men that came off that ship? Now to my mind, Fletch, men is nothing but trouble. Present company excepted of course, Fletch. But these guys are stealing our women, drinking our booze, and next thing you know they'll be taking our jobs."

"Well, I'm not too sure about that, Cal. I have it from reliable sources that a number of those sailors are actually women and I'm pretty sure the bar owners down on George Street are quite happy to have them drinking their beer."

"What about food, Fletch? They're eating our food."

"I'm sure the restaurant owners are quite pleased that there is someone eating out. Things have been pretty slow downtown for the last couple of weeks."

"I'm not talking just about the ones who came to shore. What about the ones still on the boat? Have you thought about how they are gonna feed a boatful of people on the St. John's wharf? I heard that a bunch of them went out to the Atlantic Grocery warehouse and cleaned them out at gunpoint. There's no new food coming in to the island and I'm worried that there will be people starving in Newfoundland this winter. It's happened before, Fletch, and there's no reason that it won't happen again."

"You bring up some interesting points there, Cal, but I'm afraid our time is up for today. So, let's get to these ideas again tomorrow at 1:30 when your buddy Fletch will be back to hear the island's concerns. Have a good day everyone."

It had been a long time since anything said on his program had bothered Dave. He knew that his show catered to the base fears and ignorance of the population. His only worries at night were about how to stir up more outrage and increase his ratings, but there was something about Cal's call that had stirred a real worry deep inside.

Normally Dave would have his headphones off and be out the door within seconds of the last caller hanging up. This time he sat and ran his fingers over the volume control knob in front of him.

His producer Deb recognized his behaviour as unusual and called out from the control room.

"Everything OK, Dave?"

"I don't know, Deb, that last call just got to me. Guys like Cal call in here with the same old crap about potholes and unplowed streets and we thrive on that stuff. But he's got a point about the food in the province. If nothing is coming in from the mainland, the grocery stores will soon be empty. What's it going to look like here in the middle of the winter?"

"Maybe we should back off on this stuff. If we rile people up enough there will be riots in the streets."

Dave paused, shifted his headphones across his desk, and sighed.

"Nah, to hell with it. This stuff is gold. Our ratings will go through the roof. People will remember that they heard about it first from their buddy Fletch. Now, I don't know about you, Deb, but I'm heading out to pick up as many canned groceries as I can stuff into my car. Maybe I'll even go out twice. See you tomorrow."

The next day, Dave opened his show with concerns about the island's food supplies.

"Good afternoon, St. John's, and anyone else out there within the range of my dulcet tones. It's your buddy Fletch and today we are going to talk about food. Specifically, I want to know if you think there will be enough for us all to survive this winter."

The phones lit up immediately and opinion was unanimous that Newfoundland was in trouble. The only question left was whose fault this whole fiasco was. No one had suggestions for how the problems could be dealt with, but callers had nothing but loathing for the city's mayor and council, the Canadian navy, the premier and his cabinet, and even the monkeys of any species in Ottawa who had caused all these problems. Someone hadn't done their job properly and someone was going to have to pay.

Dave's program had hit a nerve. It was as if no one had thought of the possibility of food shortages until it was mentioned on the radio. Rumours started to surface that there were elderly and shut-in people in the city who were already in trouble. Facebook messages saying that some expert had predicted mass starvation over the winter were shared thousands of times.

As soon as Fletch's show was over there was a run on the grocery stores. By evening every shop in the province had bare shelves.

The premier held a press conference in time for the evening news begging the population to keep calm.

"We are going to be alright. The only thing that will get us into problems is if we all panic. There is enough food in the province to feed us all at least through the winter and I'm sure that things on the mainland will settle down before we really run into trouble. My ministers of fisheries and agriculture are aware of the problems we may be facing and are hard at work planning as we speak."

When a reporter raised his hand, the premier added

that he wouldn't be taking any questions at that time.

That night, a television news anchor described the premier as visibly shaken and noted that he didn't have the confidence to face any questions.

After playing the premier's recorded announcement, the host introduced a professor of history from Memorial University to comment on the province's situation.

"Dr. Hudson, do you think that there is a real possibility that there could be food shortages in the near future?"

"Well, Garth, as you know, we aren't strangers to nutritional problems. As recently as the 1940's people on this island died from starvation. We can grow root vegetables and hardy plants like cabbage here, but our soil and climate are not conducive to large scale intensive agriculture. I believe it's a real possibility that we may be in for serious problems as early as this winter.

"The premier spoke about things settling down on the mainland. When people say things like this, I just have to wonder if they've seen the same reports from the rest of the planet that I have. It looks to me like the world outside of our island is beyond repair. It seems there will be no food or assistance coming to us for the foreseeable future. We're going to have to look after ourselves and we need solid leadership."

The interview went on with no new information and the same opinion repeated in different words. The host finished with an unhelpful summary.

"Well, you heard it here from one of the province's experts, it sounds like we are in for interesting times."

The next morning there were long lines in front of every grocery store in the province. At some locations, owners and employees told the crowds that nothing was left inside. At others, the doors were simply locked. As tempers rose, a number of stores had their windows broken.

Municipal police and the RCMP were called out. In most cases they were able to quickly convince people to quietly move away. Police management could see how things were progressing and sent squads of officers to establish a presence at food wholesalers. By the time crowds of people showed up, the buildings were surrounded and safe. The police left small detachments of guards in place with a contingency plan for rapid deployment of more men should the need arise.

Fletcher was back on the air the next day with the same topic. He knew there was still more mileage he could get from the people's wrath.

"It's Fletch here again and I think that we have some unfinished business left over from yesterday's show. I'm sure you've all heard about the riots at the grocery stores around the province yesterday. Well, folks, I'm just as upset as you about the lack of food, but I think your anger is pointed in the wrong direction. Those people running the food stores are doing the best that they can. They're normal working folks just like you and me. The problems come from a lot higher up. Our governments haven't done enough preparation for this kind of a situation. I think that someone needs to be held accountable and heads should roll."

As Fletch spoke Deb was in his headphones.

"Dave, I think you'd better go to commercial. I've got the mayor on the phone and he doesn't sound like he's in a good mood."

"Just a second, folks, my producer tells me that we've got the mayor on the line."

"Hello, Mr. Fletcher?"

"It's me, Mayor Foster, you're on the air, thanks for joining us."

"On the air? I wanted to have a private word with you."

"These are important days with important issues and I think the people deserve to know what their leaders are thinking."

"All right then, I just wanted to point out that some of the things you've been saying on the radio are not helpful right now. Everything is fine in St. John's and the people need to believe that council and government have the situation under control."

"Under control? Have you been watching the news, Mr. Mayor? We've been cut off from the rest of the world and the people are worried that we will run out of food. It's only a matter of time until we have riots in the streets of our fair city."

"There you go again. It's talk like that that stirs up trouble. Nobody is thinking about riots or disturbance until someone like you plants ideas in their heads. I'm just asking that you use a little restraint here."

"So you're saying that people should just trust you that everything is going to be fine? I'd like to know what plans you have for when the food is gone or when we have no gas or electricity. It's time for strong leadership in the city and in the province."

"Are you suggesting that you could do a better job?"

The mayor regretted his words as they were coming out of his mouth. This tin pot radio personality who didn't have a clue how government worked had goaded him into saying far more than he had intended. Fletcher jumped in before he could say anything to change the direction of the conversation.

"Well, sir, the last time I checked, the government of this city was based on democratic principles and it wouldn't surprise me at all if our citizens just might think I could do a better job."

"As you said, Mr. Fletcher, these are times that require leadership and as mayor of this fine city I have more important things to do than argue with a radio talk-show host. Good afternoon to you."

The mayor's line went blank and Fletcher was on a roll.

"Well, listeners, that was certainly an interesting call from our illustrious leader. It doesn't sound much to me like he has any kind of a plan or any interest in communicating with his constituents. Our lines are open now and I'd sure love to hear what you make of this latest development."

All four lines on Deb's console lit at once and she spoke into Fletch's headphones.

"You've done it now, Dave. I hope you are ready for what's coming next. I've got a feeling we're going to have an interesting half hour ahead of us."

"Dat you, Fletch? It's me Jake. How's she hangin?"

The speed with which he continued made it clear his question was rhetorical.

"You'd make a fine mayor, Fletch, and I know that me and the wife and young fellow would all vote for you. Sure, there are thousands who'd be happy having a straight talker like you running things. We've had enough of politicians and their lies. It's time we had someone who cares for the common people."

"Now I'm going to stop you right there, Jake. I'm perfectly happy right here in the studio. We all have our roles and I don't have the least bit of interest in politics. Still, I must thank you for your vote of confidence, it's quite flattering."

"Hello, Fletch, am I on?"

"You are indeed and I can recognize the pleasant voice of Cal from your first words."

"Fletch I just have to re-echo again what your last caller was saying. We needs someone like you in city hall. Anybody can see the arse is coming out of her and it's time for the people to have their say."

Despite Fletch's protestations of disinterest, the show continued with a barrage of opinion that the host was the only one who could save the city. The enthusiasm of the calls increased as the minutes ticked by. One elderly woman suggested that Fletch would be nothing better than a traitor if he refused the obligation of power that was being thrust in his direction.

As the last caller hung up, Fletch slumped in his chair with Deb's taunting voice in his headphones.

"'Mayor Fletcher.' It has a nice ring to it. You need to be careful what you suggest when the mob is broiling. I've got a feeling this is going farther than you might expect."

Dave threw his 'phones across the table and stalked out of the studio without looking at his producer.

CHAPTER 7
ON THE ROAD

John was surprised by how many abandoned cars he saw as he got farther out of Ottawa. He reasoned that the roads inside the city were relatively empty because people who had decided to drive were able to get some distance before getting sick enough to have to stop.

Most of the cars were pulled off on the side of the road. Perhaps the drivers developed progressively worse symptoms until they couldn't continue. He slowed down and noticed that about half of the cars had corpses behind the wheel. There were also dead people lying on the road close to their vehicles.

He was just wondering what horrors might befall families trying to escape when he spotted a young girl with a stuffed bear in her arms standing in the road beside a parked vehicle.

John slowed with the intention of inviting her to join him. As he pulled in close, she turned towards him and retched, bringing up a large volume of bright red blood. There was no question that the girl would soon be dead and he worried that he still might be susceptible to the disease if he contacted a large enough dose of the virus.

With tears in his eyes, he slowly pulled around the doomed child and continued down the road. The girl's condition reinforced the reality of how widespread this disease had become. It was obvious that no one in her car had survived. If anyone else in the family had lived they surely would have stayed with the child.

To distract himself from the realities of the road, John turned on the radio. In this area of southern Ontario he knew that the dial would normally be jammed with stations vying for attention. The first noise was pure static and he slowly scanned across the radio frequencies for stations. He was just about to give up when a Dolly Parton song came through the speakers. It wasn't the kind of music he liked, but he couldn't remember ever being so happy to hear a song. The only thing that would be better would be a disc jockey coming on with some reassurance that there were others doing well.

After Dolly Parton there was Toby Keith and then Merle Haggard. Of all the music to survive, it had to be country. Still, he kept the radio on with the volume up. It took six songs for John to realize that a prerecorded loop was being played and there was no one to talk in the station. The disappointment hit him hard. He felt like a friend had let him down.

John looked at his watch and wished that he had picked up some extra batteries during his looting. His first reaction to the thought was that he'd find another place with batteries and then he wondered why he cared about the time.

His first glance at the watch had been to see whether he should stop to have his lunch. He had to laugh at himself as he considered why it was important to eat at noon.

The only reason was because that was when he'd always eaten. There was no one to join him for his meal and there was no reason to eat at any time other than when he was hungry.

He reflected on how completely the past was gone. Ideas of communal meals and appointment times were no more. Survival was what mattered now; everything else was unimportant.

As this percolated through his mind another thought arose. The natural conclusion to this kind of thinking was that everything of beauty and grace in his life was no longer of significance. There was no need for him to talk unless he found new friends, but did that mean that he should stop talking? If he went silent, it would only be a matter of time before he couldn't speak. John resolved to eat his lunch at noon and to stop at a picnic area and get out of the car for his meal.

At ten minutes to twelve he saw signs for the Voyageur Provincial Park. Once again, he signaled when he pulled the Mazda off the road.

He opened his road map and saw that the park bordered on the Ottawa River. There was no one at the ticket office and for the first time ever he was disappointed by his free admission to a park.

Other than three staff vehicles pulled up in front of the office, there was no evidence of anyone having been in the area recently. He drove slowly along the narrow roads appreciating the untouched beauty on both sides. It went through his mind that this scenery might represent the future.

He decided that there was no reason for him to hurry. He would explore the park and find the most scenic spot to stop and eat. Perhaps he'd find a place with a clear view of some rapids.

After fifteen minutes of exploring, John spotted a raised picnic area with a spectacular view of the Ottawa River. The grass looked like it hadn't been cut for a few weeks. Nature would return this spot to a more natural looking grassland before long.

He parked the Mazda and pulled a can of beef stew and his camping stove from the seat behind him. Once the stew was heating up, he would return to the car for a can of juice and perhaps some fruit for dessert.

The combination of the roar of the river and his concentration on lighting the stove kept him from hearing the approach from behind.

"Don't turn around or I'll blow your head off."

John lifted his hands from the stove to show he was unarmed.

"Just relax," he said. "I have no weapons and I don't want to fight with you."

"Sit down and don't move."

"Sure, I'll do what you say. There's no need to make this into a problem. Maybe you and I can help each other."

John heard the door of his car open.

"Where are the keys?"

"I've got them right here in my pocket."

"Throw them over your shoulder, and I'll be on my way."

"Listen, I've got lots of food and supplies. There is enough to look after both of us. Why don't you just join me and we can maybe get through all of this together."

"I can see your car is full, that's why I'm taking it.

Now, throw those keys my way. Do anything stupid and you'll regret it."

John pulled his keys from his pocket and tossed them over his shoulder.

"Are you alone? I don't think there are many of us left and we need to work together."

"Shut up and don't turn around."

The pitch of the voice made John realize his assailant was likely a teenager, possibly even a girl. He wasn't even sure if he or she even had a weapon, but he didn't feel lucky enough to chance calling anyone's bluff.

"I've heard that Newfoundland may be unaffected by all of this and I'm originally from there. With two of us we'd have a better chance of getting there."

"You're nuts, man. Who would ever want to go to Newfoundland? There's nothing there. I've got buddies in Ottawa and I've been walking that direction for three days."

"I've just driven out of the city and as far as I can tell there is almost no one left there. If you want to get away from the disease, you're going the wrong direction."

"Don't try to tell me what to do, old man. I'm taking your car and heading for Ottawa."

This was the first time anyone had called John an old man. He was only twenty-six and it was becoming clear that he was dealing with a teenager. As well, this kid hadn't had the sense to take one of the vehicles that were abandoned on the highway. It was a nuisance to lose his car and all the supplies he had gathered, but he was relieved that he wouldn't have to put up with this lunatic for much longer.

"Take my car and get going. There is a siphon in the

front seat so you can get more gas from another abandoned car before you run out. You know how to use a siphon, don't you?"

"What do you think I am, stupid?"

John bit his tongue as he was beginning to think that this was an accurate description of the kid.

The car door slammed and the engine started. John didn't bother to look around. He was just happy no one had shot him or slit his throat. Getting another car and more supplies was a minor inconvenience.

As he returned his attention to his boiling stew, his biggest regret was that he hadn't brought utensils or a drink from the car. John collected a pile of maple leaves and used them to lift the can off the stove. He decided to move to the edge of the water. This way he could easily get a drink and he was happy to be away from the picnic table. His tolerance for man-made articles and other people was at an all time low.

As he poured the stew into his mouth, he reassured himself that there must be some decent people left. Surely the disease hadn't taken all of the good from the world.

After he'd eaten and cooled his feet in a shallow pool at the side of the river, John walked to the outhouses at the edge of the picnic area. He paused for a moment in front of the door labeled with the word "men" and the universally recognizable symbol. He looked around, smiled and opened the women's door. As he sat, he laughed at his foolish demonstration of power and freedom.

Despite all of his bravado, John still looked both ways as he came back out through the door of the women's outhouse.

He decided there was no value in carrying the stove

with him. He needed a complete new set of supplies and getting new cooking equipment wouldn't take much extra effort. The walk out to the park's front office was much longer than he had remembered. As he walked along the tree-lined road, he became aware of a beauty to the green filtered light that he'd missed driving in. Bright yellow birds flitted from branch to branch as he passed. He'd never noticed before how many of them moved in pairs. He stopped to take it all in and realized that the only deaths he'd seen were human. There were live horses and cattle along the road and no evidence of any dead wildlife.

The door to the park's office was open and his first thought was to find the keys for one of the trucks parked outside. A quick search through all of the rooms and then an exploration of every desk drawer was unsuccessful. He found road maps of Ontario and Quebec and a backpack that would certainly be helpful.

In the staff lunchroom he found a large bottle and three cans of carbonated drink. In the refrigerator there was a Tupperware container filled with lasagna and a flat tray with half of a chocolate cake with "ppy ement" written in icing. All of this went into his new backpack, along with a fork, knife, and spoon from a drawer.

Back on the highway John had time to think over his situation. In a way, he had been given a second chance to prepare for his trip east. This time he would be more careful in his choice of vehicle. He would take the first car or truck that he could find, but use it only until he could find a vehicle that he really wanted. There was no reason to compromise on his transportation. Once he had his new ride, he would head into Montreal and stock up again on food and supplies.

CHAPTER 8
HOME ON THE FARM

Conditions in Bay Roberts didn't change quickly. The canned food in the grocery stores disappeared as fast as it did anywhere else around the province, but locals soon came to the conclusion that there would be enough food. Farmers continued to sell at roadside stands but were quickly convinced by local grocery stores that they could unload their produce for a good price without any of the effort they normally put into sales.

It wasn't long before security problems began to crop up on the farm. The first two times it was apparent that locals had come into her gardens and made off with a few potatoes. Joan reasoned that people were hungry and if they needed a bit of food, she wasn't going to worry. There was plenty to go around.

The third incident was different in kind and scale. The morning after the attack, one of her hired hands reported that a field had been almost completely destroyed. There were tire tracks through the soil and nearly all of the cabbage had been taken away. The plants that hadn't been cut were ruined because vehicles had run over them.

When she asked around, neighbours reported that

three pickup trucks that no one recognized had been seen roaring through the community the night of the vandalism.

She had heard stories that gangs from St. John's had looted a number of grocery stores in the area. Enough incidents had occurred that store owners were beginning to post armed guards. Rumours spread that food shortages were becoming so serious in S. John's that desperate inhabitants of the city were coming out to the outports in search of something to eat.

Joan was quite certain that she knew who had taken the potatoes the first night, so she approached the boys she suspected.

"Hello, boys. I'm not going to say that you fellows have been stealing my potatoes, but I have a pretty good idea that you guys know your way around my fields."

"Missus, we would never dream…"

"Hold on, boys. You are best to just be quiet and listen to me. I'm sure you'll be interested in the proposition I have for you."

"Yes, ma'am."

"I have no doubt that whoever took my potatoes did so for a good reason. We all have to eat, and I wouldn't be surprised if your families are having worries about finding enough food this winter."

"Yes, ma'am."

"If you boys can find another two of your friends and between you guard my fields and barns at night, I'll make sure your families have enough to eat for the rest of the year. Does that sound like a reasonable idea?"

"Yes, ma'am."

Joan showed the boys the areas they were to watch and gave each of them an air horn and instructions to discharge them off at the first sight of any intruders.

The three unfamiliar pickup trucks returned a week later and were immediately spotted by the new young guards. At the sound of the air horns, the field was swarmed with locals brandishing everything from pitchforks to shotguns. The trucks made a hasty retreat and weren't seen again in the area.

Joan kept the boys watching over the fields until all of the vegetables were harvested and then hired armed guards to watch the feed and animals.

She contacted the head of the Cattleman's Association that oversaw the operation of the local pasture and invited them to her farm for a working dinner. The pasture had been traditionally used as a communal summer holding ground for local farmers with a few cattle, sheep, or horses. In recent years the number of animals in the area had declined drastically and much of the fertile pasture ground wasn't being used.

They agreed on a plan to put most of the underused grassed area of the pasture into vegetable production. The Cattleman's Association and Joan would share in the new vegetable business. She would contribute seeds, expertise, and equipment and the association would provide the land and labour. It was too late to put in crops this year, but they would be ready for next spring.

A short-wave radio operator who was friends with Joan told her that he was hearing reports from around the world that were even more worrying than what they had heard when the international television and radio networks were on the air.

His colleagues from United States, Brazil, Germany, and Japan agreed that the pandemic had started in Canada and had likely reached every continent on earth. There were no reports of illness from Antarctica, but even if the scientific research stations there were unaffected, there was a limit to how long they could survive without returning to infected areas to replenish their supplies.

The short-wave operator pieced together a story that the disease had broken out in Germany just after the first Canadian deaths and then quickly spread through Europe.

Affected individuals started with symptoms that suggested a mild flu and progressed to bloody vomiting. It seemed that there was a wide range in the time it took for people to die after contacting the disease. Some individuals were dead within a day or two of exposure and others took a month or more to even develop signs. Evidence suggested that very few people survived once they had even the mildest symptoms. The progress of the disease made it clear that the virus was being passed without the need of direct contact. Being in the general vicinity of an infected individual was enough to spread the disease.

The speed with which television and radio stations went off air was evidence of how fast and completely the pandemic had overcome populations. The short-wave operators who had survived reported that there were very few people left. Most estimated that far less than one in a thousand people were still alive. Others suggested that the real survival rate was even less than one in a hundred thousand.

The operators who were still on air all reported that they were alone. None of them were interested in finding other survivors. Their common opinion was that coming together with other people only increased their chance of getting infected.

There were surprisingly few reports of any kind of civil unrest. It seemed that people were too frightened to go into the streets or anywhere they might contact others. Some early rioting and looting was reported, but it was short lived. Police and military presence weren't evident anywhere.

The short-wave operator from Wyoming had a different take on events. He had lived alone before the disease started and made it clear that he had been warning about something like this for years. He refused to tell the other operators exactly where he lived and warned that he was extremely well-armed and would shoot anyone who tried to find him. He claimed to have stored up enough food to last fifty years and had air filtration systems that would keep him safe from the toxic gasses that he believed would inevitably make their way into the environment.

His information was the least useful of anything that was on the air. He was so far removed from any population that he had nothing helpful to add about what was happening in his part of the world. Most of his time on air was spent ranting about how this whole debacle had been deliberately planned by a consortium of Jewish industrial magnates who were now safely living in a mountain retreat somewhere in Israel.

The most disturbing messages were from Japan. An operator there had been in contact with other short-wave enthusiasts in Asia and had heard that the disease had devastated Australia, New Zealand, and the Philippines. Even more worrying was his report of a loud bang and severe tremor that he suspected was an atomic accident. Since the explosion, his own electricity had failed and the lights around his apartment in Tokyo had gone out. The only reason he was still on air was that his equipment was run on solar batteries.

All of this news made Joan realize how lucky Newfoundland was to have avoided the disease. It seemed that the island might be the largest unaffected population left on the planet. The pandemic had come on so quickly and completely that there was no research-based information to help predict how long the danger would last.

It was possible that the virus could burn itself out by using up all its possible hosts or it might linger on in animals that would carry the agent without showing signs. If the latter was true it could mean that the disease could still show up in Newfoundland years or decades after the worldwide plague subsided.

Joan decided she would make her farm into an impenetrable fortress and not worry about the rest of the province or planet. The news from around the world made her realize that the virus wasn't something she could hide from. If it made its way to the island, there was little she could do.

CHAPTER 9
SIZE MATTERS

Small, isolated outport villages coped with the challenges of the pandemic better than St. John's. They had looked after themselves for centuries and being cut off from the rest of the world was just one more difficulty to overcome.

Trepassey was located about sixty kilometres from the city, but, as far as the residents' attitudes about life, they might as well have lived on the other side of the world. Shortly after the disease outbreak, an emergency measures official from St. John's visited the small town to make sure they were ready for anything that might come up.

When asked, the mayor admitted that the town didn't have an emergency preparedness plan. The official asked what they would do if the town's main water supply was cut off. The mayor admitted that that very thing had happened just six months earlier. They didn't bother telling anyone in government because the deputy mayor had a backhoe, and a bunch of local guys dug up the line and repaired it with some material they happened to have on hand.

The official asked what they would do if their electricity was cut off. The mayor suggested it wouldn't cause much trouble because just about everyone in the community had a generator. The power often went out in Trepassey and it wasn't something the people worried about.

The discussion continued in the same vein with the mayor having ready answers for any catastrophe the official could dream up. It was only when asked what would happen if a giant tsunami wave crashed over the town that the mayor was stumped. He admitted that he didn't know what they would do, but quickly added that he wasn't sure having a plan written down in the council office would make much difference.

The same attitude was common in small communities throughout the province. They had seen many hard times over their history and they had little faith in government as a source of relief when things went wrong.

The larger centres didn't have it as easy. The inhabitants of the big towns and cities knew that they relied completely on an intact support and supply system to keep them alive. There was far too little food produced in the immediate areas to maintain their populations.

Within six weeks there were people starving in the city of St. John's. The early deaths didn't cause much concern because the old and very poor people who went first had been invisible until this final indignity anyway.

Even those who did manage to find enough food to survive the first few months knew that the city would soon be unlivable if any of the public utilities failed. If the removal of sewage or supply of water stopped or even if garbage wasn't promptly collected the population would suffer.

Perhaps it was the realization of this reality more than the slow accretion of deaths in the invisible underclass that led to unrest in St. John's. Within two months of the outbreak, people started moving out of the city. It was a trickle at first, mostly retirees going back to family homes in the outports. As food became scarcer, the numbers moving across the island increased.

Restaurants had been the first businesses to feel a real pinch. The complete lack of tourists quickly closed a number of downtown establishments. The eateries that remained open found it difficult to get any variety of fresh food on their menus.

The failure of restaurants foreshadowed problems in many other businesses in the downtown. People understood that difficult times were ahead and they stopped spending. Places specializing in souvenirs didn't stand a chance, and they were soon followed out of business by high-end clothing stores.

Financial ruin spread quickly from the downtown into the rest of the city. Rumours that the province would soon be out of gasoline ensured that no one was buying vehicles. Problems got worse as the employees of the failed businesses lost their jobs and curtailed their own buying.

Fletcher was quick to pick up on the decay and made it his pet topic when nothing else scandalous was on his radar. The tone of his shows shifted to the point where nearly everything he spoke of had an undertone of disgust at the mismanagement of the city.

When the fourth car dealership closed its doors, Fletch suggested on air that those out of work should be protesting at city hall. It was obvious to him that incompetence of the city leaders was at the root of most problems.

The protests started with a few unemployed waiters and mechanics and quickly grew to hundreds of angry citizens greeting the mayor and council members at every meeting or event they attended.

After two weeks of demonstrations, the mayor held a press conference to announce that he was resigning from his position. As an independently wealthy man with a new young trophy wife, he decided that the prestige of his position was no longer worth the stress involved.

The council held an emergency meeting and installed the deputy mayor into the head position. A senior councilor was voted in as the new deputy mayor and plans were made for a by-election.

After his resignation, the mayor moved out to his extravagant summer home on the ocean-front cliffs near Portugal Cove. His first project once out of politics was to install an eight foot wall around his property. He refused any interviews with the press and wasn't seen again in the city of St. John's.

On the first show after the mayor left town, Fletch started by suggesting that the mayor's resignation was just a good start. The new mayor and full council were complicit in the incompetence that had put St. John's into such a precarious position. The city would be better off if all of them resigned.

The first call that day resuscitated the theme of Fletch's responsibility to the community.

"Fletch, boy, it's Sophie. You remembers me, I phoned in, say, maybe three years ago about the vet chargin' so much to fix me poor little cat.

"Indeed I do, my dear. How's your pussy cat doing now."

Fletch looked across the glass at Deb in the control room and rolled his eyes.

"Well, sir, she's dead, the poor dear. Got run over by a truck not a week after I called you. I do miss that cat."

"And what are you calling about today, Sophie?"

"It's a wonderful thing that good for nothing mayor is out of the way. But it's time for a change now and you are our man. Will you be running for that council seat?"

"Do you think I should, Sophie?"

It was Deb's turn to roll her eyes.

"Yes I do. And I'll tell you what, sir. If you don't run I won't be listening to your show or anything on your station any more or buying anything from the people that are sponsoring you."

"Whoa now, Sophie, we can't hold the good folks who make sure that this show comes into your home every day responsible for what I decide to do."

"I don't care, sir. That's just what I think and that's what I'll do. Good day to you."

Sophie slammed down the phone and there was a stretch of dead air that Fletch and Deb would never normally allow. After a full three seconds of silence Deb hissed into Fletch's headphones.

"Wake up, Dave. You've made a mess now. You're going to have answer that next line and find a way to get yourself out of this. Line three is somebody from outside of town. Maybe you can steer things in another direction."

"Sorry, folks, we're back. We had a bit of a technical problem there, but we're on again, and I have Dave from Holyrood on the phone."

"Hey, Dave, It's Dave. How are things today."

No one called him Dave on air. He was Fletch, a separate character who only existed on the radio. It was always important to him that he was someone else when not at work. He swallowed his indignation and hoped the rest of the show would float by quickly.

"Dave boy,

There it was again.

"I'm not from St. John's, but I do spend a lot of time in town. The wife and I are in at least twice a week and that's where we used to get all of our groceries. We've seen the change in the city and I'm pretty sure you're right that the problem is with management.

"I may not be the right guy to be saying this. I can't vote in St. John's elections, but I'd have to say that Sophie was right on the button with her comments. You owe it to us common people to get on council, and I don't mind turning off your show or walking away from your advertisers to make sure that it happens."

"Well I appreciate that vote of confidence, Dave, but I'm just not sure that I'm the man for this kind of position. There are many talented people in St. John's who could do a much better job than the old or new mayor. I'd just like to wait and see who presents themselves as a new alternative."

"It disappoints me to hear that kind of talk out of you, Dave. Didn't you say you could do a better job than the mayor just a little while ago? And now you're suggesting that you may not even run for council? I'm hanging up now, Dave, but I have to admit this is the first time that you've really disappointed me."

The floodgates opened. Every line on Deb's console was blocked for the rest of the show and every caller had the same message. Fletch had to run for council or his audience would abandon him and his sponsors.

Dave was sweating by the time the last caller hung up. From the control room Deb slowly twisted her head in a manner that unmistakably said "I warned you about this." They had worked together for three years and there was no need for them to speak. Each knew exactly what the other was thinking.

As Dave walked down the hall towards the exit, the manager of the station came around a corner and stopped in front of him.

"Mr. Fletcher?"

The manager hadn't called him by his full last name for about two years.

"Yes, sir?"

"I hope you can spare a minute to step into my office. We have some rather important issues to deal with."

"Yes, sir."

Fletch followed the manager down a dark hallway and through a door into a large room with a window on the parking lot. The sky outside was noncommittal. It looked like the rest of the day had equal chance of being warm and sunny or brimful of rain.

"Sit down on this chair."

"Yes, sir."

"You've been with us here at the station for quite a while now, haven't you?"

"It will be three years next month, sir."

"And in that time, Mr. Fletcher, I'm sure you've come to understand what goes on at a radio station."

"Yes, sir, I believe I have."

"Just in case you have any misconceptions about how

things do work, I will explain everything to you now. A radio station depends on three factors. Those are, in order of importance, the advertisers, the audience, and the material we put on the air.

"Each of these elements depends on the other two. The advertisers need an audience and, to a somewhat lesser degree, an interesting product. If any of these three elements fails, the whole system will collapse. Do you follow me so far?"

"Yes, sir."

"I listen to our radio programs and I carefully watch the success of our advertising sales crew. As you can imagine, the current climate in the province is not conducive to attracting advertising. You may have noticed that the Ford dealership, which normally is one of the main sponsors of your time on the air, is no longer with us. The time slots that were reserved for selling cars are now filled with promos for other shows we produce. Do you know how much money we get for airing promos, Mr. Fletcher?"

"Nothing, sir."

"That's right, Mr. Fletcher, nothing. And that nothing is what I am supposed to use to pay your salary."

The manager was working himself into a bit of a lather. His ears had become quite red and more and more spittle was spraying from his lips.

"Despite the loss of advertisers, we are continuing to survive. You still have a job and a paycheck. But, and this is a big but, I listened to your program this afternoon and that program was a problem for all three of the elements of radio.

"The show itself was a mess. You weren't yourself. I could feel your confidence slipping as the hour wore on. There was dead air and your callers backed you into corners. If your performance was the only problem, I wouldn't be so concerned, but you let the show mess with our advertisers and our audience. You allowed everyone who called today to threaten the basis of our existence.

"And this whole mess is of your making. You got the city going about problems in government and then you had to tease them with silly ideas that you could do better. Your pride got in the way of common sense and you've backed yourself into a corner.

"Can you see where I'm going with this, Mr. Fletcher?"

"I'm afraid I do, sir."

"The only way for you to get out of this debacle is for you to run for council. Your audience called your bluff and I'm in line behind them. Unless you file your nomination papers for city council by tomorrow evening, you are fired."

Fletch swallowed hard and looked at his shoes.

"I understand, sir."

"You can leave now. You have some work to do this evening."

"Yes, sir."

Dave stood and moved toward the door.

"One more thing, Mr. Fletcher. I'm expecting a real effort out of you. You'll also be fired if you don't win that seat."

Dave was in a dark mood as he started his car. He mumbled to himself.

"Dammit, dammit, I don't want to be a friggin' politician. Talking to those idiots out there for an hour and a half a day is all I can stand."

His first thought was to type up a resignation letter and bring it in to work the next morning. He ran through clever opening lines and protestations about how much he had done for the station and how his program was the most listened to in the province. They couldn't replace him. It wasn't just anybody who could instigate outrage and manipulate public opinion like he could.

Driving home he passed two shuttered car dealerships and considered the consequences of the current economic conditions. He didn't have any special skill beyond what his present position required and there were no new jobs anywhere. Most people felt lucky if they could keep the work they currently had.

Maybe he could be a politician. If he could win he could have it both ways. He would have a new job that his particular skill set might be useful in. Once he had a position on council, he'd quit his radio gig. The thrill he used to experience on air was gone and there was no real possibility of him moving up at the station. If he was on council, he'd have less work, get a paycheck, and he was certain there was room for him to advance. If he was going down this road, he was going all the way, and he wouldn't be satisfied until he was mayor.

Back home in his basement apartment Dave considered his way forward. His first concern was the physical process of filing his nomination. He needed someone to sign his papers and then he would have to put together a campaign team.

Outside of work, David Fletcher was a very shy man. His free time was spent reading and watching television.

He avoided crowds of people and disliked eating in restaurants. The only real friends he had in St. John's were his colleagues at the station. When he thought of them he admitted they were really more acquaintances than friends. Deb was married and he knew she had two girls because she was always calling them and had their pictures all around the control room. He wasn't even sure if any of the others at work were married.

Deb would sign his papers if he asked politely. He had to admit that she was always helpful. The guys in advertising should have the skills needed to run a campaign and if he could convince the kid who just started doing graphic arts to make some posters, he would be all set.

Dave's salary didn't provide much more than he needed for his food and lodging. He'd put a little away over the years, but he had no intention of dipping into his savings to get on council. The station manager was the only person he knew with enough money to bankroll a campaign, but there was no way he was going to owe that jerk anything. He knew the way that the guys in advertising did things. They always had some kind of spoils from their work that they flaunted around the office.

When big contracts were signed, the boys would invariably have an enormous bottle of cheap booze on conspicuous display. He had no intention of buying anything for them, but he was certain that he could convince them that there was a real advantage to having a friend in politics that could make sure the potholes on their streets were attended to.

The graphic arts guy might not be so amenable to this approach, but he was sure that the promise of friendship and fulsome praise of his artistic abilities would buy him all the poster designs he needed.

The next morning he brought in a cheap box of chocolates for Deb and she was quick to agree to nominate him. Her only comment was that she knew this run for office was important for both of their jobs and he didn't need to think that his pathetic attempt at chocolate bribery made any difference.

The graphic design kid immediately agreed to help out. He was obviously thrilled at the idea that his creations would be seen in public.

The advertising department surprised him the most. When he brought up his proposal to Mac, the senior ad man, he insisted that they step outside to discuss things further.

With his bright checkered sports coat barely covering his ample gut, Mac pulled out a cigarette once they were on the parking lot.

"Fletch, my man, I think we can work something out here. First off, there's no need for you to involve anyone but me in your planning. The rest of the boys are busy, you know, chasing down contracts and besides they don't have the experience that I have."

Dave had to agree that no one in the building had been around as long as this guy.

"I can run your campaign and do a lot more than just design a strategy. If you are willing to promise to scratch a few backs, I'm pretty sure that I can get a couple of my big advertisers to pay for exposure for you on billboards and TV. We won't worry about the other radio stations."

"That sounds good. What would I have to do for these

guys?"

"Nothing just now. You would only have to remember that some of these companies need a little special consideration from city council from time to time. You're a resourceful man and I'm sure you could make things happen once you're in power."

"Sounds pretty simple to me. So that's all you need?"

"There is one more thing. I'm sure you've heard the news about the halfway house that is being planned for drug addicts up in my neighbourhood."

Fletch was familiar with the project he was referring to. It seemed to him a progressive move by the city to sponsor such an undertaking. He told Mac that he knew about it.

"Well, I'm uncomfortable with the idea of a bunch of addicts running around in my corner of the city. They're nothing but scum and I don't want them anywhere near my house. If I'm going to help you get on council, I'll want that whole idea shut right down."

Fletch didn't agree with the adman's characterization of the proposed facility, but this seemed like a small compromise to ensure his plans went ahead.

On his afternoon show, Fletch let it slip that he had thought hard about the calls that had come in the previous day and decided that it was his civic duty to run for council. Every call that came in backed him completely and many suggested that anyone in the city who thought they could beat Fletch was out of their mind.

No one in the office complained when he and Deb took an hour off after the show to drive down to city hall to formalize his entry into the race.

CHAPTER 10
NOW FACE EAST

John had only walked a half hour when he came across a pickup truck on the side of the highway. This wasn't what he was looking for, but it would do until he found a more suitable ride. When he reached the side of the truck and looked through the closed window, he could see a corpse lying across the front seat and flies buzzing around the interior.

He didn't look to see if there were keys in the ignition before walking on. John glanced at his watch and was surprised that it was already past four o'clock. It didn't seem possible that so much time had gone by since he had pulled into the park. The passing time, the dead man in the truck, and the empty highway ran a chill through him.

There was a vulnerability inside him that hadn't been there since his troubles began. Until this point there had always been something other than himself he could count on for comfort. His apartment and then the little Mazda were places where he could feel safe. Now he was on an open highway with nothing. He had no idea what or who lurked in the trees that ran along the sides of the road.

As the sun made its way closer and closer to the treeline he worried that the night would come without him finding a secure spot to stop. There were houses along the road, but he worried that desperate people might be hiding inside.

When he had walked far enough to be out of sight of the truck, he stopped and sat by the side of the highway. He wondered how he had ever thought he might make his way back to Newfoundland or even the Maritimes. Even if he did get home, what were the odds that the disease hadn't moved in ahead of him?

As his spirits fell, he wondered how much of this disaster was his fault. He was the one who let the monkey go, and it was because of him that the virus was now running rampant across the globe. He didn't deserve to survive. So many people had died who had nothing to do with the outbreak. Sometimes the world wasn't fair.

He stumbled down off the pavement into the ditch and opened his backpack. Even though he wasn't hungry, he started into the chocolate cake. He had mindlessly made his way through over half of the dessert when he heard a throaty roar coming down the road towards him.

John put down the Tupperware container and stepped back onto the pavement. Coming towards him was a high powered vehicle that was being driven hard. His worries fell away and he stood respectfully on the shoulder and stuck out his thumb.

John assumed the red Mustang was going full speed when he first heard it, but as the car approached and moved to the far lane, it became apparent that it could still go faster. The smell of exhaust lingered after the car sailed past and disappeared over a hill.

John worried that the behaviour of the Mustang driver was a sign of what the disease had done to those who survived. It was apparent that there were very few people left in his part of the world, and many of them felt their survival depended on their ability to stay away from others.

Perhaps it would take more time for people to get over their fear of the disease. He had come to the conclusion that he was resistant. He didn't fear infection. As these thoughts went through him, he remembered passing the vomiting girl on the road. It was so easy to second guess his own motivation. Had he left her because he knew she would die or was there still some deep seated fear of contagion?

His prospects for finding a vehicle before dark were decreasing and John needed a plan for the night. He walked another twenty minutes deep in thought when another lane to a farm came up to his right.

He considered the house and wondered who might be inside. Farmers usually had guns to deal with predators, and in these drastic conditions he was sure they wouldn't hesitate to shoot an intruder – especially one who might carry a lethal disease.

Walking in by the lane seemed too vulnerable an approach, so John climbed a wire fence a hundred meters before the turn and made his way through the cornfield next to the road. Moving through the dense green vegetation was claustrophobic and he was relieved when he stepped out into an area of cut lawn. It was obvious that the grass hadn't been attended to for over a week, but he wasn't confident this meant no one lived in the house. In times like this, lawn mowing wouldn't be anyone's top priority.

He walked quietly along the edge of the corn to a large barn that was set in behind the house. The big red sliding doors on the back were open and he carefully moved up and peered in.

The barn was filled with about forty black and white cattle that immediately set up a chorus of bellowing. He stepped inside the barn and moved into the shadows waiting for someone to check on the animals. It took him a full half hour to convince himself that no one was coming. The cattle gradually stopped their calling but started up again when he moved out from his hiding place.

John grew up on a farm and with his experience in vet school, he knew these animals were malnourished. Two of the cows were lying down and didn't make an effort to rise when he walked by them. The dull look in their eyes and their dry skin indicated that they hadn't seen food or water for some time.

His worries about being discovered diminished as he considered how many farm animals would be in the same situation. The cows obviously weren't affected by the virus, but, like the pets in the city, they were still victims of the disease. John walked through the herd and undid each cow from its stanchion. The grateful animals immediately ran from the barn and started eating the grass around the building. He hoped that they could find water somewhere nearby.

The two animals that he had seen lying down didn't respond when he untied them. His first thoughts were the diagnostic ideas that had been drilled into him at school. These animals needed intravenous fluids and perhaps some help getting to their feet. As he ran through treatment ideas in his head, it became clear to him that he wouldn't be doing anything for them. There were likely hundreds if not thousands more animals nearby that were suffering the same fate. It was impractical to think he could do anything to help them.

Despite the strong evidence that there was no one alive on the farm, John was hesitant to approach the house. He decided to spend the night in the hayloft above the cows' quarters and see if there was any movement or light overnight. He made himself a nest in some loose hay and settled in with the rest of his cold lasagna and chocolate cake. The sweet smell of his bedding eased him into a restful sleep.

John woke with the sun and was pleased that he didn't remember any dreams from the previous night. He drank down a can of pop for breakfast and stretched as he walked out the barn doors in his underwear. This time he had no concern for whether anyone saw him.

The cows were gone and there was a wide swath of corn knocked down. He assumed that the single line of wire around the crop had been electrified in better times but now was useless at stopping the hungry animals.

After pulling on his pants and shirt he walked directly to the farm house and knocked on the door. It took him three tries before he felt it was appropriate to turn the knob. The door wasn't locked and there was no response when he walked in. A quick tour through the building confirmed that there were no people either alive or dead in the house.

He sat down on a comfortable couch in the living room feeling more relaxed than he had in days. It was something like a reflex that made him try to turn on the television. As he pushed down the button on the remote he laughed at his own stupidity to think there might be any programming still going. But the television didn't even turn on.

His first thought was that the batteries in the remote were gone and then he wondered if there was electricity in the house. He flicked the light switch by the door and nothing happened. When he tried three other switches, he got the same results.

He remembered that the refrigerator at the park was working. There hadn't been any noise from a generator, so he assumed that the electrical system had been intact. Just a short distance down the road things were different. He wondered if this location got its power from a different line or if something had changed in the short time since he'd left the park.

It struck him that so many things that he had taken for granted throughout his life required people to maintain them. If there was a small problem in a power generating plant or in any of the transmission lines, electricity would be lost and there would be no one to restore it.

John spent the rest of the morning sitting on the couch and reading old copies of *People* and *National Geographic* that were piled under a coffee table. Just about everything he read about in People was meaningless now. The carryings-on of celebrities and politicians meant nothing to anyone, and there was a good chance that most of them were dead. The *National Geographic* stories were divided into pieces about interesting cultures and natural phenomena. The cultures might be gone, but the deserts and forests would be unchanged. The only differences would be that there was no one to admire them and no one to ruin them.

There was a battery-powered clock on the kitchen wall, and at noon John looked through the kitchen cabinets for food. The place was well stocked; he estimated there was enough canned food to last a single person for well over a year. He opened a can of peas and one of mushroom soup and ate them together cold.

After lunch, John began exploring the farm. There was a shed next to the barn with two tractors and a number of implements. Everything was clean and looked ready to start work in the fields.

He climbed aboard the smaller tractor and, after a few tries at different buttons and levers, got it started. It took him nearly half an hour to drive back along the trails through the farm to what appeared to be the end of the property. Just before the land ended there was a wide stream of clear water. He parked the tractor and walked another half hour upstream.

Just at the point he was ready to turn back, he spotted a half dozen of the dairy cows drinking. The sight made him as happy as anything that he had seen since he left the city. This place was a relative paradise.

Back at the house John found a large pile of firewood. There was a woodstove that could keep everything warm in the winter and would be adequate for cooking. That night he dug a half-dozen large potatoes from the garden and snapped off some fat cobs of corn from the field.

He found matches in the kitchen and soon had a fire roaring out behind the house. While the flames danced he sat and watched. With little effort he jammed the back legs of the chair he'd brought out from the kitchen into the soil. The resulting angle was perfect. The light of the setting sun crinkled through the leaves of the trees that framed his view. Down the opening between the vegetation he could make out the back lit silhouettes of insects. The hypnotic quality of the endlessly changing pattern of their flight was only interrupted by an occasional swallow swooping though. The mellow glow of the flames and the quiet activity in the sky warmed him as much as the fire's heat.

As the flames died down, he pulled the husks from three cobs of corn and rubbed and picked at the strings until everything was bare and clean. His original plan was to boil the potatoes, but seeing the coals glow red he decided to find some foil and wrap them for roasting.

There was a pump in front of the barn, and he soon had a pot filled with water and corn sitting snugly amongst the coals. As his supper cooked, he wondered whether he might be best settling in more permanently at the farm.

There was everything that he needed here. The garden was full of vegetables he could preserve, there was water and there was wood for fuel. If he was careful, he might even be able to bring some of the cows back to the barn. It shouldn't take too much effort to maintain a few cattle for milk and meat.

He continued to fantasize about his future on the farm. Perhaps he could go out and find a woman somewhere to join him and they would start a new family here. Staying would be so much easier than moving down the road.

The corn boiled and juice oozed out of the potato wraps. This was the first meal of fresh food he'd had for a while, and he couldn't wait to taste it. He unwrapped a potato onto his plate and fished out a cob of corn. Both were too hot to put in his mouth, and the smell made him salivate as he waited.

He tried the corn first and was immediately disappointed. This was obviously a low sugar, cow corn, nothing like the varieties that people normally ate. The vegetable left a starchy residue in his mouth. He ran into the house and brought back a salt shaker, but his food remained tasteless.

John gave up on the corn and started into his potato. It was hard; obviously it hadn't been in the heat long enough and when he tried to eat it, it was tasteless. Disappointed with his meal, he moved back into the house and found a can of baked beans. He punctured a small hole in the top and tossed it onto the coals.

Beans were a big step down from his hopes for fresh vegetables, but he was content to have something warm. Rather than sit watching the glowing embers, he decided to take a walk around the barn. The sun had gone down and the night was filled with a different soundscape than he was used to.

There were no roars of planes or automobiles and no sudden reports from explosions or guns. At first, the night seemed silent, but when he stopped and listened he could make out rustling in the grass. He wasn't sure if it was from small animals or the wind, but either way, there really wasn't silence. When he sat still longer, he could make out singing frogs from some distance away and the occasional cry of a nocturnal bird. He heard one coyote call from so far off that the sound could have been an illusion. There was nothing he could hear that sounded connected to humanity.

John was lost in the quiet noise of the night. He couldn't decide if the atmosphere of this new reality was comforting or frightening. The world had returned to a more natural state, but he wondered what room there was for him.

Recovering from his thoughts, John realized that he had forgotten about his supper. He walked back around to the fire pit and fished the can of beans out from the coals. He realized that he would need a can opener to get at his meal and it took him twenty minutes to find one. It bothered him a little too much that the previous owners of the house had put the opener in the back of the drawer full of forks, knives, and spoons rather than in a separate drawer as he would have done.

He had enough foresight to bring an oven mitt and in no time he had the lid off the can of beans. He was hungry from the anticipation of fresh vegetables, but the beans were another disappointment. They had a sooty taste and when he looked carefully into the can he could see a burnt black perimeter around the inside of the container.

The warm can of ginger ale that he'd brought from the park was the best part of his supper.

John decided it was vital for him to retain as much structure as possible by keeping up habits he had from previous times even when they didn't make sense. He pumped a bowl full of water to brush his teeth, wash his hands and clean up the utensils that he'd used during the meal. It would have been easy to leave the washed articles out to dry, but it was important to him to find a towel and dry them.

Carrying on in the same frame of mind, he searched the drawers of the master bedroom for a pair of pyjamas. Once he was dressed appropriately for sleep, he settled in under the covers.

The next morning, John had a can of pineapple for breakfast and made hot chocolate from powder he found in a kitchen cabinet. He decided to pour the fruit out into a bowl rather than eating from a can, and he ate his meal sitting on the front porch.

It was a gorgeous day; there was dew on the grass and a slight breeze blowing through the weeping willow that stood in front of the house. He wondered about the people who had lived here before. There was no car or truck on the premises so he assumed that they had decided to escape the region. The toys he found in the bedrooms of the house suggested that there were two small children who had lived here. They must have left before anyone got sick or perhaps they drove off with some of the family already infected. Either way he wasn't optimistic that any of them would now be alive.

The fact that the family had fled made him reconsider his plan to settle down on the farm. The meal from the night before made him realize how unequipped he was to survive in a rural setting. He was kidding himself that he could look after cattle and have a stimulating existence here.

As he considered his future, he thought of the man

that he'd seen the day before driving his tractor. There was no question that the man was deluded and now he wondered if he was falling victim to the same fantasies.

The thoughts confirmed his earlier decision to move east. There was no future here, especially this close to where all the problems started. Perhaps there would be a better world in Newfoundland or even the Maritimes. He would spend one more day on the farm enjoying the peace and making another attempt at eating fresh food before he put together a few supplies and continued his eastward journey.

Perhaps it was the lack of pressure on him to prove he could do anything at the farm that made his second day so much more successful. He ate fresh peas, beans, and tomatoes with crackers from the pantry. None of his food was burned and he found spices to add a touch of variety to his cooking.

He spent the morning walking back over the farm and then explored the house for material that might be useful. By suppertime he had a duffle bag filled with canned goods and his cleaned out Tupperware container filled with fresh vegetables. His strategy was to find interesting food and not to worry that he needed great volumes. He was confident that there would be more supplies along the way.

John slept soundly that night and after a breakfast of powdered orange juice and fried vegetables, he secured his bag to the back of the smaller tractor. Before he left he checked the fuel level and pumped it full from the gas tank behind the implement shed.

The tractor started with a snort and he was back on the road heading east.

CHAPTER 11
YOUR WORSHIP

Three days after Dave had filed his nomination papers, Mac poked his head through his office door, winked and clicked his tongue.

"Fletch, my man. I've put together a few things here," he indicated a thick sheet of papers under his arm, "laying out how we are going to get you on council and what you'll be doing once you're in power."

Dave wasn't completely comfortable with the way his sentence ended but rationalized that there would have to be some compromises to run a cost-free campaign.

"You've been busy, Mac. Leave that with me and I'll have a look through everything tonight."

"Fletch, Fletch, Fletch. Do you think we are going to be running some second-rate, under-baked, half-hearted affair of a campaign? If that's what you are thinking, you're badly mistaken, my friend. We will be having our first campaign strategy meeting tonight over supper at the wings joint across the road. The good folks over there owe me a few favours, so the meal will be on me.

"It will just be the two of us. I've already been talking to the young fellow in design, and he's put together some pretty good work. I had a few suggestions and he'll have acceptable logos and signs for us within a day or two. You don't need to worry about him any more."

Dave couldn't remember telling Mac that he'd approached their colleague in design, but he thought the issue was better left unexplored.

"Six o'clock on the dot. We'll have a few drinks, some wings, and I'll explain everything about our campaign. See you there."

Mac backed out as if being sucked away by some giant vacuum cleaner before Dave could even say goodbye.

That afternoon Dave had a fish farm operator on for a short interview and then asked his listeners for comments. Opinion was evenly divided between those who thought this was a wonderful employment opportunity and a strange alliance of those who felt it might take real fishermen's jobs away and the environmentalists who worried about disease and runoff problems.

Dave spent the rest of the afternoon sitting in his office thinking about his future. He realized that he hadn't looked into how much city councilors were paid, and wondered whether he would be able to afford to quit his job. He convinced himself that he wasn't going to become a typical politician, but there was no question that his life was going to change.

He arrived at the restaurant a few minutes before six and found a table in a quiet corner. Mac was a clever guy, but he wondered why he would hold a strategy meeting in such a public place.

Mac burst through the door at three minutes after the hour and immediately started up a conversation with the young girl at the front. He held her hand and looked intently into her eyes for the twenty seconds they were together. As he let her arm go, she blushed and motioned to a door at the back of the room. Mac strode across the restaurant, rapped once, and disappeared from view.

Dave ordered a beer to fill in the time his co-conspirator was gone. It was close to ten minutes later that Mac made his way to their table.

"Fletch, how good to see you here." He extended a hand for a meaningless but robust shake.

"It's too bad you ordered that beer before I settled in. I've just had a word with the manager and let him know that our campaign would be using his premises for meetings and that no one should be seated in our immediate vicinity. There won't be any charge for the meal, but I can't guarantee you won't have to pay for that pre-contractual beverage. I did say he could be certain that this place would have a friend with a capital F in the halls of city power. Let's order some wings, I'm starved."

Mac waved over the young girl he'd spoken with and rhymed off four kinds of wings and ordered more beer. Dave was certain that the girl at the front didn't usually take orders from the tables, but Mac had a way of rushing things through to completion before anyone could see what he was doing.

"That's done. I hope you agree with the wings choices I've made, Fletch. I'm a bit of a regular here, you might even say a connoisseur, and I can tell you which flavours are the best. There is no time to waste with picking out food. We have more important things to be at tonight, don't we?"

"I suppose..."

"Glad to see that we're on the same page. Now, before we start there is just one formality that we need to get out of the way."

Mac fanned out three pages of densely blackened paper.

"This is our contract of understanding. You just sign this and we can begin."

"Mac, I thought this was going to be a simple process. You are my campaign manager and I'll make sure there's no halfway house in your neighbourhood."

"Do you remember, my friend, that I said we wouldn't be running any half-assed campaign?"

Fletch didn't remember this, but he meekly nodded.

"This little paper is just to make sure that you get to be councillor. Have a read through if you wish. I don't think there's anything in there that should be any surprise to you. Go ahead, read it."

"I think I will."

Dave reached across the table and started in. The thing read like a caricature of a legal document. It was filled with phrases like "the heretofore mentioned" and "the party referred to in the previous clause." It took him some time to get through the dense verbiage. This wouldn't likely stand up in any court, but it was a chance to see what Mac understood their relationship to be.

The first section repeated three times that Mac was to be the only agent who dealt with the upcoming campaign. It suggested that if any other individual was brought on, they could not be paid, and that such an action could jeopardize the relationship between the candidate and the previously referred to campaign manager.

The next piece emphasized that the manager would be free to comment either on record or off record to any third parties in a manner that would not damage the candidate's chances of success in the election.

Dave found all of this foolish and unnecessary but not bothersome enough to comment on. He knew from the start that one of the costs of having Mac work with him was that he would say whatever he wanted to whoever he wanted. His consolation was that he knew Mac would do nothing to decrease his chances of having a friend in a position of power.

The question of the halfway house was dealt with next. The only surprise was that the document required Dave to explicitly state his position during the campaign. He found this odd, but, again, he wasn't greatly surprised.

The most troubling part was the bit on the last page that required Dave to stay at his job on the radio.

"What's this about me having to keep working? I was hoping to be away from this mess and to not be under the thumb of those jerks in management anymore. I want to be away from that talk show crap and be myself and free to change a few things."

"Fletch, Fletch. Do you understand why you are running for council, and why you have a near lock on winning that seat?"

Dave raised his arm and pointed across the table, but Mac was too quick for him to get a word in.

"Don't answer. That was what we call a rhetorical question. The reason you are going to win is because of what you do and who you are on the radio. People aren't looking for someone with clever ideas. No Alfred Einstein is going to get elected anywhere. What the people want is someone like you who asks the questions that get them hot and bothered. They don't care for a second if you have any answers.

"What you have to do in this campaign is to keep asking questions. Keep suggesting that everyone in power is crooked and that they don't have any plans. Don't stop long enough for anyone to ask what you intend to do. If you get stuck, you'll know what to say from what your callers are saying. You need to stay on the air and you need to be Fletch. Nobody knows or cares about David Fletcher.

"And my advice is that you stay Fletch once you get on council. You will have a way into the minds of the public that no other politician can possibly come near. Your show will go through the roof. The fools out there will think you can do what each one of them wants, and all you have to do is throw them a bone from time to time and talk about how delicious it is.

"If you are worried about your financial position, just forget it. I predict that once you get elected you'll be able to write in that number at the bottom of your contract that says how much they pay you. When you get onto council, you just gently suggest that you might move over to another station and the boss will be kneeling at your feet.

"Now, you and I have jobs to do. Both of us will be working on publicity. I will be behind the scenes, getting people to know Fletch just a little better. I've explained to the boss how beneficial it would be to the company to have one of our own in power and he's agreed to free up a couple of our big billboards. As soon as the young fellow has adequate designs ready, your lovely face will be out there for everyone in the city to see as they drive to work.

"There's a printing shop that's been having some zoning problems, and I've convinced them to do up our lawn signs. Of course their difficulties will evaporate once you're in city hall.

"Your part of the job will be mostly just tweaking what you are doing already. I don't want any more spineless crap like today's show about things like fish farms. How do you think talking about fish is going to get you elected? Your time is too valuable for the next three weeks to talk about anything but the election. All of your effort on the air needs to be spent getting people to talk about what a mess we are in and how it's all because of poor management. You don't need to say that much yourself, just set him up with a leading question and John Q Public will do all of your work. This is most of what you've been doing since you got here anyway. Now all you need to do is focus that public discontent."

"What if someone runs against me?"

"Yeah, well… I don't think they will. Anyone would be nuts to want to get on council with the way things are right now. Present company excepted.

"If someone is foolish enough to take you on, you can just shift the focus of your show over to the deficiencies of that unfortunate individual. The people who phone in to your show are your people. This is a truth that not many recognize. Those folks on the phone aren't your average citizens. Everyone listening may think they are, but these are your people and you have to use them."

Mac ate nearly two thirds of the wings and through the continuing orders of beer, he somehow managed to drink twice as much as Dave. As the adman had predicted, the only bill that came at the end of the meal was for Dave's first beer.

The tone of the show didn't change that much. Every program was a relentlessly single minded assault on real and imagined problems in the city. The common sentiment from the callers was that it would take Fletch's magic touch to straighten everything out.

Two weeks before the election, Dr. Louise Jones from Memorial University announced her candidacy for the vacant council seat. In her nomination speech she made it clear that the only reason she was running was that she feared the "unfettered populism" of David Fletcher.

Fletch was onto Dr. Jones like a dog at a rotten fish on the first show after her announcement.

"Good afternoon, good people of St. John's. I'm sure that you've all heard that a Dr. Louise Jones from the university has decided to run against me. Now I've never heard of this Mrs. Jones – wait now, I should be careful with the Mrs. business. A lot of those university types aren't married, at least not to a man, if you know what I mean."

Deb was standing in front of her console with fire in her eyes making a slicing motion across her throat. Fletch tipped his head toward the ceiling and waved.

"I suppose that she's adequate at whatever she does over there at the university, but just the fact that I've never heard of her makes me wonder what credentials or experience she has to be a true servant of the people. We've got

Norm on the line."

"Is that you, Fletch?"

"Yes, boy, I'm here, you're on the air. Do you have something to say about Mrs. Jones?"

"She's got some nerve running against you, boy. That's all I want to say."

"Before you go, Norm, do you think that teaching at a university is the right kind of preparation for a position on council?"

"No, sir and that I do not. I've got no idea what they do up there at Memorial. As far as I can tell they're all just smoking drugs and chasing girls. From what I hear, half of the fellas up there are chasing boys. You wouldn't find me dead in that place."

"Thank you, Norm, for contributing your considered opinion this afternoon. I wouldn't be surprised that there are a lot of people who share your concerns about the university. You know they say a little learning is a dangerous thing. If that's true, what does it say about a whole lot of learning?"

"We're off to a quick start this afternoon. I have Carl on the line from town. Do you have anything to add to our discussion today Carl?"

"Indeed I do, sir. Like Dr. Jones, I am a professor at the university and I have grave concerns about your characterization of the school and Dr. Jones in particular."

"You have trouble with my characterization do you, sir? I suppose you folks up at Memorial like using big words like that so the ordinary guy can't understand you?"

"Please allow me to state my case in a civilized manner."

Fletch snorted into the microphone.

"Please do continue, Dr. Carl. I assume it is 'doctor,' isn't it?"

"You are correct in your assumption. If I may continue."

"Oh please do. This is fascinating. People in the real world don't often get a chance to hear someone quite like you."

"I will ignore your innuendo and continue."

"My innuendo? I didn't think you could see that over the radio. This is wonderful fun, please do go on."

"As I was trying to say, I have concerns with your apparent opinion that knowledge is somehow a problem. Dr. Jones has a PhD in political science and a deep understanding of how governing entities like city council can operate in an efficient manner that will provide the most benefit for the largest number of our citizens. Particularly in light of the global catastrophe of the Ottawa virus, we, in what may be the largest surviving population on the planet, must have sober and carefully considered governance."

"That was all very fascinating, Dr. Carl. But if you are ready to come up for a breath of air – I'm sure my listeners would appreciate it as much as your lungs would – I'd like to ask you a few questions."

"Certainly, Mr. Fletcher. I would be more than happy to deal with any concerns you might have with my position."

"First of all, Dr. Carl, we've established that you and Mrs. Jones work together. You obviously know her well enough to even know what subject she teaches. I have to wonder if there is any romantic attachment between you and Mrs. Jones."

"Just a minute, sir. This is outrageous, Dr. Jones is a colleague of mine and I happen to be happily married. Dr. Jones is a single woman and neither her nor I have had any relationship beyond what would be expected of academics working together."

"I'm glad you cleared that up, doc. So you're saying she never showed the least bit of interest in you as a man."

"Certainly not."

"Well that's helpful, she's not married and she isn't interested in men. I think we can all draw our own conclusions."

"Now just hold on."

"Sir, I'm the host of this program and I will decide what things need to be held on to and when. I'm frankly a little disappointed that you would phone in to my program as a shill for one of your friends at the university. That strikes me as a very serious conflict of interest. Good afternoon to you. sir."

Dave pushed the disconnect button on his phone console and winked at Deb in the control room. She shook her head but couldn't help smiling.

Deb was at the same time relieved and disappointed that no one else supporting Dr. Jones had the courage to call in. A part of her enjoyed watching Dave eviscerate anyone who disagreed with him on the show. For the next hour the calls were either congratulating Dave on what a great job he'd done with buddy from the university or saying they couldn't wait to see him at work in council.

Following Mac's advice, Dave refused to be interviewed on any of the other media outlets in the city. Dave's home phone number was unlisted, so Dr. Jones' campaign manager had to phone the radio station to propose a public debate. Mac had instructed the switchboard to send this kind of call to him. He politely refused the invitation, explaining that Fletch had all the publicity he needed. The only way he would debate Dr. Jones was if she agreed to appear on his program. Her campaign manager wisely refused the offer.

The next day, Fletch informed his public that his opponent had been offered a debate on his show and had refused. This was such an obvious sign of weakness that he wondered out loud how she even had the nerve to stay in the race. As much as the Jones campaign team tried to clarify the actual situation, most of the city had already decided what had happened.

The election was a bit of an anticlimax. Turnout at the polls was the lowest that the city had ever seen for a by-election, but Fletch won by a landslide.

The success of Fletch's radio program soared after his election to council. He began each show with his reports from City Hall. He concentrated on inefficiencies in city government and the frustrations he had as the sole honest man in the system. His most vicious comments were reserved for the new mayor. On every program he attacked the man for his inability to rule and always threw in wild insinuations about his personal life.

Two weeks after the election, the new mayor had a nervous breakdown and resigned. Fletch's callers went into overdrive insisting that their hero was the only man fit to run the city.

Protocol directed that in a situation where a deputy mayor moved up to the office of mayor and then resigned, the councilor with the most votes in the previous election would take his place. The person in this position was Russ White, a reasonably successful real estate agent. He was a shy man whose original candidacy for council nine years earlier had been as the result of a bet after a night of heavy drinking.

White rarely spoke in meetings and wasn't a member of any committees. The idea of becoming mayor terrified him.

At the council meeting after the previous mayor's resignation, the city clerk spoke and outlined the rules for succession. City staff would explain everything to Mr. White before the next meeting and a formal transfer to his new role would be arranged.

At the end of the meeting White moved over to Fletch's chair and asked if he would stay behind for a moment. Once the chambers were cleared, White got down to business.

"Mr. Fletcher... you know, I never know what to call you. Is it Dave or David or Mr. Fletcher?"

"Fletch does just fine. How can I be of assistance?"

"You just heard the clerk say that I'm supposed to be the next mayor. I would just as soon get a poke in the eye with a sharp stick. And I suspect that you would be just as hard on me as you were on the last mayor. I don't need that."

"Ah, Russ. There's no need to worry. I don't go after

anyone that doesn't deserve it. I'm sure we could work out some kind of understanding."

"Well, that's decent of you, but I don't want to be mayor. I won't take the job. I've been listening to you on the radio and I think you are the only one who can do it. What would you think if I proposed you for mayor? All I'd ask is that you leave me alone on the radio."

"Russ, my friend, I think we can work together very comfortably. Let's head downtown and see if we can find a spot with available beverages that's still open."

At the next council meeting, Russ White rose before the city clerk could begin the formalities of presenting him the mayoral chain. The councilor explained that he would not take the position of mayor and rather would move that David Fletcher take his place.

A small group of citizens in the public gallery rose to their feet and began chanting "Fletch, Fletch, Fletch." One of them held up a bristol board sign with "Mayor Fletch" clumsily written in red magic marker.

The clerk warned the crowd that they would be removed if they continued to disrupt the meeting and began to explain proper protocol. The role of mayor should be passed down to the candidate with the next most votes in the last election and Mr. Fletcher had not run in that election.

Russ White rose for only the second time in his tenure and asked the council if they were going to be bullied by one of their employees. He suggested that it was important for elected officials to be allowed to act as they felt proper.

A second councilor stood, agreed that the clerk should

not be directing important work of the council and seconded Mr. White's nomination of Fletch for mayor.

The clerk was acting as chair until a new mayor was in place, but realized that trying to stop the momentum of the occasion would jeopardize her continuing employment. This was not the time to be looking for new work.

The chair accepted the nomination and asked the council if they wished to have further discussion before a vote was taken.

Fletch rose immediately.

"I would first like to thank my two esteemed colleagues for their nomination for such an important post. I am a simple man with little ambition..."

At this point a female councilor and the clerk both coughed a little closer to their microphones than would normally be expected.

"...but, it appears that a mantle of responsibility has been placed on my shoulders by the people of our fair city. I have never desired to be mayor, but if this is the wish of the public I believe it would be a foolish mistake for us to ignore their desires. Who knows what misfortune would come to anyone who flew in the face of the obvious wishes of the people."

The crowd in the balcony rose again and roared their approval.

The clerk asked again if there was further discussion before the vote. A number of councilors squirmed in their seats, but none of them looked in the direction of either Fletch or the clerk.

Although a number of the councilors sighed as they raised their hands, the motion was passed unanimously. David Fletcher was the new mayor of St. John's.

CHAPTER 12
GET ME TO THE CAR ON TIME

John passed a number of vehicles on the side of the highway. About half of them didn't have dead people inside. As he drove by the third unacceptable car he realized that his tractor would do for the short term and there was no need for him to compromise until he found the perfect ride.

His mind wandered as he slowly made his way down the highway. His progress reminded him of times that he had been held up by sauntering farmers. Now there was no one to complain about his speed. His thirty mile per hour trajectory seemed appropriate. He realized there were hundreds if not thousands of cars within the range of his tractor.

After a short period of fantasizing about a high powered sports car - perhaps a Corvette or some foreign rocket, he realized that he needed to be practical. A sturdy, dependable car like a Mercedes Benz or BMW would be good; something top of the line and something that ran on regular gasoline. He knew there were some very good diesel powered cars, but he was concerned they might limit his ability to find fuel.

As he narrowed his search to a high end German car that was in good condition, he realized that what he needed to find was a Mercedes Benz dealership. Why should he settle for a used car when there were buildings full of new ones?

As he was wondering about how to find an appropriate car dealer, he saw a sign saying the next exits were to the town of Hudson. He'd never been there before, but he was sure this was a big enough place to have the ride he was looking for.

He wandered along a number of empty streets before he realized that random driving was an inefficient way to find his new car. There was a monotony to the strip malls and gas stations he went by and he had no idea what direction he should be heading.

He drove past the tourist centre before it occurred to him that there might be useful information inside. No one minded his slow U-turn across the four lanes of pavement. The small parking lot was empty and he pulled up right in front of the double glass doors. The tractor shuddered and snorted as he pulled the clutch to shut down the engine.

The street was silent other than the odd harmony from the wind whistling through overhead wires and the flapping flags of country, province, and town. He waved at a friendly looking dog that ambled by. The tourist office was neatly maintained with boxes of geraniums under the two front windows. Signs in French and English invited him to come inside. It bothered him to break the glass in the doors of such a neat establishment, but he couldn't think of any other way in.

The local paper was on prominent display on the front desk next to a pile of town maps. It was dated three weeks earlier and he wondered if this was an indication of when the last issue was put out or when the tourist information shop had closed.

The list of concerts and social events saddened him as he realized that none of these affairs would happen, and it was unlikely that anything like them would occur for years. It surprised him that there was nothing in the entire issue about the problems in nearby Ottawa. Was this a question of ignorance or wishful thinking?

Running through the ads at the back of the paper, he was disappointed that there was nothing mentioning a Mercedes dealership. There was an outdoor store advertising an end of summer sale and he decided to write down the address. Looking for a pen and paper to make some notes, he noticed a phone book just under the counter.

A quick look through the yellow pages gave him all the information he needed to find anything he would want in Hudson. He wrote down the addresses of all of the stores and dealerships that interested him and went to work finding the locations on the complimentary town map.

He put the phone book neatly back under the counter and pushed a large hard poster against the defect that he had broken into the glass in the front door. The place looked almost as vacantly neat as when he had first arrived.

The tractor started with his first push on the starter and he ambled across the city with his marked up map on his knee. Even with the traffic lights out and no sign of other vehicles on the roads, John stopped and looked both ways at every intersection.

The Mercedes Benz dealership was an impressive example of modern architecture, with two stories of glass across the front. He cringed as he fashioned an entrance of destruction. For a person who had followed rules so closely for his entire life, the path of vandalism and devastation that he was leaving weighed heavily on his conscience.

The showroom featured a convertible sports car, a large SUV, and a white behemoth the looked like a jeep on steroids. He poked his head through the windows of the larger vehicles and took in the new car smells. John was no automobile aficionado. To him the cars looked quite similar. Just as he was thinking of making his choice by colour he notice a rack of pamphlets sitting next to a desk.

John picked up the information about the cars in front of him and settled in behind the wheel of the sports car. The passenger's side would have been more comfortable to read in, but sitting in the driver's seat gave him a sense of control.

The white monster was an AMG c63. It was designed to force its way through the toughest terrain in decadent comfort. It looked like the kind of thing that some tinpot dictator would be driven around in. The black SUV was a GLE, a slightly smaller model that looked more like a normal car.

The fact that the GLE would stand out less appealed to him. The last thing that he needed was to attract attention. His final decision came down to the practical notion of fuel efficiency. The GLE could get him to the Maritimes on a single tank of gas. The price of the vehicle made him momentarily consider moving on to another dealership. He shook his head as he realized that money had nothing to do with this transaction.

Congratulating himself on his clever and rapid ownership of a vehicle, he slid inside. As he ran his fingers over the rich leather seats, he realized he had no way to start the motor.

It took forty minutes of searching before he came across a drawer in a salesman's desk that held a fob labeled "showroom cars."

The GLE made a satisfying throaty roar when he pushed the start button and he was relieved to see that the gas tank was nearly full. He sat wondering how the cars had been brought into the showroom for a few seconds before he put his vehicle into drive and smashed through the plate glass across the front of the dealership.

All this car shopping and vandalism had worked up an appetite and he headed for the grocery store that he'd seen on his way across town. After breaking in, he started with a quick meal of an apple with nachos, salsa. and cheese. John had been through all the planning and execution of putting together a car full of supplies before, so it didn't take him long to fill the back seat with hardy fruit and non-perishable food.

Back in the car, he took some time to look more carefully at the dashboard console as he idled in the grocery store parking lot. The massive screen had views from cameras all around the vehicle as well as a radio and a GPS. He tried the search function on both the AM and FM radio bands and wasn't surprised to find nothing.

More for fun than expecting any response, he touched

the GPS symbol and said "where is the nearest camping store?" He nearly jumped out of the car when a female voice gave clear navigational instructions. All the forms of communication he had tried had been out of order and it seemed odd that the most recently developed of all was still in operation. Satellites were made to work without much human intervention and it was apparent that at least some of them were still functioning.

John stayed in the parking lot and continued to ask directions to random addresses in the city and then to places he had lived throughout the country. The woman's voice was the most reassuring thing he had heard in over a week.

He was largely satisfied with the non-food provisions that he had chosen the first time in Ottawa. Although he hadn't had the opportunity to try everything out camping, he was satisfied that his choices were appropriate.

He folded the map from the tourist centre and addressed the GPS unit.

"Is there a name that I can call you?"

"I'm sorry, I did not understand. Please speak slowly and try your request again."

"That's OK, I'll call you Louise. Louise can you tell me how to get to a camping supply store in Hudson, Quebec?"

"Drive straight ahead for one hundred meters and turn left..."

John was thrilled with his new electronic companion.

The only change that John made in his original list from Ottawa was to add a firearm. He would still get another crossbow, but even if he never used it a rifle or handgun would at least work as a deterrent for anyone who tried to take advantage of him.

Like in Ottawa, he was surprised to find that the first outdoor store he went into had all of its weapons gone. It seemed there were a few people who had at least initially survived the virus in Hudson, but those who had were armed and keeping out of sight.

It was late in the afternoon by the time John had completely loaded his Mercedes. He decided to stay the night in Hudson, and his growing complacency with breaking into business establishments made him decide to find a hotel.

He was tired from all of his gathering of provisions and settled for the first Holiday Inn he came across. This time there was no hesitation to smash through a glass door and his new hammer made the process simple.

He brought his camp stove and some spaghetti and sauce in from the car and soon had a hot meal prepared in the restaurant. Once everything was ready he moved to the centre of the room and had a leisurely meal at a fully set table. He didn't bother to look in the kitchen for anything more than his own food.

The power was out and he found a room on the ground floor. He had no interest in climbing stairs and worried about being trapped above street level. His first inclination was to break down the door, but he decided he'd be civilized and find a key at the front desk. A thorough search showed that the only way in was with a piece of credit card shaped plastic that had to be electronically loaded. Without power, he had no way to make himself a key.

The door kicked in more easily than he thought and he was soon asleep in a comfortable bed with clean sheets.

The next morning John roamed around the ground floor of the hotel and found a cake in reasonable shape under a glass display counter in the restaurant. It had survived the time since the hotel had emptied and served as a tasty breakfast.

On the ride out from Hudson to the main highway he saw only one man on the street. He ran into a building as John's vehicle approached. The Mercedes was a powerful machine, and John was soon cruising along the Trans-Canada Highway at over 120 kilometres per hour.

There were very few abandoned cars on his side of the divided highway, but as he approached Montreal there were more and more on the side leaving the city. John played with the options on the GPS panel trying out different voices. He settled on a female British accent and kept up a discussion of various routes across the country as he drove. Despite her new inflections, she remained Louise.

John had never been to Montreal before, and he decided this would be an opportunity to see some sights when there would be no crowds. He had heard of the St. Joseph's Oratory whose supposed healing power had cured all sorts of problems. His late co-worker Beth had been a true believer Catholic and had spoken many times of her visits to this wonderful building. Louise was quick to provide him directions.

The church was located at the base of Mount Royal and he made his way to a large parking lot at the side of the building. He was intrigued to see a number of cars parked close to the church. He stopped a little way back from the other vehicles and walked along a curved pathway to the front. From the landing there were steps divided into three sections that rose to the front doors. The centre section was roped off with a sign advising it was reserved for supplicants. As he approached the top of the left set of stone stairs John could make out a large white sign fastened across the front doors. When he was close enough he could read a roughly lettered message saying: "None will be turned away in times of trouble."

He stood with his ear against one of the heavy front doors. There were voices inside laughing. He had a sudden thought that he should have brought a weapon and then reconsidered with some embarrassment. The welcoming sign and friendly sounds from within encouraged him to step inside.

A group of people turned at the creak of the door and waved to him in welcome. A slim bearded man in a robe strode towards him.

"Please come in. All are welcome in this holy place."

John had attended Protestant churches as a child but he had never stepped inside a Catholic church. He was initially intimidated by the moist coolness of the room and the eerie sight of crutches and canes lining the walls. The echo of the priest's voice and the wonder of so many people together moved him.

"Father, I am surprised. I have come from Ottawa and this is the largest group of survivors that I have seen. How is it that so many from your church are still living?"

"We are all of this church now, but we originally come from many places. Amongst us are the homeless and the wealthiest of the city. We are joined together as those who have been spared by God. We understand the blessing we have been given and we believe that in this place we can live together in peace."

"How many of you are there?"

"There are fourteen of us living here now, but others are welcome to join us at any time. We would be pleased if you would choose to stay."

"But, how do you eat and how will you survive the winter?"

"We are a congregation of many skills. There are those of us who know the city well and can find food. As we speak, there are six of our flock out foraging for sustenance. You might be surprised how many gardens there were in Montreal. Perhaps you noticed the vehicles parked outside of our church. We have a mechanic who lives with us who has procured a fleet and maintains it."

"How long do you think you can survive like this?"

"Come with me to a quiet pew at the side of the sanctuary."

They moved across the church and sat together a little away from the rest of the crowd.

"You say you came from Ottawa. How many have survived there?"

"It's hard for me to say, but it seemed there were very few living people when I left."

"We have a medical researcher with us who is skilled in statistics and he estimates that there are less than one in ten thousand in this city who have survived. Of course there are others besides us who still live here, but most are frightened to go anywhere where there are other people. Our doctor has hypothesized that the survivors with us are individuals with outstanding immune systems. He worries that we still may not be safe. We lost another of our group just two days ago and we really have no idea how long people might take to develop symptoms.

"If it would give you peace, I would be happy to take your confession."

"Thank you, Father, but I'm not a religious man. I have only come into Montreal as a kind of post-apocalyptic tourist. My hope is that things are better in Newfoundland or the Maritimes. Before the radios went down I heard rumours that Newfoundland was able to close off the island before the disease arrived."

"Come outside with me and walk a while."

They stepped out through the doors and went down the steps. At the bottom they strolled along a curving road that was lined with expensive houses.

"Fancy neighbourhood here, Father. Why don't people move into some of these houses?"

"These are troubled times and much care is required for us to survive as individuals and as a community. The city is a dangerous place now. Have you been shot at since you entered?"

"No. Are your people getting shot at?"

"The virus has spread more than disease in our city. Most survivors are filled with fear and distrust. It isn't uncommon for our food foragers to be attacked on their rounds. One of us was shot last week and died from his wounds. This is why we send out large groups looking for food. Unfortunately they sometimes must defend themselves."

"Wow. This all makes me even more anxious to get out of the city. Have you considered moving your group to some remote country location?"

"We may take that step eventually. Perhaps we may move to a more rural setting in the spring so we can begin to grow our own food, but for now there is an abundance of provisions in the city that we can take advantage of. You asked why we didn't move into the big houses in the area. These are trying times and it's important that we learn to trust each other. By having individual residences, I worry that our people would become selfish of their possessions and start to quarrel. Our present arrangements force us to live communally and rely on each other."

"It sounds to me like you've thought this out well. It's lucky that these people found a priest to lead them. I can only wish you the best of success. Considering everything you've said, I think I'll be leaving Montreal before night."

"I didn't get your name, son."

"I'm John. And what should I call you, Father?"

"Back in the church, I offered to hear your confession. It would help me immensely if I could confess something to you."

"Of course, go ahead."

"Please understand the nature of a confession. Whatever I tell you, you must never repeat to anyone."

"I have no trouble with that."

"John, I'm not a priest and like you I'm not a believer. Until this disease came along I was a hard core atheist. At this point I don't know what I believe or don't believe, but it seems to me that the people who are with me need something. I was a professor of political science at McGill University and something made me come to this church when everyone around me was dying. I'm not really sure that it was anything more than curiosity.

"There were two other survivors in the building when I came and they were completely lost and without hope. When I tried to reassure them that something would work out, they assumed I was a priest. I didn't bother to correct them and when others came, I somehow took on the role of comforter. I found this robe in a room up near the front of the church and since that time I've been a priest.

"I really don't have a clue what I'm doing. I haven't dared to hold a formal service and I've explained it by saying this is not the time for ordinary church functions. I worry every day that someone will discover what a fraud I am."

John stopped and put an arm on the other man's shoulder.

"Father, I think you are doing a wonderful job. If there is such a thing as God's work, you are certainly doing it. These people are lucky to have someone as wise and considerate as you leading them. If there is a future for anyone, it will be because of people like you.

"You haven't invited me, but I would be honoured to share a meal with your people before I go. I have plenty of food in my car and I would be happy to help with anything."

"Of course you are welcome for dinner, but keep your food. We're well supplied and I doubt that you will find any meal within miles as delicious as what we have here. Our foragers are putting most of their efforts into finding fresh fruits and vegetables. You won't get much meat, but we have some fabulous cooks in our congregation."

John stayed for the best meal that he had eaten since he had left his family in Newfoundland.

CHAPTER 13
POWER

Fletch's first two orders of business as mayor were to stop the halfway house planned for Mac's neighbourhood and to straighten out the zoning difficulties experienced by the printing shop that donated his signs.

Neither of these actions required a vote by council. The city manager looked after both problems directly after he understood that his job would be secure and his name would stay off the radio as long as he co-operated with the mayor.

Dave called the councilors individually into his office and explained his plan for the city. There were going to be difficult times ahead for the citizens of St. John's, and in order for them to be occupied and happy they would need an enemy. The people of the mainland would do in the short term, but it sounded like most of them were dead anyway. What the city needed was someone else to blame their problems on.

He went on to explain that he would hate to have to shift any guilt onto the shoulders of his colleagues on council. As long as they co-operated with him, there was no need for any of them to be vilified on his radio show.

As well, there were easier targets. He would start with the federal government and move on to the provincial government when necessary. What he didn't tell the councilors was that an idea of taking over governance of the whole province was starting to develop in his mind.

Not one of the members of council stood up to Fletch's ultimatums. They figured it was best to be on the side of the man who was an obvious winner and had the power to decide the fortunes of them all.

Fletch made it clear to staff that he considered his radio program an arm of city government. His original plan was to fire the city's public relations director, but when he spoke with the woman it was obvious she would say anything he wanted. Perhaps she could be useful.

The day after his first council meeting, Fletch began his assault on the federal government.

"Good afternoon, everyone. It's your buddy Fletch on the air on this beautiful Thursday afternoon. I'm comfortably settled into my new gig as mayor of this fine city, and I've been thinking about our needs in the new world. There are difficult times ahead for us, my friends, and we will have to do some belt tightening. And where do you think we should start? Well, I've asked myself that same question, and the answer that I've come up with is government. I'm sure you'll all agree with me that most of what government does is just to hold us back.

"Now, as you all know, there are three levels of government in the country – federal, provincial, and municipal. But the way things are, we have to ask ourselves, what does the federal government really mean?

"Like a lot of other bad things, this disease we are all

so worried about has come out of Ottawa. No surprise in that, is there?

"I'd like someone to explain to me right now what Canada means. We are cut off from the rest of the country we used to be a part of, and now they have nothing to offer us. From what I've heard, most of them are dead.

"So what did the federal government ever do for us? Let me think now. They sure did put up a lot of big expensive buildings that we paid for in the city, but what are they really doing? There's the passport office. Nobody needs a passport anymore. We aren't going anywhere, my friends. There's Fisheries. What did they ever do for anyone? The only useful thing I can think of is watching fishermen from other countries. Last I heard there are none of them left. The only other thing they do is to harass our own honest fishermen. We could certainly do without them. Then there's the penitentiary. That's federal and a lot of good it's doing. We are looking at food shortages for the honest people of this province and the government is handing out our precious resources to criminals. Do you think that's right? Of course there's also the taxation office. What do they do? They take our money and send most of it back to Ottawa – which, if you've been paying attention, you'll know practically doesn't exist any more. The little bit of money that does come back pays for all these useless offices.

"So, friends, what do you think we should do about this? Our lines are open and I'd love to hear your ideas and suggestions. We'll head to a commercial, and when we're back I'm sure we'll have a lively afternoon.

"We're back, and I have Obe on the line from way out

in Northern Bay. How are you today, Obe?"

"Good day to you, your Honour, thank you for taking the time to listen to me."

"Obe, there's no need for that kind of talk here. We're all friends. I'm still Fletch. But, in case you are interested, the proper way to refer to a mayor is your Worship."

"Well, your worship boy, I'm glad that someone is finally going to do something about DFO. I've fished all my days, and I had hoped that my boys would carry on in my steps. But DFO and the government scientists have mucked that up completely. Ever since the moratorium, kids around the bay have been kept from doing what they really should be at."

"So where are your boys now Obe?"

"Well, they are a twin Fletch. Clever lads. The older one was working in Fort Mac. We haven't heard from him since the disease came, and I'm worried that he might be gone. Now the missus says he's probably just not able to get to a phone, but it doesn't look good to me."

"I'm sorry to hear that, Obe. How about the other one?"

"He's a doctor in St. John's. But both of them would have been far ahead if they'd stayed in Northern Bay and taken up the fishing. And I blame all of that on Fisheries. Fishing is a rough business and all the feds do is make it harder for us. I say run them out of the province. We'd be far better off without them and probably save a pile of money."

"Well, Obe, I can't say that I disagree with anything you are saying. It's high time that we rid ourselves of the burden that Canada has placed on this fair island. Thank you for calling in today. And now we have a regular caller that I think you'll all recognize on line two."

The show went on with nothing but the federal Department of Fisheries being discussed. Not one caller suggested that there was anything of value that the department added to life on the island.

As the last caller finished, Dave stretched his arms and pushed his shoulders back. Before he turned he could feel Deb's strong fingers dig into the muscles of his back.

"Now that feels good. What brings you out from your little lair to my desk?"

"You aren't slowing down a bit, are you? I figured that once you got to be mayor, you would ease up a little. Don't you realize that you are in power now and maybe you should stop telling people how bad things are?"

"Deb, Deb, I've thought this all through. The people expect certain things from Fletch and I can't just change who I am just because I'm mayor. If I ease off or slow down, people will realize how little food they have and they'll move on to the next rabble-rouser before we realize what's happened."

"Well Dave – and I'd like to think there is still a Dave in there somewhere – there's one thing that you may want to consider in this campaign against the federal government."

"And what would that be, my wise and helpful producer?"

"You realize that the military is federal don't you? Do you remember that there is a fully armed frigate in the harbour? Who do you think their loyalty lies with and what do you think they will do if the sovereignty of the country is challenged? They've already shown that they are ready to come into the city and take what they want. Don't fool yourself into thinking that the local police would stand a chance against them. Remember, too, that most of the police force in the rest of the province are employed by the federal government."

Fletch was uncharacteristically silent after her outburst. He fiddled with the cord of his headphones for an extended period before he meekly answered.

"You've got some good points there, Deb. I've always said you were a fine producer. I'm going to have to keep you around."

The next morning Fletch drove up to City Hall and called his public relations director into his office.

"Mary, when I first took on this job, my inclination was to fire you. I've always looked after my own image, and I've done it directly on the radio. I'm not sure I need any more help with publicity."

"I completely understand your concern, sir."

"But, Mary, I've seen you at work and you are clever with words. I think we might be able to help each other."

"I'm more than willing to do what I can, sir. I've worked at public relations all of my career, and I must confess that I haven't seen anyone much better at it than you."

"Why thank you, Mary. Now I have a job for you this morning. I'd like you to go on down to the harbourfront and see the captain of the *St. John's*, whatever his name is."

"He's Captain Pickford, sir."

"Yes, Captain Pickford. I'd like you to invite him for a

meeting at my office tonight, say at eight o'clock. Sometime after everyone has left for the day."

"Very good, sir. I'm on my way now."

That evening after everyone had left, Dave waited inside the locked front doors of City Hall. At precisely eight pm a tall muscular man with short red hair stiffly approached the entrance. He wore regular street clothing, but the man's manner made Dave assume this was the Captain of the *St. John's*.

He unlocked the door and leaned through the opening.

"Good evening. You must be Captain Pickford."

Pickford extended his hand and moved inside.

"I am. Please excuse the informality of my attire. Your assistant insisted that I dress as a civilian for our meeting."

Fletch thought he'd decided well when he kept Mary. She understood the sensitivity of the meeting and the importance of no one knowing that the mayor was meeting privately with the Captain of the *St. John's*.

They exchanged pleasantries as Dave led the naval officer to the elevators and then to his office.

"Please have a seat, Captain. Can I offer you anything to drink?"

"We are outside of regular hours and I am not in uniform. If you have Scotch I wouldn't be averse to a drop."

Dave poured them each a generous glassful and got down to business.

"These are strange times, Captain. I'm sure you've heard the reports from the mainland. The best we can figure is that very, very few people are still alive in the rest of North America and likely in the world."

"That is also my understanding of the situation, Mr. Mayor."

"Please, call me Fletch. We have important things to talk about, and I'm hoping that you and I will become very helpful to each other."

"Alright, Fletch, what's on your mind?"

"Tell me, Captain, who do you work for?"

"As you no doubt realize, I am an officer in the Royal Canadian Navy and, as such, work for the Government of Canada and ultimately the people of our great country. When I began my career in the armed forces I swore an oath of allegiance to the Queen of Canada and her heirs and survivors."

"We heard some early reports out of England that indicate things are just as bad there as in Canada. What do you think the chances are that the Queen or any of her heirs or successors are still living?"

"I have thought of this, Mr. Fletch. I think it's fair to assume that it's very unlikely that there is anything left of the monarchy."

"You mentioned the federal government. You take orders from the Department of Defence. This disease started in Ottawa. Do you think there is the slightest chance that there is anything left that resembles the Department of National Defence let alone the Government of Canada?"

"It certainly appears that there has been a complete breakdown of the chain of command. Since we have been in St. John's, I have tried to contact my superiors without success."

"So is it fair to say that you are your own commander

at this point?"

"That is how I understand the situation."

"Now see, Captain, to me this presents a serious problem. I'm no scholar on political systems, but my understanding is that military dictatorships are generally bad. As well, I'm not sure how you intend to pay the men on your ship."

"These are both points that I have given much thought to."

"Any legitimate military force requires some kind of oversight from a body elected by the people, and the city is in a position that we could pay your sailors."

"That sounds fair to me, sir."

"I have a proposal for you, Captain. Please, hear me out, and then you can go away and take your time considering what I suggest. You and I have problems that I believe we can solve together. I am in charge of a city in a time when security is critical. We need a way to keep infected outsiders from coming to our island and spreading the disease and we need a way to keep the locals in line if things go south and panic breaks out. You need civilian oversight to keep your power legitimate.

"What I am proposing is that we put you and all of your crew on city payroll. You will become the man in charge of the military arm of our government. I don't think it should be difficult to convince the militia in the province and the RCMP to work under you. I'm sure they will all see the need for some central control of armed forces in the province."

"There is some logic to your suggestion, but why wouldn't this fall to the provincial government?"

"That is an excellent point, Captain. There are a number of reasons for you to align yourself with the city. First, you command a ship called the *St. John's*. Doesn't it seem reasonable that this ship should be affiliated with its namesake city? Second, the provincial government knows nothing of enforcement. They have only the Royal Newfoundland Constabulary under them and it is basically a St. John's organization anyway. Their ignorance of military matters would mean that you would be constantly tied up in mountains of red tape. The final reason is that most of the people in this province and almost all of the financial power are in this city. The people of St. John's will want self governance and they will not be stopped."

"You do present an intriguing offer, Mr. Mayor. I'll do as you suggest and take your ideas back to the *St. John's* to consider."

CHAPTER 14
MORE DEADLAND

As soon as John finished his meal in St. Joseph's Oratory, he walked out to his car with the priest.

"I have enjoyed your visit, John, and our discussion has been most helpful to me. When you start your car, you may notice that your fuel tank is completely full. I had one of the men top it up. You do realize that a Mercedes Benz GLE should be driven with premium fuel? You need to be careful which vehicles you siphon your gas from."

This was no ordinary priest. Despite his unusual ecclesiastical provenance, there was no question that he was the most helpful religious leader that John had ever encountered. He felt confident that the community of the St. Joseph's Oratory would continue on and perhaps even thrive. In a way, what was happening there was a miracle that outshone the healings suggested by the canes and crutches hung around the church.

On his way through the city, he saw a single woman running into a building and another man with a rifle standing in front of a grocery store with broken windows. At one point he made out two figures on the roof of a five-story building. They looked to be young and armed, but he didn't slow down to be sure. The chilling darkness of the place went far beyond the atmosphere that the setting sun was implying. Louise took him efficiently back to the highway and this time he didn't stop or even hesitate going through intersections.

As he left the outskirts of the city, he decided he would spend the night in his car. He pulled off at the first minor exit he found and took smaller and smaller turnoffs until he was in uninhabited countryside. When Louise complained that he was not going the right direction to get to Quebec City, John explained that this was a minor diversion to find a safe place to sleep.

He pulled the car into a thick grove of trees and shifted material behind him so that the front seat would recline. His experience in Montreal had given him hope that there were good people left with reasonable strategies for survival. If his plans for Newfoundland didn't work out, he might return to the church group. Despite his optimism, he didn't sleep well that night. The overhead rustling of leaves was erratically interrupted by coyote howls, and at one point there was a loud sound that he was sure was a gunshot.

The next morning as John boiled water for his oatmeal, he realized that he didn't have a specific plan for how he would get to Newfoundland. He had travelled from the island to the mainland a number of times when he was younger and had always come through Sydney. Before that moment, he had carelessly assumed that he would take the same route.

The only reason anyone travelled through Sydney was for the ferry. There was obviously going to be no routine movement from Nova Scotia to the island. The ferry would either be tied up uselessly in Sydney or permanently in Newfoundland.

In order for him to get to the island he would have to find some way to cross the ocean. It was a long sail from Sydney to Port aux Basques. In the north Atlantic this wasn't a trip that he could make in some vessel that he could commandeer and pilot himself. The only option was to find someone alive in Nova Scotia who would take him across. The more he considered the idea, the more he realized that it was impractical.

He concluded that his only real chance of getting home was to head north to the Strait of Belle Isle, a small stretch of water separating the north shore of Quebec from the northern peninsula of Newfoundland.

John took out the Quebec road map he had picked up at the tourist centre in Hudson. The closest community to Newfoundland was Blanc Sablon. He was surprised to see that driving to that town would involve a long diversion north into Labrador. He told Louise of his plans and asked about the route he should take and the distance involved. She first suggested he should drive to Sydney, but when John reminded her that the ferry wasn't running, she gave details on Quebec route 389 and the Trans Labrador Highway. She told him the trip would be just under 2,200 kilometres from where he was and estimated it would take him thirty-one hours.

Consulting his road map, John decided he could do the trip in four days. Stops in Baie-Comeau, Labrador City, and Goose Bay would divide the drive into nearly equal sections. A check in the GLE's manual confirmed that his vehicle could do each of these drives on less than a tank of gas.

It was well after ten am by the time he got back on the main highway. The route to Quebec City was monotonous. It was all four lanes and designed for efficiency rather than scenic considerations. There were more cars abandoned on this stretch of road than he had seen since leaving Ottawa.

As he crossed to the north shore of the St. Lawrence River, he considered whether he should go into Quebec City for a visit to the beautiful old walled section and take one last opportunity to pick up supplies. He slowed down at the first exit and then moved on. He had everything he wanted, and there was no need to expose himself to the dangers that cities presented.

A little farther on, he pulled off by an apple orchard and enjoyed fresh fruit with his lunch of crackers and tinned ham.

It was after seven pm when he reached the roundabout that directed him into the small town of Baie-Comeau. He crossed a bridge and drove down the main street. The place was filled with featureless aluminum warehouses and strip malls. When he saw the sign for a Comfort Inn, he considered breaking in for the night. As he pulled in off the highway he could see three human corpses in the parking lot. A fierce looking, floppy jowled dog stepped out from behind a pickup truck and was soon joined by a pack composed of everything from a husky to a poodle. The lead dog sniffed the air and confidently walked towards John's car. A large black animal near the back of the group carried something wet and red in its mouth.

It hadn't occurred to him that animals would inevitably clean up human remains if no one was left to bury the dead. The thought convinced him to sleep in his vehicle just outside of town rather than trying to find another hotel to stay in.

The dark came on quickly after he'd finished his supper. This time he had no appetite to look for anything fresh to eat. The canned stew that he opened was completely tasteless.

Even though he was stiff from his hours in the car, he limited his time outside in the dark to a short trip to relieve himself. He wasn't sure if the barking and howling he heard was from dogs, coyotes, or wolves, and it worried him to consider what they were celebrating. Beyond the canine sounds he could make out nothing but silence.

As the darkness deepened he decided to end the day with more conversation with Louise about the preferred routes to various towns in Quebec. He turned on the car's auxiliary power and immediately the radio came on. He was reaching to switch over to GPS when he heard a faint suggestion of music. The sound oscillated on and off, but it was unmistakably "Bang a Gong." He hadn't heard the tune for years, but memories of high school dances rushed into his head. The song had been an antique even when he was a teenager, but its rhythm and melody had always appealed to him.

John played with the controls wishing that he had an old fashioned car radio with a tuning nob so he could accurately zero in on the active wavelength. With some time and patience he improved the reception and then leaned back to enjoy the music. He assumed that some abandoned station with generator power had left a loop running.

The song ended and John was amazed to hear a man's voice verifying that this was T Rex he'd been listening to and next up was "Born to be Wild" by Steppenwolf. John's first reaction was to wish he had music like this to listen to on the unchanging miles he'd driven since Montreal. Next, he wondered if this was a real man in a radio station or a tape that included introductions from a recently deceased disc jockey.

After the organ and overdriven guitars of Steppenwolf died away, a commercial for a law firm played and the man's voice returned. He sped through the name of the station and listed off a series of repeaters.

"They don't make music like that anymore and it sure looks like they won't be making much music of any kind for a long time outside of our wonderful island. Newfoundland has always been able to provide our own entertainment, and I'm sure we'll continue to amuse ourselves even if we're alone. Now here's a blast from the past with Great Big Sea."

John couldn't control his excitement. He banged his fist into the dashboard and honked his horn. Newfoundland had survived. The way the disc jockey talked, it sounded like things were almost normal. There was no suggestion of despair in his voice. The world was looking better. John had a safe place to escape to and most of a plan for how to get there. Another few days of driving and a short trip across the straits and he'd be safe and home.

When John woke the next morning every muscle in his body ached. Hours of driving and two nights sleeping in a car seat had taken their toll. With the horrors of the previous day deeply stuck into the back of his mind, he started the car and began a search for fresh food and refreshment.

On his way back into Baie-Comeau, he pulled off the bridge and drove down to the river. With a yell, he stopped the car, peeled off his clothes and jumped into the cool, clear current. He was treading water about ten meters off shore when he realized that he had left his car with keys inside and the door opened. Surely, his experience in the park outside of Hudson should have taught him something. The realization crushed his gleeful mood and he started for the shore in a stumbling panic. Not a person or animal was in view as he stood panting by the side of the vehicle. Things were definitely looking up, but he would have to remember to be careful for the rest of his trip. One moment of inattention could ruin everything.

John had a breakfast of fresh fruits and vegetables from gardens he found down side streets in the town and set about the task of refueling his GLE. He thought this would be a minor inconvenience until the priest's reminder that his car took premium gas came back to him.

John had never been a car aficionado. He appreciated beautiful vehicles and the comfort of something like the one he was driving, but he really didn't know much about how they worked. He knew that if anything went wrong with his car, the only option would be to find another one.

Now there was the question of getting the right gas. Of course, he'd always seen premium fuel at gas stations, but he had no idea what that meant. Was it absolutely necessary to use this fancy fuel in his Mercedes? He knew there was no way he could get gas from pumps at the service stations. His only source was siphoned fuel from abandoned cars. How was he supposed to know which cars had premium gas in them?

Louise would be no help with a question like this, and he sat discouraged for a while. Maybe he had made a big mistake when he unknowingly took a vehicle that required special fuel.

After a few minutes of brooding and self-doubt, he decided that the reasonable approach was to find the fanciest looking cars he could and assume that they would have premium gas inside.

There were plenty of cars on the streets of Baie-Comeau, but most of them were quite ordinary. He spotted a big BMW in front of a pizza place and immediately got out his siphon and gas can. He was disappointed how quickly he was able to empty the BMW. When he poured his siphoned fuel into his car, it only put the gas gauge up to the quarter full mark. It took him another three cars go get enough gas to fill his tank. For all of this effort, he still wasn't certain that he had premium fuel. He could only hope that the best looking cars in the town had provided what he needed.

Louise directed John back to an intersection with a sign saying that a left turn would take him to Fermont, Port Cartier, and Sept Iles. A short drive through an industrial section of town brought him to another turn to highway 389 and Fermont. Continuing straight would have brought him on to Sept Iles, which was in the direction he wanted to go, but the highway ended well before Blanc Sablon.

Less than a kilometre after the turn, the landscape changed completely. The straight highway lined with controlled confers was replaced by a curving and undulating road with poplar, birch, and rock edging in close to the shoulders. The change made for an interesting if somewhat slower drive.

The transformation of the scenery emphasized John's feeling that he was finally on his way to Newfoundland. A disheveled moose crossed the road just after he passed a red sign with a picture of a telephone receiver and the letters SOS. His first thought was that he must be careful, because he was so far from any possible assistance. It didn't take long to realize that he was no farther from help than when he had been driving through what had once been heavily populated sections of Quebec.

About three hours into his drive there was a sign with large lights and the words "Barree quand les feux clingnotent." John's French wasn't good, but he could decipher enough to understand that flashing lights meant the road was closed. Just as he was wondering what would cause a road closure here in the middle of nowhere, he looked up to see an enormous grey structure. A wall of cement that suggested a Roman aqueduct on steroids towered up in front of him. The concrete rose up over a hundred feet and was lined with massive oval topped concavities.

Another sign announced that this was the Manic 5 power station. No doubt manic meant something different in French than what it suggested in English. He pulled off and looked up at the structure, thinking for all the silence around it the name was appropriate. With no one maintaining the dam, it was just a matter of time before something failed and tons of cement would collapse and unleash millions of gallons of water on the surrounding environment.

It was time for a midday meal, but John wasn't comfortable stopping in the shadow of the dam.

Immediately after Manic 5, the road turned to gravel. For the first time in his journey he had a real feeling of being in the wilderness. It seemed appropriate to get flour from the back of his car and fry up bannock. He had no doubt that the road was based on old voyageur trails, and heated beans and bannock would be a perfect compliment to the place's history.

The road narrowed and got even more convoluted than it had been before the dam. There were no signs posting a speed limit, but he seldom got the GLE over sixty kilometres per hour. About two hours on from the dam, the slow progress and rough ride convinced him that Louise's suggestion of an eight-hour drive was hopelessly optimistic. His back ached and his hands were tired from grasping the steering wheel. He was just about ready to pull over for a break when the pavement returned.

The road wasn't any straighter, but the ride was improved immensely. His spirits rose enough for him to start asking Louise for directions to places he knew he would never visit again.

The trip to the Newfoundland border from Bay-Comeau was just over five hundred and sixty kilometres and John decided he would stop and celebrate at five hundred. He was a stubborn driver and hadn't got out of the car since his lunch. Louise's display told him they were nearly there when the gravel returned.

There was only about an hour of driving left to Fermont, but the rough surface frustrated him enough that he refused to stop and get out.

John had heard stories about Fermont when he was a kid growing up in Newfoundland. An uncle of his who worked in the mines in Labrador City came home with stories of a strange town just across the border.

Fermont sat on a rich iron ore vein that was just about as far from Quebec civilization as you could get in that province. In order to convince workers to come to this remote site and stay, the company had built a huge mall like structure for the miners and their families. Under one roof there were apartments, a shopping mall, an ice rink, a swimming pool and a boxing ring. Everything everyone needed was under one roof.

The problem with indoor Fermont was that it was too complete. The families of miners found they had no reason to ever leave the complex during the fiercely cold northern Quebec winters. The result was one of the highest suicide rates in any community in North America.

John was curious about what the Fermont mall looked like, but he'd seen enough abandoned buildings, and the place's history had a darkness that strangely mirrored the devastation of the present. He couldn't imagine what he would find inside.

He didn't even slow down going by Fermont. It was only a short drive to Labrador City where he would be finally in the province that he'd set out for. Still, he realized he was a long way from being back and safe on the island portion of the province.

CHAPTER 15
MILITARY DECISIONS

Walking back from City Hall to the *St. John's*, Pickford was amazed at the life he saw on George Street. While most of the restaurants in the city were suffering, the bars on this stretch were thriving. Music blared from open windows and groups of girls in torn stockings and tight, low-necked T-shirts wandered by in packs. He knew from previous visits to the city that the street really came alive much later than this. If George Street had ever suffered from the realities of the disease, it seemed it had recovered.

No one paid attention to him as he made his way down to the harbourfront.

Strolling along out of uniform, he relished his temporary freedom from the heavy responsibility that came with his position. He also knew that he would soon have to respond to the mayor's offer. His choice could put him in a place of power that he had never hoped for or dreamed of.

Once on board the ship, he received the Duty Officer's report and retired to his quarters. His decision could wait until the next morning.

Captain Pickford started most days with reports from his weather man and the officer who had been on the bridge through the night. Even though the *St. John's* wasn't at sea, he insisted that all of his briefings were to continue. Since being docked, the weather was of little consequence and nothing beyond minor scuffles between bored sailors was reported.

He waited until nine am before contacting the provincial government. The mayor's suggestion that the federal government was a thing of the past was plausible, but he felt that the next logical place for his allegiance was with the province.

Pickford didn't know anyone in provincial politics in Newfoundland, so he started with the phone book. There was a listing for the office of the premier and he dialed the number. An aloof sounding woman answered articulately.

"Good morning, I'm Captain Pickford commanding officer of the HMCS *St. John's*, and I wonder if I might be able to speak with the premier."

"I'm sorry, sir, the premier is currently preparing for a meeting with cabinet this morning."

"Thank you, ma'am. Could you tell me when I might be able to talk with him?"

"Indeed, sir. He will be in the house this afternoon and he has a press conference this evening. Tomorrow he has a meeting with some poultry producers and the minister of agriculture and then he is scheduled to be in Marystown the following day to open a new welding room at the shipyards. If you would like to leave your number, I could have his assistant call you back later in the day."

"Yes, thank you. As I mentioned, I am from the HMCS *St. John's*. I'm sure you have heard of her. She's the navy frigate in the harbour. I have some rather pressing business that I would like to speak with the premier about."

"I understand you are captain of a boat in the harbour, but, sir, you must realize that there are many people who want the ear of the premier. He is a very busy man, and he can't just talk with every boat captain who calls in."

Captain Pickford was a patient man, but he was fast reaching his limit.

At three that afternoon a call came in to the captain.

"Captain Pickford, this is Matt Ryerson. I'm the premier's executive assistant and I understand that you called us this morning."

"Mr. Ryerson, I need to talk with the premier concerning an issue of provincial security."

"If you are aware of a threat against the premier, I can put you through to someone on his security detail."

"No. You're not getting this. The province is in a precarious position vis- á-vis the pandemic, which has apparently devastated most of the planet. You require a plan to keep the island secure. All it would take is one infected individual landing here to cause complete devastation. I have a fully equipped frigate in the St. John's harbour and I might be able to help."

"But you're with the Navy aren't you? The armed forces are national entities and we would never pretend to encroach on matters under federal jurisdiction."

"Don't you understand that there is no federal government? You and the people you work for need to see that there are things that the feds were once responsible for that you will have to start looking after."

"The premier is very sensitive about questions of federal-provincial authority. Constitutionally, our government has no dealings in matters pertaining to the military or defence. I will make him aware of your concerns, but I can almost guarantee that his positions will reflect what I have been saying."

Pickford hung up the phone without saying any more and dialed the number that David Fletcher had given him.

"Hello, the mayor here."

"Mr. Mayor, it's Captain Pickford speaking. I would like to get together with you again. I've thought about your suggestion and I think that we can work something out."

The negotiations didn't take long. Neither Fletch nor the captain were men who worried about bureaucratic details. At the next city council meeting, the motion to add the crew of the HMCS *St. John's* to the city's payroll was passed unanimously.

The main problem plaguing the city was a lack of food. The stock of anything that came from outside the province was being used up quickly. Even some who could find food were beginning to show signs of malnutrition. There was a healthy supply of fish, but fresh vegetables and wheat-based products were becoming scarce.

As well, anyone who worked for companies based outside of Newfoundland was not being paid. Among those not receiving compensation were all employees of the federal government.

For the first month of the island's isolation, federal civil servants were given cheques produced on the island with a promise that the government would be good for them. Real problems began when a provincial credit union decided that since the federal government no longer existed, they would no longer accept their cheques. The rest of the banks in the province quickly followed suit.

Fletch kept up his radio assault on federal civil servants, but by the time his audience was enraged enough to march on the Fisheries office, there was no one there. None of the employees were interested in coming in to a job that offered no likelihood of pay.

The day after the futile move on the Fisheries office, Fletch got a troubling call on his show.

"Mr. Fletcher?"

"That's me, and who might I be speaking with?"

"My name's Mike. I'm not sure if you know how difficult it's getting for some of us in the city to eat. I've used up pretty well everything in the house, and there is nothing left in any of the grocery stores. I know that there are people living near me who are sick from lack of food. It's not even winter yet, how are we supposed to survive?"

"I can sympathize with you, Mike. These are difficult times and all of us are going to have to do some belt tightening."

"This isn't a question of belt tightening, sir. This is a question of starvation. I'm not sure how I'm going to be able to find anything to eat by the end of the week. My wife's brother is in the pen and those lowlifes in there aren't worried about getting a meal. No, sir, they're living high off the hog. Perhaps I'd be best to murder someone so that I would be looked after."

"Now, Mike, don't you think that's a bit of an over reaction? Things will work out. We Newfoundlanders always find a way around things. I'm going to have to let you go, Mike, there are lots of people lined up to talk today."

The next caller said he had originally called in to complain about the potholes in his section of the city, but now that he'd heard Mike's call, he would like to second his suggestion that the inmates at Her Majesty's were getting off easy.

The rest of the show was dominated by people with opinions about jail conditions. The least rabid response was that the province should let all the drug offenders out and concentrate its resources on keeping the city safe from the most violent criminals. Many suggested that the place should be abandoned and locked up. The animals inside could look after themselves.

After the show, Deb approached Fletch in the hall outside of their studio.

"Why did you let them go on about the pen so long? You said it was federal, but you know that the place is the province's responsibility. All you had to do was to tell everyone to phone up the provincial justice department. People went away thinking that this somehow had something to do with you."

"Deb, you heard that first guy saying that he was worried about having enough food? That's our real problem. I don't care what people are upset about as long as it's not the food. But you are right. Tomorrow, I'll tell them it's the province's fault."

Fletch's next show concentrated on the inefficiencies

of the provincial government. He reminded his listeners of the previous day's discussion of jail conditions and suggested that everyone should phone their member, the minister of justice, and the premier.

When Dave arrived at his office in City Hall there was a message waiting for him to call the premier as soon as possible.

"Mr. Premier, this is the mayor of St. John's, how can I help you this afternoon?"

"First off, Mr. Mayor, I must congratulate you on your rather meteoric rise to political power. We haven't had the opportunity to speak since your election and I realize this has been an oversight on my part."

"No offence taken. I'm sure you are a busy man."

"Mr. Fletcher, I must take issue with some of the things you have been saying on your radio program. We in power all try to do the best we can, and those of us at different levels of government must sometimes scratch each other's backs. There is no need for any of us to make life more difficult for the other."

"Mr. Premier, I don't need anyone scratching my back. I'm sure there is some specific reason that you are calling me today."

"Yes, I'm concerned about you stirring up of passions around the situation at Her Majesty's Penitentiary. We have one hundred and eighty prisoners housed there at this time and I have no idea of how we are going to feed them. Your rhetoric only makes the situation more difficult."

"That's not my problem, Mr. Premier."

"And I suppose you think you could do a better job

with the prison?"

"Without a doubt. You are in way over your head."

"So what would you think if the government decided tomorrow to hand over jurisdiction of the pen to St. John's?"

"I'd be perfectly happy with that, but I know you don't have the spine to let it go."

"Watch me, Mr. Fletcher, just watch me."

Two days later a motion was presented to the house of assembly to transfer the jurisdictional responsibility for Her Majesty's Penitentiary and the St. John's Lockup to the city. The opposition leader protested that this move marked the beginning of the fall of the institution of provincial government. There were difficult decisions to be made, but passing such important institutions off to city government was an abdication of responsibility.

When the vote was called, all government members and half of the opposition supported the motion. There was general relief in the chamber when the burden of prison maintenance was off their shoulders.

The speed of the transfer was unusual for government. Within a week, all of the funds allocated for maintaining the St. John's prisons were moved to the city, and all staff were told that they had a new employer.

Immediately after the provincial vote, Dave held a meeting with Mary, Mac, and Captain Pickford.

"Thanks for coming in this evening at such short notice. I'm sure you've all heard that we will be looking after the St. John's prisons. This may seem like a burden, but I'm sure there's some way that we can twist this so it works in our favour."

"So are we getting the money they used to run the pen?"

"We are, Mac. Otherwise I wouldn't even look at this."

"Well it seems simple to me. We find some way to run these places for less money and laugh all the way to the bank."

"But, Mac, there are a hundred and eighty people in the pen. We need guards and we need to feed everyone inside. Despite what some of my lovely callers think, we can't just shut the doors and let those people starve."

Mary was the next to comment.

"My suggestion is to have a hard look at who is in there. If they aren't a danger to society, we should let them go. It's too bad we couldn't just banish them from the city. They're probably not going to hurt anyone, but I don't want them in my neighbourhood."

"Mary, you may have stumbled onto something there. You know, in the navy we have problems with misbehaving sailors. One of the frustrations on a ship is that you have to keep them close at hand. I can't tell you how many times I've wished that I could leave some troublemaker behind in Sudan or Australia. Perhaps we can banish some of them. What would you think about taking the very worst of them and sending them off to the mainland?"

Dave sat up straight and tapped his pen on the table.

"Good plan, Pickford. I know how we can sell this too. We make a big announcement that we will be taking the most serious offenders in our jails and giving them passage to Nova Scotia. We can present this as a kind of experiment. We say that we'll drop them off in Sydney and check on them again in six months. This is a win-win situation. We get rid of these animals and we have canaries in Nova Scotia to see what the disease situation is. If they die, it's no great loss, and, if they survive, we'll know that the mainland is safe for us to travel to again."

The captain spoke again.

"This sounds good to me. If we send the worst of them to the mainland, and let the minor offenders go with a warning that they will be off to Nova Scotia at the first whiff of trouble, we should be able to get the prison population down to maybe a couple of dozen. I think it would be a good idea to keep a few so that we have more to send off to check on the mainland later."

"Now, this is the way to run a city. I appreciate all of your wise counsel, and I'll be announcing our decision on my show tomorrow."

Two days later, sixty inmates from Her Majesty's Penitentiary were released. Before they were let go, Captain Pickford addressed them all in the prison's cafeteria.

"The city has decided to allow all of you gentlemen to go free. We have concluded that you are not threats to anyone and perhaps should not have been in prison in the first place. I wish you all the best of luck, but I leave you with one warning. We will be keeping a close eye on all of you, and if there is the slightest suggestion that you are causing trouble we will apprehend you. When we do, we will not be returning you to Her Majesty's. We will be sending you to the mainland. I'm sure you've all heard of conditions there, so keep that in mind as you leave today."

Three days later, seventy of the most violent offenders

were moved by police van from the prison to locked rooms on the HMCS *St. John's*. Once they were all aboard, the frigate made a quick trip to North Sydney. Sailors armed with machine guns watched as the men were unloaded on the Sydney wharf. Each of them had a small bag with the possessions that they had stored while in jail. The officer in command told the questionably liberated prisoners that the *St. John's* would return in six months.

The response from the men was a series of catcalls and middle fingers. As the boat left the wharf, the men dispersed into North Sydney in small groups.

As the *St. John's* approached the island of Newfoundland, the Executive Officer received a call from Captain Pickford on shore, ordering him to anchor just outside the Narrows for seven days. He had been reluctant to have his vessel leave port without him on board, but now he wasn't willing to take the chance that his beloved ship had brought virus back to the island.

CHAPTER 16
HOME PROVINCE

As John drove along the highway that skirted Labrador City, he wondered if it was possible that the disease hadn't reached such an isolated centre. The first exit to the town didn't look promising, but he turned in the next road when he saw a Walmart and Tim Hortons. The stores gave him comfort, but he soon realized that there were no more people in this city than any of the other places he had been through. If the virus had reached Labrador City, it was unlikely anywhere else in the world had been spared.

He wandered up and down the streets until he came to a small motel called the Two Seasons Inn. His back ached and his arms were sore from sitting and driving so long in the car. He reasoned that if there were any survivors here, they would be of a friendlier sort than those in the big cities, so he would take his chances staying at the Inn.

For the first time, he felt no hesitation breaking the glass of a front door. He was too tired to put together any kind of proper meal but took an odd satisfaction in finishing up the pop, chips, and candy in his room's mini bar. The bed was soft, and he slept dreamlessly for the first night in a long time.

John woke with the sun, optimistic that his life had turned around. Just two more days of driving and he would be within sight of the island of Newfoundland. He was certain that he could find some way to cross the narrow channel from the north shore of Quebec unnoticed.

As a celebration of his sunny mood, John decided that he would have a special breakfast. He had picked up instant pancake mix and maple syrup way back in Hudson and hadn't had the patience to use them yet.

He whistled as he undid the uselessly locked front door. His car was parked close to the front, and he didn't see the girl until he pointed his fob at the vehicle.

She looked to be about eighteen years old and must have been hiding behind the Mercedes until he came out. She hesitantly raised her hand to the level of her face and slowly moved her upper arm back and forth from the elbow.

John swallowed and coughed before he could manage any words.

"Good morning."

"Hello, sir. You aren't from here are you?"

"No. No. I've just driven in from Ontario. Do you live here?"

"I do, sir. I'm Mandy."

"Hi, Mandy. I'm John. Please call me John. When you say 'sir' it sounds like you're talking to my father."

"OK, John, I'm pleased to meet you."

Mandy was skinny with stringy blond hair and a triangular face. It was obvious that she hadn't washed or changed her clothes in a long time.

"Is there anyone here other than you, Mandy?"

"No, sir. I've been walking around town for two weeks now looking for someone to talk to. I haven't found anyone."

"Did people die or did they move away somewhere?"

"I think a few people drove off to cabins in the bush, but the ones I saw packing up were already coughing. As far as I can tell, anyone who coughs dies."

"But there are no dead people in the streets or in cars."

"If you go down to the hospital, you'll see lots of dead people. They're in the parking lot piled up. It's the same at the arena. I don't know why people would go to the hockey rink to die. I think that most people just tried to hide in their houses.

Everyone got scared as soon as the problems started. I haven't had the nerve to go into any of them. I've been sleeping outside since my parents passed."

"So, you're the only one left in the whole town?"

"Until right now, I haven't seen a living person for three weeks. Yesterday I saw a bear and I'm not sure, but it looked like it was dragging a dead kid out of town. I didn't get close enough to really see, but it scared me pretty bad. You can't believe how happy I am to see someone alive."

She moved one step toward John and raised both arms before abruptly stopping and looking at the ground.

She was just a scrawny kid and John didn't feel the least bit of attraction, but rather an overwhelming sense of protectiveness.

"Hey, Mandy. Look at me. We are going to be all right. I've been listening to the radio and it sounds like things are still good on the island. I'm driving down to Blanc Sablon and then making my way over to safety. You can come with me if you like. We're going to be OK."

Mandy's tears overcame John's sense of awkwardness and he moved forward and put his arms around her. At first contact, she broke into heavy sobbing and let her inconsequential weight fall against him.

"Hey, Mandy, how would you like some pancakes?"

This return to the mundane of everyday life pulled her back together. She stood back from John and nodded enthusiastically. He opened the vehicle and pulled out his cooking set and pancake ingredients.

"This will be a special meal. We'll be using Two Seasons deluxe bottled water in our cooking this morning."

The pancakes were somehow both burned and undercooked at the same time, but neither of them complained. Their conversation lightened as they told each other their stories and dreams.

John explained that they had two important jobs before they started on the road east and south. First, they had to find the fanciest cars in Labrador City for fuel to siphon into the Mercedes and then they had to go shopping for new clothes for Mandy.

They drove around town looking for likely sources of premium gasoline. Luck was with them when they came across another car just like theirs that had almost a full tank.

"Now that we have our gas, I'm going to show you how we shop in a world where no one else lives. Show me your favourite clothing store in Lab City."

Mandy gave directions and they pulled up at a fashionable place in a strip mall. John took his hammer from the back seat and walked to the front door.

"Here's my key and here's how we open the door."

He leaned back and demolished the glass in the doorway with one smash. Mandy raised her hands over her face and looked away as John reached through the new opening to unlock the door and pull the ruined frame open.

"After you, mademoiselle."

Mandy couldn't help but laugh and strut just a little as she walked into the shop.

"Take your time and pick out three or four of the nicest sets of sensible clothes that you can find. It's not stealing if you aren't taking it from anyone and as far as I can tell there is no one here but us. I'm going to use my little key on the convenience store just over there, and I'll get us a couple of cans of pop and some bars for the drive. Next stop, Goose Bay."

The five hundred kilometres from Labrador City to Goose Bay flew by. Although the road twisted and turned for most of its length, it was completely paved. Near the halfway point they stopped like tourists to admire the dam at Churchill Falls. John didn't share his worrisome feeling that without human maintenance, these giant concrete structures would soon disintegrate.

They both cheered at every mileage sign for Goose Bay and got out and danced around the car when they entered the town.

Mandy had been to Goose Bay a number of times before. She had an aunt and uncle there, but never suggested that they should try to find them. Goose Bay had the same dead feel as Labrador City and every other community that John had come through.

As they drove the main road through the town, John pointed at a large blue structure labeled the Hotel North.

"How about if we pull in here for the night?"

"Can we find another place? That's where my parents always took us. I'm not sure I can handle the memories just now."

John understood and kept driving until he found a place called the Royal Inn and Suites. It seemed over-optimistically named, but it would do for the night. They pulled up next to the door and John reached back for his hammer.

"I'll just open up the front door here at reception and we'll find ourselves some rooms."

Inside, John was pleased to see that the place used regular keys.

"Looks like the rooms are in that building behind us. I assume the ones starting with a one are on the first floor and the twos are the ones above. I'll be staying in room 107. What would you like?"

Mandy looked down at the floor, rubbed her right foot in a small clockwise circle and didn't answer.

"OK, how about if I just get you room 106? I assume that will be next to mine."

"John, can I stay in your room? I won't be a bother, and it's not like I want to sleep with you. I just don't want to be alone for another night."

John coughed nervously and looked down at his key.

Mandy was great company and he'd enjoyed their talks in the car. He brushed away the next thought that she also was cute in her own way. Mandy was just a kid and something deep inside him drove away any romantic notions.

"OK, you can stay with me. But don't worry about me trying anything stupid. I'm about ten years older than you."

Mandy didn't answer, but smiled up at him with her head tipped down.

The room had only one bed and despite Mandy's protestations, John spent the night on the slightly too short couch. He changed into pyjamas in the bathroom and Mandy was snoring softly as he settled in for sleep.

CHAPTER 17
CONSOLIDATION

As the fall descended, conditions in St. John's rapidly worsened. Most companies that manufactured food products ran out of imported raw materials and had to close. Funeral homes were kept busy as more and more people succumbed to malnutrition. The prices of the food that was available skyrocketed, and only the richest were able to afford the diminishing supplies.

More and more people left the city for long-forgotten rural family homes where they hoped to find relief in a simpler way of life. Whole sections of St. John's were abandoned.

The one commodity that actually increased in availability was seafood. Because interprovincial marine trade had ended, supplies of marine fuel were plentiful enough for inshore fishing to continue. Since there was no market outside of the province for their catch, there was a local glut of fish and shellfish.

In the war of words between Fletch and the provincial government over who was to blame for the food shortages, he had one big advantage. The national broadcasting corporation collapsed. Like other federal employees, the reporters and technicians working for CBC were not paid. Some of the more idealistic workers kept coming in, but eventually there were too few employees showing up to continue television and radio broadcasts.

The premier went on the surviving private television station to urge the population to remain calm. He admitted that finding enough food for the first winter was going to be a challenge. In response, his agriculture department had prepared information about growing vegetables indoors and all limitations on hunting and fishing in the province would be lifted. He assured his listeners that there was enough electricity and oil for everyone to heat their houses, and it was his firm belief that the province would survive as long as no one panicked.

Dave continued to monopolize public attention and made it clear that provincial politicians were the main culprits for everything that was going wrong. Egged on by his listeners, he insisted that government should have had a plan in place for food shortages.

One of Dave's chronic callers phoned in to say that he was not going to be paying any of his provincial taxes. Dave responded that no one in St. John's should be paying anything to anyone but the city, because the city was the only body that provided any real benefit to the public.

The movement spread like a rumour in a senior's home. Businesses put cards in their windows announcing that they weren't collecting taxes. When word got out that police had showed up at one establishment telling the proprietor he would be fined or jailed if he didn't submit the taxes he owed, almost every business owner in the city joined the movement.

The premier and minister of justice met and reluctantly concluded that it was impossible for them to force tax collection in the face of such a united front. Their solution was to lay off provincial employees, particularly those who worked in St. John's.

The provincial government workers' union called a strike vote within days of the first layoffs. The results were a near unanimous call for action and the provincial government was soon crippled.

Dave was back on the attack as his opponents stumbled. He insisted the strike was more evidence of incompetence and lack of leadership. The province was falling apart and it was all the fault of the premier and his government.

Dave's next move was to arrange secret talks between Captain Pickford and the RNC's chief of police. Pickford invited the chief to a sumptuous meal on board the *St. John's*.

"Chief, it's good of you to come out here and meet with me. These are difficult times in the city, the province, and the world. They are especially complicated for those of us who are charged with maintaining order. Civilization as we know it is on the brink of collapse, and we are the last bastions of stability. It is those of us in the military, the RCMP, and the RNC who hold the greatest responsibilities."

"Captain, I don't like talking much about the situation we're in, but I think you are one of the few who appreciates our frustration. What I'm going to say now is just for your ears, and if you repeat any of it I'll deny we ever talked."

"I get it, Chief. We are all exasperated, and it is nice to have a chance to unload on someone who understands. You can say what you like. You have a completely sympathetic audience here."

"This whole mess is from the absolute incompetence of the premier. I can't say that I think too much of our mayor, but that is one thing he's correct about. You can't just let the public decide they won't pay taxes. Government should have immediately sent us in to deal with the first few troublemakers. We have semiautomatic rifles and shotguns, but if the politicians had their way our weapons would be locked up so tightly we could never get at them."

"I'd have to agree with your assessment. This whole mess with the strike was completely avoidable. One thing I'll give the mayor is that he lets us loose. I'll guarantee you that if the city had trouble raising the funds it needs, my men would be on the streets and fully armed."

"You're lucky, Captain. I sure don't get the support it seems you have."

"You know, Chief, this province is too small to have more than one security force. It's a waste of resources to have two separate systems. I've actually been thinking about talking to the union about whether your men could move over to work for the city."

"Whoa, whoa. Just hold on a minute. I don't think there is any reason to go to the union over something like this. Perhaps you and I could work something out. I'm confident that the men would fall in with any changes I suggest."

"You think you could swing something like that,

Chief? Now, the only ones we'd really be interested in at first are the RNC that are on the Avalon. I'm not sure how we could look after a police force on the other end of the island."

"Leave it with me, Captain. I'll have a talk with my senior officers, and we'll get all the men together and discuss it. If they are in agreement, we'll all move over to city jurisdiction. Now, in order to do this we'd have to be able to tell the men they would get the same pay they are getting now."

"Listen, if we can arrange that all the police forces in the province are under one umbrella, pay isn't going to be a problem. I can guarantee you that."

The captain and chief shook hands. Pickford reported back to Mayor Fletcher and the chief said nothing to anyone in government.

The RNC chief of police had little trouble convincing his senior officers that they would be better off working for the city of St. John's. They decided to present their plan to everyone on the force as a finished deal and suggest that anyone who wasn't happy with the new arrangement could transfer to Corner Brook on the other end of the island.

The chief called an emergency meeting at RNC headquarters and almost everyone cheered when the suggestion was made. They were fed up with the lack of direction from the Minister of Justice and unhappy being forced to continue on as essential workers during a strike. Only one secretary asked for a transfer to Corner Brook.

The day after the meeting, the RNC chief went on Fletch's radio program to announce that his force had moved to city jurisdiction. Callers phoned in with congratulations. A number of provincial employees who were home on strike called to say that they wished that the city would take over their departments.

At the next meeting of city council, one brave councilor asked who had given the mayor the authority to take on a new police force.

Dave replied somewhat disingenuously that it hadn't been him who had asked the RNC to move over to the city. The police force had made the overture to his office, and he felt that, for the sake of the security of the province, it was important to embrace this change.

The councilor agreed the move was appropriate, but felt it should have been voted on at a council meeting before any announcement was made. As well, he expressed concern about where the city would find the money to pay these new employees.

Fletch agreed that it was important for the council to make decisions of this sort and said he would appreciate if someone would make this motion. The deputy mayor was quick to move exactly the words that the mayor suggested, and it was passed unanimously.

"Now, to your question of how we are going to pay for this new arrangement. You are certainly correct that we will need more funds to operate an expanded city government. I have a suggestion for how we can do this. I propose that we levy a twenty-five percent tax on everything that is bought or sold in the city.

For such a momentous change, there was little discussion around the council table. One councilor asked for some clarification and more details. The mayor had thought the concept out and had convincing arguments ready.

Under the new tax regime, anyone selling anything, whether it was goods or services, to anyone in St. John's would have to submit twenty-five percent of the value to city hall. St. John's residents who bought items outside of the city would be required to pay the same tax.

When a councilor asked if this new scheme would be complicated to run, the mayor responded that the simplicity of it was one of its most attractive features. The entire taxation system currently in place would be dismantled. There would be no more tax collectors on government payroll and citizens wouldn't need accountants to help them figure out how much tax to pay. The only ones to lose would be those parasites (as Fletch put it) that made their living off of the tax system.

Under the new scheme, the city would contract tax collectors who would keep a small percentage of the money they took in. The city would pay them nothing and provide no office space for them.

Concerning enforcement, Dave suggested that penalties for withholding taxes would be particularly severe. The RNC would make a concerted effort to catch a few cheaters when the system first went in place and the offenders would be banished to Nova Scotia. Everyone understood that a trip to the mainland was the equivalent of a death penalty and few would risk this to save on taxes.

The motion passed and the next day, ten city workers from the finance division were given their pink slips.

Dave used his radio program to introduce his new plan to the city.

"Good afternoon, listeners. It's been an exciting few days here in the capital. The provincial government is in a worse mess than ever. The RNC has finally come home to where they belong, and we have a new taxation system that was voted in by city council last night.

"Now, I know that no one likes to talk about taxes. But just hear me out before you jump to the phones. We've talked a lot on this program about the inefficiency of government - it's the main reason that I got into politics in the first place - and there is nothing in government more inefficient that the collection of taxes. We pay taxes on everything that we buy or sell and then at the end of the year we are all taxed again based on how much income we earn. All of this tax collection requires thousands of bean counters, and, if that's not bad enough, it's so complicated we have to hire people to figure out how much tax we have to pay.

"Our new system will get rid of all the extra baggage. There will be no more income tax. There's no federal government to pay tax to, and, as you know, the people of this fair city have agreed not to pay provincial taxes. All that we are going to do is to increase sales tax a little and there will be no more figuring out how much you owe the government.

"You might ask, Fletch, why do we have to pay taxes at all? Well, my friends, everybody knows these are dangerous times. We all have relatives that we've lost because they were exposed to the dangers of the mainland. We need protection and that protection isn't going to come free. If you don't want to pay for the safety of Newfoundland, that's fine. We are going to give the people who don't love this province a one-way ticket to Nova Scotia. In these difficult times, everyone is going to have to pull their weight. This is St. John's, the most wonderful and safest city in the world, and you can love it or leave it.

"So, I hope you understand that paying this new twenty-five percent sales tax is important. We will be watching carefully that everyone helps out. The RNC will be keeping an eye on things, and we will be setting up a twenty-four hour tip line where you can let us know about your neighbours who aren't doing their share.

"Tell me what you think of this new system. I'm your mayor and eager to hear what my citizens have to say. Give me a call now to talk about our new fair tax system."

Deb made sure that the first three callers were regulars who never disagreed with Fletch about anything. Dave could suggest burning the city to the ground, and they would wonder why no one had thought of this before. Predictably, they concluded that the new system was a big improvement, and the new mayor was making St. John's great in a way it had never been.

Caller number four took a completely different tack.

"And we have Al on the line from right here in the city. Go ahead sir."

"Mr. Fletcher, I'm a first time caller, and I'd like to comment on the new tax regime."

"Just the fact that you call me Mr. Fletcher gives you away as a newcomer. We don't stand on formality here. Tell me how I can ease your mind today."

"My concern with your proposed new system is..."

"Sorry to butt in, but I have to correct you right off the

bat. This isn't a proposed new system. This is how taxes are being collected starting today. But please, go ahead."

"As I was going to say, my concern is that citizens will no longer be able to take advantage of the advice of tax professionals. A certified accountant, when properly utilized, can markedly ease the tax burden on anyone who chooses to take advantage of their services..."

"Al, just hold on for a minute. I'm going to make a big leap here and assume that you are an accountant."

"Yes, sir, I am a certified professional accountant in the employ of Burnside, Loudwater, and associates."

"You just said that anyone can use your services, didn't you?"

"That is correct, sir."

"So am I to assume that your services are free?"

"Of course not, sir, there is a reasonable fee for the assistance we offer."

"Ladies and gentlemen out there in radioland. This man has just provided all of the evidence we need to see how unfair the old tax system was. If you were rich, you could afford to pay someone like Al here to find a way for you not to pay your share of taxes. We all know that's what accountants really do. We need some way for everyone, rich or poor, to shoulder their fair burden of the cost of our society.

"I don't want to be rude to poor old Al here, but in my opinion, the sooner parasites like him are out of the system the better. Before I let you go, do you have any last comments for our listeners, Al? Al? Well it looks like Al has been called away by one of his worried wealthy clients. Whose next on the line, Deb?"

The rest of the show went well for the mayor. The next caller complained that he had heard a rich neighbour bragging about how he hadn't paid a cent of tax on his new boat sized recreational vehicle. Dave assured him this kind of thing was going to stop. The call and Dave's response incited a number of others to phone in with similar stories.

Dave summed up saying that it was obvious to him that the public supported the new tax system. He was proud of how his listeners were always the first to step up to help the city.

As the 'on air' light in the studio went off, Dave turned to Deb in the control room.

"And they're always the first to complain when things aren't going perfectly for them. We're going to have to work hard to keep them occupied."

CHAPTER 18
CLOSE TO HOME

Mandy was up and dressed before John woke. As he stretched and wiped the sleep from his eyes, she offered to get the cooking set from the car and start up some breakfast. He reached into his jeans on the couch and tossed her the keys to the car.

He changed and washed his face with the bottled water from the mini bar. Looking in the mirror, he wondered if his four day stubble made him look more mature or just like a hobo. There was a razor in the amenities set out beside the sink. John shaved, washed his face, and combed his hair. He checked that the tank of the toilet was full of water and relieved himself in comfort.

Mandy had the cookstove going by the time John came out of the bathroom.

"Don't you look spiffy this morning. Sit down and I'll have pancakes for you in a minute."

Mandy's cooking technique was far ahead of John's, and they had perfectly formed golden pancakes for breakfast. It was still early in the morning by the time they had filled the car with gasoline and were on the road.

They both remembered the turnoff to the Trans-Labrador Highway that they had passed a few kilometres before they came into Goose Bay. This section of the highway would be their last day of driving before they got back to the island of Newfoundland. The road was mostly paved and much straighter than what they had driven to that point.

John didn't turn on the GPS, as the only possible complication was the turnoff to Cartwright about half way along the trip. Other than that, it was a simple full-day's drive to Blanc Sablon.

The ride went without complication. They stopped at the Cartwright junction for a lunch of canned stew and then explored the settlements of Port Hope Simpson, Mary's Harbour, and Lodge Bay. There was no evidence of life in any of the communities.

Just a little over an hour after leaving Lodge Bay, they came to the town of Red Bay.

They turned into the settlement and made their way to the edge of the strait. John jumped out and touched the toes of his shoes into the water. When Mandy joined him, he pointed across to the clearly visible far shore.

"Mandy, look at that! That's where we are going. We've made it!"

"Looks pretty rough on the water, how are we getting across?"

"This isn't the narrowest place, we have to go on a bit farther. Get back in the car, I want to introduce you to someone."

Mandy frowned as they settled back in the Mercedes. John turned the car back on and started up the GPS.

"Mandy, this is Louise. She has helped me find my

way this far. Louise, how far to Blanc Sablon?"

The GPS screen displayed a map of the road from Red Bay to Blanc Sablon, and Louise informed them the trip was eighty kilometres and would take one hour and twenty minutes to drive.

"There is, or I should say there was, a ferry in Blanc Sablon that went over to the island. I'm certain it will be shut down now, but we will find some way to cross. It shouldn't be hard to get a little boat somewhere around here."

They drove around the community and got out to look at the whaling station museum. Another time, John would have liked to see the display, but their final destination was too close to spend time on sightseeing. Outside of the museum a parked truck had a red plastic sea kayak strapped to its box.

There was one set of tourist cabins that they noticed, but John suggested that there would certainly be a place for them to stay closer to the narrowest section of the straits.

The road turned inland for a short distance and came back on the water at West Saint Modeste. They saw a larger resort with a number of cabins but decided to drive on further. The picturesque towns of L'anse-au-Loup, L'anse-Amour, and Forteau all went by with more and more tourist accommodations. They didn't stop until they reached their final destination.

The ferry terminal in Blanc Sablon was a modest affair. An industrial looking grey building with a discreet sign indicating its purpose stood just in front of a utilitarian looking wharf. There was no ferry tied up.

The lack of a boat only added to the loneliness of the scene. The place was dead in every way, and just across the water was life and safety. John reflected that at least the crew of the ferry made it to a safe haven.

They spent a few minutes in silence looking across the water before Mandy spoke.

"Can I use your key to get into a grocery store? I think this deserves a bit of a celebration, and I can make up a fancy desert for us. There are loads of blueberries around here, and with some special ingredients I can whip up something you'll never forget."

They drove back to the grocery store, and Mandy laughed as she smashed in the front window with John's hammer. He had become used to this way of entrance, but Mandy's easy delight in destruction bothered him a little. Once they had the ingredients she wanted and found a patch of blueberries, they followed the signs to the Motel Blanc Sablon.

John insisted on opening the front door, but as soon as they got inside it was apparent that they wouldn't be staying there. The room had a choking odour of decay and before he rushed back outside John could make out four dead people sitting in chairs in the lobby. He couldn't imagine how they all could have died in the same place and ended up sitting together.

He staggered out to the car and looked around for Mandy. She wasn't in the parking lot or sitting in the vehicle. As he looked back into the hotel, he could make her out standing in the middle of the lobby.

John ran back to the front doors and into the hotel. Mandy was standing over the corpses and running her hands through the hair of what had been a middle-aged woman.

"You'll be OK. All we have to do is get across the water. We'll all be OK."

John didn't speak but grabbed Mandy around the waist and lifted her off the ground. She seemed almost weightless as he carried her out into the fresh air.

"Mandy, it's time for us to get supper. You promised me a special dessert."

"We could share some with the people inside. They look hungry to me."

Mandy had a far away look in her eyes that John hadn't seen before.

"When we were in Goose Bay, there was a hotel you didn't like, and I agreed to go somewhere else. There is something about this hotel that I don't like, so it's my turn to say we have to move on to another place."

"OK."

Mandy got back in the car without complaint, and they drove back down the road to the Northern Light Inn. John was pleased to see that besides the main hotel, there were a number of cabins. By having their own building to stay in, he could be sure they wouldn't have dead roommates.

John asked Mandy to stay in the car as he broke into the main office and found keys for one of the outbuildings. When they drove up to the cabin and started unpacking their food and gear, Mandy seemed completely back to her normal self.

John set up the cooking equipment and they made up a spaghetti dinner with a can of flaked ham added to the sauce. John cleaned up the dishes and pots as Mandy went to work on the desert.

The blueberry crumble[1] with caramel sauce that Mandy put together and cooked in a frying pan with a tin foil cover was delicious. By the time they were finished eating, the sun had gone down. John suggested another trip out to the ferry terminal.

They parked and turned on the radio to listen to evidence of a more normal life on the other side. As the sky darkened, they could make out lights on the far shore.

"You know, Mandy, it doesn't get much better than this. Sometimes I think the happiest times in our lives are when we are looking forward to something. It's like the joy of kids waiting for Christmas morning. A lot of times the actual day and the presents are a bit of a letdown. Tomorrow morning we'll find a little boat with an outboard motor, and, before you know it, all of this will be just like a dream."

They sat in silence for a long time watching the water and the flickering lights of their destination.

"Well, missus, I don't know about you, but I've had a long and exciting day. I'm just about ready for bed."

They drove back to the Northern Light Inn and settled into their room. John found water to wash and brush his teeth and again changed into his pyjamas in the bathroom. When he came out Mandy was sitting on the edge of the bed. John hadn't seen what she wore to bed the previous night, but this time she was illuminated by a candle that she'd placed on the nightstand.

Mandy had on a silky blue camisole that hung from her slender shoulders by thin spaghetti straps. The soft material clung to her in a manner that accentuated every curve and bump. John reddened and looked down at the floor.

"What's wrong with you, have you never seen a girl in a nightie before?"

John's colour intensified and he continued to examine the carpet.

"No, no, there's nothing wrong. That's quite a nice outfit. Did you get that shopping in Goose Bay?"

"Of course I did. Do you think it's pretty?"

Mandy put her hands behind her head and pushed her hair up suggestively. John couldn't respond, and Mandy started to laugh.

"Don't be so silly. I'm just teasing you. Do you think I'm going to eat you?"

She waited for a response, but John still couldn't answer.

"Now, John, there's only one bed in this room again and there is going to be no nonsense about you staying on a couch. You get in the other side, and we can both get some sleep. We have an exciting day coming up tomorrow and both of us need our rest."

"OK."

John moved quickly around the bed without looking directly at Mandy. He pulled up the covers and settled in with his back towards her.

"Good night."

"Good night, John. Sweet dreams."

In no time the sound of Mandy's slow breathing made it clear that she had drifted off. John couldn't clear his mind. The next day would be his escape from the horrors of the mainland disease. Still, he worried if there was a possibility that he or perhaps even Mandy might be carriers. Was it possible that one or both of them could ruin the lives of hundreds of thousands of people by their selfish attempt to save themselves?

Every time he managed to push these thoughts away, he returned to the vision of Mandy sitting on the bed in her slinky silk. Until that night he had forced himself not to consider her that way, but through her efforts it was becoming more and more apparent that she was an attractive woman.

John managed to keep from checking his watch, so he had no idea how long he tossed and turned before sleep took him away.

He dreamed that he was back in Ottawa at the monkey facility. He was playing volleyball outside of the building, but only he and Beth were on the court. She was wearing a white T-shirt that she had tied together half way up her stomach and a pair of very short shorts. When she served, the dream shifted to slow motion and her long blond hair splayed out behind her as she leaned back. John was mesmerized by the way her body moved through every aspect of the serve. The ball didn't come with any speed, but he couldn't draw his attention away from her quickly enough to get anywhere near it.

Beth waved her finger in his direction.

"You're a naughty boy, John. I can see what you're looking at."

John smiled as he picked up the ball and prepared to hit it back.

"Well there's no one else left here to look at, so I guess you'll just have to put up with me."

"We need to get back to work, Johnny boy. Time for the showers."

In the dream, John looked around and realized that there was no one else standing outside the monkey building. The parking lot was filled with cars and every one had a driver with his head tipped back and mouth open.

Beth took John by the hand and led him to the steps of their building. He entered the passcode, and they walked inside. The showers were just inside the entrance, and Beth pulled him toward the door marked for women. John hesitated, and Beth looked back at him.

"Don't be silly. Do you think I'm going to eat you?"

John knew that he'd fantasized about being in the showers with Beth before, but in his dream it all seemed wrong.

She pulled her T-shirt over her shoulders and shimmied out of her shorts. Her body was magnificent, and John's growing excitement was encouraged when she pulled off his pants.

Beth started the showers, and they began by lathering each other's hair and gradually moving the suds down each other's bodies. John moved behind Beth and began caressing her breasts.

"You are certainly making sure that those will get clean."

"John!"

"I'll get you clean alright."

"John!"

The voice was insistent and it seemed to come from somewhere outside. John felt like he was moving up into the nozzle of the shower and suddenly he was in bed with Mandy. His upper arm was draped over her, and he was enthusiastically massaging her chest. He smiled and continued for a short while before he realized where he was, and that his dream had faded. He pulled back across the bed and retrieved his arm.

"I'm so sorry. I was having a dream. No, a nightmare. No, a dream. I was having a dream."

"I'll bet it was a good one."

"Well it was a dream that's for sure. I'm so sorry about this. I didn't mean to do anything like that. This wasn't my plan. You are just going to have to believe me."

"John. Don't be so silly. That was nice. Come back here and put your arm around me. It makes me feel safe. I haven't had anyone to look after me for a long time. Come back here."

"Really?"

"Really. And it's pretty obvious that you were enjoying this as well." She nodded suggestively.

John's excitement had settled down, but he followed her request and reached back over her shoulder. This time he took her forearm in his hand.

"That's nice. Now just lie there for a while and don't say anything. I really need this."

John relaxed and settled in against Mandy's back. He had to agree that this felt as comfortable as anything he had experienced in months, maybe even years. Within fifteen minutes, both of them fell asleep. When John woke some time later, he was still draped around her and had a firm grip on her forearm.

He lay still feeling Mandy's back move with her breathing. Thoughts of escape to the island drifted away, and he felt he could happily spend the rest of his life in this bed. Mandy flexed her shoulders and put her free hand over John's.

"Good morning, John."

"Good morning."

"Can you do me a favour?"

"Sure, anything. What would you like?"

"Get on top of me."

Mandy pulled away from John and shifted onto her back. He followed her without hesitation and straddled the leg that was nearest him. As he gradually settled his weight on her she kissed him on the cheek. He returned a kiss to her lips and pushed himself up onto his elbows. As he opened his mouth to comment she put a finger across his lips and shushed him.

They continued to kiss and it was hard to tell who first moved a tongue into the discussion. Involuntarily they began to rock against each other and run their fingers along each other's sides.

John reached down and ran his fingers up Mandy's legs. She stopped her grinding motion and pulled his arm away.

"Now hold on there. The idea here is that we are friends just giving a little comfort to each other. If I want any more than that, you'll be the first to know."

John had never understood women. He'd had girlfriends before, and Mandy's actions really didn't surprise him. Despite his initial disappointment, deep down inside he was pleased that she had stopped him when she did.

He smiled at her and ran his hand across the top of her head.

"Sorry about that. I just got carried away. We have a lot of things to do today. How about we have blueberry pancakes for breakfast again this morning?"

CHAPTER 19
IT GETS MORE COMPLICATED

As fall deepened, it became obvious that St. John's was running out of food. The two grocery stores that stayed open had armed guards around the clock. All they had to offer was fish and the small amounts of locally grown potatoes and vegetables they could manage to get from local farmers. The prices for produce were astronomical.

The RNC was kept busy with reports of burglary. In almost every case the robbers made off with only food. Even the hospitals weren't immune from break-ins.

Striking provincial government employees felt the shortages acutely. Many of them lived from paycheque to paycheque, and, when reduced to strike pay, found it impossible to be able to afford any of the meager supply of food that was available.

Tempers flared on the picket lines and two weeks into the strike, a manager from a Department of Highways depot was shot in the leg as he left his house in Mount Pearl. Police investigated the assault, but no charges were ever laid. After reports came in of gunfire at the Health Sciences Centre, most of the employees who had been going in as essential workers refused to come back.

At the provincial government headquarters in the Confederation Building, the number of protesters on the picket lines rose. City council held long debates about how much responsibility their newly acquired police force had in keeping the provincial politicians safe.

For the first week, members were given an escort through the picket lines, but, as the number of protesters and the exuberance of their complaints increased, many of the politicians decided that it was not worth risking their lives to come in to work.

The premier contacted all members of his party and arranged a covert meeting at the house of the Minister of Health. The place was chosen because of its remote location and members were encouraged to carpool to avoid raising suspicions around the gathering.

The meeting went long into the night with most members who were not in the cabinet suggesting that their jobs weren't worth the potential danger to themselves and their families.

When it became apparent that no amount of reassurance would convince the majority of the party to return to the house of assembly, the member from Corner Brook announced that he was going home. In his opinion, St. John's was the most dangerous place on the island and it was time to abandon the city.

The premier, whose home riding was in Gander, didn't immediately speak against the Corner Brook member's opinion. Two members from St. John's asserted that leaving the city would be the equivalent of giving up. They insisted that the rule of law and the place of government must be protected if the province was to remain civilized.

The Corner Brook member challenged them, suggesting that if they felt this way, they should be the first to drive in to the House of Assembly the next morning. He finished his commentary by suggesting that all members of government should move to the other end of the province and regroup in Corner Brook.

Members from outside of the city cheered the suggestion, and those from St. John's could only sit with their heads drooped. When a politician from west of Corner Brook suggested a vote on the proposal, the premier reluctantly agreed. The proposition passed with a small majority, but there were multiple abstentions.

The Corner Brook member volunteered to find an appropriate new physical home for government in his hometown . He also offered to have his secretary phone all members of the opposition to tell them of the decision to move.

It was two days after the meeting before Fletch heard rumours of the government's move. He asked the RNC chief to look into it, and discovered that there were no vehicles trying to cross the picket line at the Confederation building. It appeared that the place had been abandoned.

Fletch tried calling the premier, but got no response on his home phone or cell. He asked the police to check on the residences of the premier and a number of cabinet ministers and found that all of them were empty.

On his show the next day, Fletch tried to pull out the truth of the missing government members. Who better to ferret out the real story than his legions of listeners?

"Good morning, St. John's, and welcome to anyone else in the province who is sitting by their radio. We've heard some interesting rumours here at the station. It appears that our provincial government has gone missing. It's been days since anyone has shown up for work at the House of Assembly. These guys and girls are being paid by us, and we ought to demand that they do their work. Give me a call if you have any opinions."

The first few calls were just the usual ranting about how this was no surprise because everyone knew how incompetent government was. None of the early callers had any useful information about what was going on. Then a call came in from the suburbs of Mount Pearl.

"Hello, Fletch. It's Lucy here. I think I might be able to shine a little light onto what's happening with our government."

"Good afternoon, Lucy, we'd all be thrilled if you could explain what's going on."

"Well, sir, my sister and brother in-law live just down the road from Mr. Rice, the Minister of Education. Now, Mr. Rice's wife plays crib with my sister every Thursday night. They have a real time of it, put out skewers of Vienna sausages and pickles, do the whole deal. But, anyway, a couple of nights ago, Mrs. Rice comes down to the sister's place and all hush hush tells her that she won't be making crib this Thursday."

"That's very interesting, Lucy, I'm sure your sister has a lovely crib night."

"Hold on now, Fletch, that's not the whole story. Now, Mrs. Rice tells my sister that she has to swear not to tell a soul, but that she and her husband and leaving for Corner Brook. Apparently the whole show of government is going up there, so she and her husband have to go with them. Now my sister's pretty good at keeping secrets, but of course she felt it was no harm telling me."

"Well thank you very much for that information, Lucy. It's important for citizens to know what their government is doing, even if they are all cowards running away from their responsibilities. So, folks, it sounds like the premier has abandoned us. I'd love to hear what some of our other listeners think about this."

The rest of the show was predictable. Not a single caller had a good word for the government. Dave wrapped up with his opinion that it was good riddance to the premier and his crew - the people of St. John's were better off without them.

Deb was out of the control room and beside Dave as soon as the last caller had hung up.

"You realize what this means, don't you?"

"I'm not sure what you're getting at."

"The premier and his gang here in St. John's were the best thing you ever had. You know that everything is going to hell in a handbasket here. Those guys were the ones that you could deflect all of the blame onto. They were your fall guys. If they move off to Corner Brook and give up responsibility for this part of the province, who do you think the people are going to look to when things get even worse?

"It's going to be you, Fletch. You are the man now. Those hungry strikers aren't just going to go home and settle down because there is no one in the Confederation Building. They are going to be looking for someone to blame all of this on and the only one I can see left is you."

"Deb, Deb, you worry too much. We've always found a way through our problems, and we will continue to. I can still talk about the government and how they have abandoned us, and we can pick up the talk about the dangers from outside the province. We've let that issue slip a little in the last while, and it's time people were reminded about the danger of someone bringing the disease to the island. It's a real concern and it'll give everyone something to think about."

Deb's worries weren't overstated. The situation at the picket line in front of the Confederation Building was rapidly degenerating. There was confusion amongst the picketers concerning who they were mad at, but there was no question that they all were furious. Fights broke out amongst the strikers and signs were thrown at innocent commuters just driving by.

The crowd gathered at the Confederation Building grew each day, and many of the new protesters weren't members of the union. The irate assembly soon changed from a regular working hours affair to a round the clock operation. The proportion of signs referencing the shortage of food increased each day.

On the fourth evening after the government's flight, a group of protesters decided that their location at an empty building was no longer effective. Two young activists stirred up the crowd with fiery speeches and led a march toward the downtown area. The crowd spilled out onto Allandale Road and headed south. The mild mood evidenced by their stop at the red light at Prince Philip Drive gradually faded as the group marched and chanted.

Other than a disagreement over which of the labyrinthine routes to the centre of the city should be taken, there was a mood of angry solidarity amongst the marchers. Word of the mobile protest spread quickly through the city and the size of the mob increased as they approached the harbour.

The first signs of violence were when a bearded young man with a scarf around his face pried up a piece of cobblestone and threw it through the glass door of a Subway restaurant. The action released layers of pent up frustration and soon bricks were being heaved through windows on both sides of the street.

A lone police officer who had stopped into the now doorless Subway for a coffee sighed, finished his drink, and made his way out into the street. By the time he assessed the situation and blew on his whistle pandemonium reigned. It's doubtful if anyone even heard his tweeting, and he soon realized that there was nothing he could do by himself to calm the crowd.

He stepped back into Subway and sat at the table furthest from the window to have enough quiet to call in for reinforcements. It caused him considerable embarrassment that the two young girls behind the counter winked at him and giggled as he tried to talk on his radio.

The police mobilized quickly and met the crowd just before they reached the city's only Korean restaurant. A sergeant with a bullhorn backed by a half-dozen mounted officers and three squad cars blocked off the road. The ranking officer ordered the mob to disperse and threatened that if the road wasn't cleared within five minutes, rubber bullets would be fired and offenders would be arrested and deported to Nova Scotia.

The final threat worked and within minutes the streets were cleared, but the precedent of downtown violence had been established.

The next morning, Dave met with Captain Pickford to discuss the previous night's downtown disturbance.

"Mr. Mayor, I'm certain that this is just the beginning of civil unrest in the city. We need to act pre-emptively to keep things under control. I suggest that St. John's needs a curfew. Even with the option of moving trouble-makers to Nova Scotia, I'm worried that last night was just the start of big problems. The people are hungry and upset. We need to act right away."

"I can see your concern, Captain, but I've always been more of a carrot man than a stick guy. What we need is other concerns to keep the people occupied. Everyone knows that if the virus gets onto the island we are in big trouble. We just need to focus people's attention on the disease."

"I don't know about that. I still think we need to clamp down on the troublemakers."

"How about this: give me one day on the radio to distract the people, and if they are in the streets again tomorrow night we can reconsider a curfew."

That afternoon, Dave got straight into his strategy at the top of his program.

"Good afternoon, Newfoundland. These are troubled times in our province. Many of you are out of work and some are hungry. If we are going to survive these difficult days, it's important for us to stand together and to be rational. Remember why we are having all the difficulties we are in. This is all about the disease from the mainland that has run through the rest of the world.

"I hope that I don't have to remind any of you how bad this disease is. It has killed almost everyone in the rest of the continent and probably in the rest of the world. We need to keep this in mind and keep our attention concentrated on preventing any outsiders from getting on to our island.

"All it will take is one infected person landing in our province to kill all of us. We have closed our airfields, but we must be vigilant over our shores. Losing focus can mean the end of life as we know it.

"Call in today and let me know about how you or your friends are helping to keep us safe from the Ottawa virus."

Deb was careful in sorting the calls. While Dave was giving his preamble, she had Vic on the line. He was one of the callers who they could always depend on for support, and she was confident he would be a safe start to the show.

"Hello, Vic. Good to hear from you, glad to see that you've taken time away from your busy life to call in."

"Fletch, boy, you've always steered us right and I appreciate that."

"Well thank you, Vic, it's because of people like you that I stay at this work."

"But, Fletch, I've got to tell you, the wife and I are running out of food. We have next to nothing in the house, and I don't know how we're going to survive. There's some fish and vegetables around, but the price has got so high that we can't afford enough to eat."

"Vic, we're working at the food problem, but right

now we have to worry about the disease. Can you imagine what would happen here if it came?"

"Well, boy, it won't make much difference if we all starve to death now, will it? We need food and we need it right now. That's all I've got to say, I'll hang up and let the others talk. I'm sure we're not the only hungry ones in the city."

Dave tried again to steer Vic back to the disease problem, but the line went dead before he could finish his argument. For the first time since he had started in radio, Fletch completely lost control of his show. No one wanted to talk about the virus. The lack of food was on everyone's minds and many callers brought up the previous night's protest. Everyone who mentioned it warned that there would be far more trouble if there soon wasn't more food in the city.

As soon as the show was over Dave called his assistant at city hall and arranged an emergency meeting of council over the supper hour. Captain Pickford was invited and gave the same opinion he'd presented to the mayor the night before. Council couldn't be convinced to agree on a city-wide curfew, but agreed to institute it if there was any violence that night.

That afternoon there were speeches on the Confederation Building picket line suggesting how meaningless their presence at an empty office space was. Speaker after speaker insisted that the protest should permanently move to city hall. A union organizer stood to say that city council had nothing to do with a strike against the provincial government, but he was booed down by the crowd. The union had completely lost control of the protest's agenda, and by late afternoon there were only a handful of protesters left at the original picket site.

By the time city councilors came out of their meeting, there was a large hostile crowd gathered outside City Hall. They slunk through the mob and hurried off to their homes.

The city manager called RNC headquarters and demanded immediate police protection. The dispatcher passed the message along to the officer in charge, and he readied the same contingent of horses and cars that had gone out the previous night.

Pickford stopped Dave and asked him to stay behind after the rest of council had left the building.

"Mr. Mayor, the council has made a grave mistake. We are going to be in for a rough night."

"You're right about that, Captain, but this is a spineless bunch we have on the council. Maybe we need to let just a little destruction happen tonight to convince them that we need a curfew."

"Leave that with me."

Pickford stopped at the top of the steps outside City Hall and watched the people below. As he stood there, three police cruisers drew up behind the crowd. He took the cell phone from his pocket and called in to headquarters.

"Pickford here. Can you tell me what's going on with the response to the activity around City Hall?"

"The sergeant couldn't get in touch with you, so he sent out three squad cars and the mounted boys are getting ready to leave right now."

"Tell the horse guys to stand down. I'm right in front

of City Hall as we speak and there isn't much going on here. We don't want to incite more problems with a heavy police presence. I'll be in shortly and look after things from here on."

"You're the boss."

Pickford made his way through the crowd. Something about his carriage inspired awe in the people gathered. No one blocked his way or taunted him as he moved towards the parked police cars.

"Looks like you've got your hands full tonight, boys."

"Yes, sir. We came down as soon as we got the order. We've been told to shut off the end of the street so no more protesters can join in."

"I'm a little worried that we may be seen as being a little heavy handed here, fellas. Forget about closing off the street. You pull back and just watch for now. I don't want any of you out of your cars unless there's real trouble. If they start destroying property, we'll send more backup. I'm going to explain this to the guys in the other cars, and then I'll be back at headquarters. You can get me there if things start going south."

"Yes, sir."

The three squad cars backed away and the size of the crowd increased as the sun dropped. It wasn't long after complete darkness that the first street signs were pulled down. A group of young guys managed to pry a stop sign out of its concrete base and began slamming their aluminum weapon against the doors of City Hall. The excitement of the violence was contagious, and soon rocks and bricks were being hurled against windows all over the downtown core. For the first time in living memory, multiple stores were looted. Small gangs of masked hooligans ran down the street hauling their booty of clothing and electronics. One of the only establishments left untouched was a bookstore. It seemed the vandals were not of a literary bent.

By the time the looting had started, Captain Pickford was back in his office. A panicked call came in from one of the officers on site reporting how badly things had gotten out of control. Pickford assured the caller that help was on the way.

He hung up the phone and slowly walked to the coffee machine in the empty squad room. He poured himself a cup and sat behind his desk unhurriedly draining his drink. It was only after the last drop was finished that he picked up his phone and called the dispatching officer downstairs.

"This is Pickford. Things have gone to hell downtown. I want everyone in, and I want them on the streets. Tell them not to hesitate to gas the buggers, and I won't be disappointed if I hear a few heads are cracked. I don't want them to bother with arresting anyone until they are done and then we'll send a few off to Nova Scotia as a lesson."

Fifty officers in full riot gear were driven to a marshaling point just beyond the protest. The men were arranged into two tight lines and began a fast march toward the disturbance behind their Plexiglas shields.

Excited young men were kicking at parking meters along the edges of the street. Every time a meter came free from the road a cheer would erupt, and a new battering ram would be applied to nearby windows. There were fires in the middle of the street from wood siding that protesters had pulled from stores.

The police in the line had only experienced scenes like this on television before. The group's commander decided immediately that there was no point in trying to reason with the mob.

"Fire six rounds of tear gas into the middle of this mess and then march them out of the downtown. We don't have enough men here to be arresting anyone yet. Just get this street cleared."

The first tear gas canister landed in the middle of a group of chanting protesters. All of them but one spread out from the gas like a splash on a windshield. The sole remaining man, who'd had a few drinks before coming down to the riot, picked up the canister and hurled it back in the direction of the oncoming force.

The police with their gasmasks, black riot padding, and billy sticks were an intimidating presence. As soon as they began advancing, one of the officers started banging his stick across his shield. He hadn't been taught this in training, but he'd seen it a number of times on television. The tactic caught on and soon the line was cracking time against their shields as they advanced.

Most of the crowd turned and ran as the police line moved towards them. Three young men fortified with liquid courage ran towards the policed brandishing various makeshift weapons. A slight man in a red plaid shirt made a half-hearted spearing motion with his four-foot piece of lumber in the direction of a lead officer. The policeman expertly turned his shield in coordination with the officer next to him. The two shields trapped the wood as the cops next to them stepped forward and rained blows across the unfortunate man's head and shoulders.

He fell heavily to the pavement and was kicked and stepped on by the advancing officers. The second attacker was hit across the forehead before he could even threaten the line with the brick in his hand. He staggered sideways and fell limply to the sidewalk. He was far enough from the line that he wasn't abused as badly as the first man, but two more policemen bounced their batons off his head as they moved by.

The third attacker was far enough behind the first two that he could see the futility of an assault. As he turned to run, one of the policemen in the front row rushed ahead of the line and hit him hard across the back of the neck. Three more officers broke away and gathered around the fallen man striking any part of him they could.

Word spread quickly through the crowd of the violence from the police and people started running from the scene. In the noise and screaming, it was impossible for the commanding officer to effectively communicate with his men. Small groups of them ran ahead and began beating protesters who were slow to get off the streets. He gradually corralled his men and sent his most respected officers ahead to stop the random beatings.

Once the noise had settled and all of the riot squad was collected back together, the officer in charge ordered his men to pick up any of the beaten protesters for delivery to Her Majesty's. This would definitely be their last riot.

A nervous young policeman ran up to his commander.

"Sir, I tried to get the guy in the red shirt up, but I

don't think he's breathing."

"Get back over to him right now and don't let anyone else near him. I'll look after this and you don't say a word about it to anyone. And that includes the rest of the men. Do you understand what I'm saying, boy?"

"Yes, sir."

The commander quickly ordered all of his men to return to the staging area with their prisoners. Those in custody were to be taken immediately to lockup and everyone was ordered to assemble at headquarters for a briefing.

As the men started moving away, the commander squatted down next to the cop watching over the prostrate man in red. He reached around his neck, felt for a pulse and turned to the young cop.

"Get me a car up here, and you and I will look after this mess."

At headquarters, the commander rushed up to Pickford's office and held a short conference behind a closed door.

He spoke to no one on the way back out to the car and explained to the young officer that they were driving down to the HMCS *St. John's* where there would be a small Zodiac waiting for them. There would be a piece of netting and some concrete bricks in the boat. The commander would help place the red shirted man in the Zodiac and the young officer would motor out beyond the entrance of the harbour, wrap the dead man in netting and concrete, and push him over the side.

CHAPTER 20
SO NEAR

After breakfast, John and Mandy drove back to the ferry terminal. They parked in front of the grey terminal building and walked towards the water. Mandy leaned in tight against John as they moved along.

"All we have to do now is find a boat and motor, and we'll be on our way. Have you ever driven a boat before?"

"I am going to guess from your question that you haven't. A real city slicker, aren't you? Of course I've driven a motor boat. I don't think there's girl in Labrador that doesn't know how to get by on the water or in the woods."

There was a fourteen foot aluminum boat with a twenty-five horsepower motor tied just around the corner from where the ferry docked.

"That looks pretty good to me. We just need to pick out some supplies from the car and we are off."

"You sure know your boats, John. Do you think it might make it easier if there was some gas for the motor?"

"OK, I give up, you're obviously the marine expert

here. Just tell me what we need to do to get over to the island."

"We need a tank full of outboard gas and a hose to connect the gas to the motor. People don't usually leave their tanks inside the boat. We'll have to find all that stuff somewhere. If we're lucky, we'll find something in the back of a pickup, or maybe we'll need to start breaking into people's garages."

They started by driving around Blanc Sablon looking in the back of trucks that were parked in front of houses. It didn't take long to canvas the entire community, and not one vehicle had a gas can in it.

The next step was looking in sheds and garages. Mandy suggested that there were clues to which places were likely to be the homes of boat owners. A boat trailer in the driveway or yard was the best way to start.

They drove through the community again looking for trailers. They saw two, and both were parked near sheds. The first building didn't have any boating equipment inside, and the second had a tank and hose, but the tank was empty.

When Mandy said it was too bad there was no fuel, John was quick to suggest they could just siphon some gas from a car. Mandy shook her head and sighed.

"Boat motors don't run on regular gas. We could find some outboard oil to mix in, but it'll probably be easier to just keep looking for some properly mixed fuel."

They got in the car and drove the short distance to Forteau and were disappointed to find no trailers in the community. As they drove farther down the road, John was starting to wonder how hard it could possibly be to travel the last few kilometres across the water to the island of Newfoundland.

Just before they entered the community of L'Anse-Amour, John and Mandy simultaneously pointed to two small houses set back from the road. There were two trailers between the houses and one had a boat strapped on.

They pulled in and were relieved to find a full tank of gas sitting in the back of the first trailered boat. John climbed up into the vessel and surprised himself how quickly he figured out how to disconnect the hose from the motor.

"You're catching on, John. We'll just try the gas in our boat at the ferry terminal, and if we can't get the motor going we'll come back for this boat and motor."

Mandy put her arm out the window and angled her outstretched hand to make her arm ride up and down in the wind current.

"Tonight, we'll be safe and then we'll start a new life."

It had taken the whole morning to find their boat and get it ready for the trip across the straights. John was concerned that they didn't have lifejackets, but Mandy teased him that a real man didn't need that kind of assurance, and that this was only a short trip across the water.

Mandy was ready to leave right after she pulled the cord and the motor roared to life, but John insisted that they needed more preparation.

"We don't have much idea how we are going to be received over there. I've heard some stuff on the radio about how important they feel it is to keep outsiders off the island. We're going to have to be careful, and we may need to stay out of sight for a while once we've landed. I think we should fill the boat with food and camping equipment from the car so that we're ready for anything when we land."

John packed the boat while Mandy put together a last meal on the mainland. They ate canned chow mein and a tin of corn in silence.

The water was calm and gulls played in the gentle breeze that blew in across the strait. John watched as groups of the birds caught wind currents and rose through the air without apparent effort. These animals had so few problems; their world was no different than it had been a year ago. The sun still rose every morning and wind still blew. Moving air under the right shape would still lift a solid body whether it was a gull's wing or a pretty young girl's hand. If the birds noticed any change, it would be the shortage of fishing boats that they could hover around, waiting for fish guts to be thrown into the water. Fishermen had always laughed at the gulls screaming and fighting over what to them was only garbage.

But real change had come for humans. Change in the form of a virus. A particle so small it couldn't be seen with a light microscope. Still, it was an agent so powerful it could kill most of the people on the earth. While the virus had spread throughout the planet, it only seemed to kill humans. Even the monkeys who brought the disease to Canada appeared to be affected with little more than a cough. John hadn't seen any evidence of problems in any other animals. There were no dead cats or dogs in the city, no rotting corpses of cattle or horses on the farms, and no dead birds where the gulls congregated on the shore of the Atlantic.

John's training in vet school made him think about the progression of the disease. He wondered how it had travelled so quickly. Was it possible that there were other means of transmission besides people coughing on each other? Could it even be that other animals besides the monkeys carried the virus without disease?

As he ran through his questions of epidemiology, his first thought was that none of this mattered any more. The disease was here, it had done its damage, and nothing could change the past.

Then he thought of the island of Newfoundland, apparently the one place that the disease hadn't landed. What were the chances that the island would remain free of the virus? All it would take was one infected animal or person and all the delusions of safety would be shattered.

He wondered again whether it was possible that Mandy or he could be disease-free carriers. Was his plan to cross the strait a selfish idea that ignored the needs of so many people? Or was it possible that his action would mean nothing in the end? At some point the virus would get to Newfoundland whether it was from people or some animal that made its way across the water. If birds could carry the virus it was only a matter of time before the island was infected.

John thought of discussing his concerns with Mandy and a memory came to him of her smiling as her arm flew outside the window of their car. She'd been through enough already, and she deserved the chance to innocently restart her life.

Mandy laughed at John as he took the empty cans from their meal and threw them into a half-filled garbage can.

"There's nobody here to empty that. You know it's just trash whether it's in the barrel or on the ground. No one is going to thank you for proper disposal of junk around here."

"I'm still civilized, Mandy, and if I was the last man left on the planet, I'd still respect the place I live in."

They stepped into the boat and John moved to the stern and started the motor again with one pull. Mandy clapped her hands and sat on the front bench. John experimented with the position of the motor and soon had a feel for how the steering and throttle worked.

A cloud of gulls followed them away from the shore, hoping that they would stop along the way to discard some fish. The sun shone and the water lapped gently on the sides of the boat. There was no rush to get to the other side and John kept the speed down low enough that no water splashed over the gunwales. He looked back over his shoulder at the receding ferry terminal wondering if he would ever see any part of the world outside of Newfoundland after today.

They were about a quarter of the way across the water when Mandy pointed out three fishing boats moving at right angles to their path. She stood to wave and bounced excitedly on the balls of her feet.

John throttled down the motor and reached forward to grab Mandy by the waist of her pants.

"Sit down and be quiet."

"But those are fishermen. Other than you they're the

first live people I've seen for days or even weeks."

"These guys are not going to want us around. Two things could happen here, either we can convince them we are just out for a ride from Newfoundland or they are going to think we are trying to get to the island from the mainland. If they think we're trying to get in from Labrador or Quebec, they're not going to be friendly."

John shut the motor down to an even slower idle and turned so that they were heading away from the three fishing boats. Over the sound of their own puttering and the roar of the distant motors, he could make out a shout from one of the other boats.

All three turned ninety degrees so that they were travelling in the same direction as John and Mandy. From the distance they were apart, John could make out a man looking their direction with a pair of binoculars. He cursed himself for leaving his own back in the car.

The fishing boats slowed to keep pace with them but didn't come any closer or make any attempt at communication. John could see the men in the boats talking between themselves but couldn't make out any of their words.

After what seemed like minutes of indecision, a man in one of the boats picked up a rifle and pointed it in the direction of John and Mandy. There was a loud pop and a splatter from a bullet ricocheting off the water. There seemed to be an unreasonably long period between the splash and the ringing of a projectile hitting the aluminum hull of their boat.

John twisted the throttle to full and turned back towards Blanc Sablon. As a second report came from behind them, John heard what sounded like a large insect flying by his head. The bug made a sound like someone snapping their fingers as it passed by.

"Lie down in the bottom of the boat. We are getting out of here. I'm running us up on the shore next to the wharf, and when we land run for the car. These guys are trying to kill us."

Neither John nor Mandy looked back as they retraced their path to the ferry terminal. At full speed the boat bounced over the waves that seemed to have increased in size since they had started. John was surprised by how much effort it took to keep the motor straight.

There were no more gunshots that they could hear, but John remained huddled down over the motor until he was within fifty meters of the ferry terminal. For the first time since their flight began, he straightened up and looked back in the direction of their attackers.

He could make out silhouettes of the three boats considerably farther away. Apparently, they were satisfied that John and Mandy had returned to the north shore. Still, John wasn't satisfied that they were safe. He pulled the boat in behind the right-angled leading edge of the wharf and forced it onto the rocks at the gentlest slope he could find.

The boat came to a sudden enough stop that Mandy pitched forward and banged her face against the gunwale. John jumped out onto the rocks and hesitated only long enough to grab Mandy's hand. The two of them rushed up to the pavement and over to the Mercedes.

When they reached the car, John had forgotten that his compulsiveness had made him lock the doors. The inconvenience was made up for by the fact that the same character defect had resulted in the keys still being in his pocket.

The car came to life with the first turn of the key, and John drove up the short slope to the main road. He headed directly for the largest hill in the community where he had noticed a boardwalk. They left the car in a small gravel parking lot and, after collecting the binoculars, walked up to the peak.

At the top of the small rise there was a bench and a statue of the Virgin Mary in a blue gown. John knew he was in Quebec, and he was happy for any kind of divine assistance he could find.

They sat panting on the bench as John scanned the straits with his binoculars. He could make out the three fishing boats perhaps a kilometre off the Quebec shore. Even at that distance he could see men on the boats scanning the shore with their own binoculars.

It was apparent that the fishermen weren't interested in coming any closer. They were no doubt aware of the dangers that mainland Canada presented, and they were unlikely to chase them beyond the water.

John and Mandy took turns watching the boats as they slowly circled. After an hour, two of the vessels headed back for Newfoundland, but the third stayed in position.

"It looks like it's not going to be as easy as I thought getting over to the island. They know that there's someone over here trying to come across, and you can bet that soon there will be more boats watching this area."

"It's not so bad, John, we have a comfortable place to stay here. Let's just settle in. There's lots of food around for the two of us, and we have each other."

John put down the binoculars and wrapped his arm

around Mandy. She shifted across the bench and leaned in tight.

"You're right. We are OK here. Let's just keep an eye on the water until it gets dark, and then we'll drive back to the hotel with our lights off. There's no need for us to give them anything to look at."

The boat didn't move until just before sundown when another vessel came to take its place. It was impossible to know if this was one of the original three, but it was obvious that the possibility of outsiders making their way to Newfoundland was being taken very seriously.

John and Mandy were so intent on watching the watchers that they didn't think of eating until the sun had completely set. When they were satisfied the night would get no darker, they walked back down the boardwalk hand in hand.

Even though they were a long distance from the boat out on the straits, John cringed when the Mercedes' engine came to life. Sound travelled far and clearly over water, especially in this new quiet environment; someone from Newfoundland would know that they were still in the area.

They drove back to the Northern Light Inn through the darkness without speaking. He wasn't sure why, but John parked the car behind the building. Mandy didn't comment and said nothing as they walked around to the front and into the room they had shared the night before.

For the first time since he had left Ottawa, John didn't wash or even take off his clothes before he got into bed. Mandy pulled off her shoes and socks and cuddled in tight behind him. Nothing was said, and they were both asleep within minutes.

CHAPTER 21
CONTROL PROBLEMS

The day after the St. John's riot, Fletch still felt confident he could maintain control of the city with his radio program.

Since Fletch had become mayor, he had only been coming into the station for his show. He would arrive fifteen minutes before air time and leave as soon as he was finished. There was work to be done running the city and everyone knew better than to complain.

Dave came in to work over half an hour early and made his first stop at the manager's office. He knocked on the door and entered without an invitation.

"Hello, boss, how are things in radioland?"

"Not bad at all. For all the doom and gloom around, radio seems to be the one thing that's flourishing. Even TV isn't doing the business we are. CBC's gone, and the private guys are having real trouble coming up with enough programming to satisfy their audience. People are moving to radio and our advertisers can see it. Our ad slots are completely full, and we have new clients trying to get in all the time. These are good days, Fletch, and we can thank you for a lot of the attention that we are getting here."

"I'm glad you can see that, boss, and I'd hate for anything to happen that would make me want to move over to another station. OZ is still running, and I'm sure they'd be happy to have the mayor on with them."

"But you're happy here, Fletch, aren't you?"

"Oh, I'm happy, but there's something that's going to have to happen to keep me that way."

"And what would that be, Fletch?"

"I was listening to the news on the way in this morning, and I wasn't real pleased with the coverage of last night's disturbance. I've always thought that we had a partnership of sorts. I'm happy to provide listeners for the station. We all know that most people are tuning in because of me. But, if I'm going to help the station, I expect a little respect in return."

"I can see what you're getting at. I can have a talk with the boys in the news room and make sure that they realize that our star performer isn't to be embarrassed by anything that comes out of this building."

"I knew that you would see things clearly, boss. Now, here's how I suggest we are going to make sure we don't have any more misunderstandings. Since there have been no feeds coming in from the mainland, I know that the boys type up their own scripts before every newscast. What is going to happen is that my publicity director down at city hall will have a look at each script before it gets read. It's not that I don't trust the news guys, but we need to be careful."

Dave paused and leaned in over his boss's desk.

"Do you have any trouble with that?"

"Fletch, my boy, the news has never been a big priority with me. It's the advertising dollars that keep this place afloat. You can change the scripts as much as you need."

Fletch rapped his knuckles across the older man's desk, turned, and walked out of the office without further comment. Deb was working in the control room as he sauntered into the studio.

"Mornin', Dave. What have you got planned for today's show? I suppose the big thing on everyone's minds will be last night's riot."

"We've got to find some way to keep them away from that. People always concentrate on the negative, we have to find something good to talk about."

Deb rolled her eyes and gave a quick shake of her head.

"What?"

"Oh, nothing."

"What do you mean 'nothing?' I saw that look. What was that all about?"

"You know, Dave, you've never been mister positive. The whole reason this show is popular is because you find things wrong and get people stirred up. Maybe now that you are in charge, it's not so convenient when we pay attention to the problems."

"If you have trouble with the way we run this show, maybe you need to find a different place to work. You know where your paycheck comes from, don't you?"

Deb looked down at her mixing desk and didn't speak for a moment.

"I didn't say I wasn't happy. I've always been on your side, but maybe once in a while you need someone to tell you the truth."

"If you are finished, we have a program to put on. It's important this morning to control who gets on the air. I don't want this turning into another shit show like yesterday. You talk to everyone who calls in and make sure you know what they are on about. Don't put anyone through who is going to be complaining about last night."

"You're the boss. We are on in two minutes. Go sit down and I'll get you a coffee."

"Welcome to the afternoon show. This is your buddy Fletch and it's a beautiful day. I think we can all agree that we've had a few stressful months here on our beautiful island. The world is falling apart, and it's only through our careful vigilance that we've managed to stay safe.

"As I was driving in this morning and looking at the sun over the harbour, it occurred to me how lucky we all are. We live in the safest and most beautiful place in the world, and maybe we just need to stop and remind ourselves how grateful we should be. So, for a change of pace today, we're not going to talk about our troubles or politics or even religion. I've been thinking that we need a break from all of this, so today I'm asking listeners to phone in their favourite Newfoundland recipes. We are going to have to get used to eating the way people did years ago, and this is a chance for us to share some of our treasures from the old days.

"And we have line one lit up with Alice from Topsail. How are you doing this morning my dear?"

"Lovely, Fletch, I'm so glad that you have decided to stop talking about politics. I get so sick of hearing nothing but nonsense on the radio."

"I couldn't agree with you more, Alice Do you have a

recipe for us this morning?"

"That's right, Fletch, I'm sick and tired of all the bad news we've been hearing about. It's disease this and starving that and then they had that riot downtown last night. Terrible goings on. I heard that the police beat up a couple of young fellas. Not that they didn't deserve it, but you have to wonder what the world is coming to."

"You're right there, Alice. Tell us about your favourite recipe, maybe something with blueberries?"

It took a couple more interruptions, but Dave did eventually get Alice to share her recipe for blueberry crumble[2]. With all of the build up it was very ordinary and a bit of a disappointment. When she finally hung up there were no lines lit on his board and he introduced a commercial.

"Deb, what the hell is going on? We never go dead on this program."

"I'm doing like you told me and screening the calls. All anyone wants to talk about is last night's riot. You're either going to have to face this one or we're going to have an empty show."

"To hell with it, let them through."

"We're back and we have all of our lines lit up now. Tell me about your favourite recipes, or if you don't have any tell me what's on your mind."

"We have a Mrs. Dalton from town on line one. Mrs. Dalton - that's rather formal for this program, we're all friends here on the air – do you have a recipe for me on this lovely afternoon?"

"No, Mr. Fletcher, I do not have a recipe for you today. There are important things going on in this city, and, as a radio host and more importantly as our mayor, you should be paying attention. Did you even know that there was a riot last night? Imagine now, a riot in the middle of the city."

"Now, Mrs. Dalton, I don't know if I'd call what went on last night a riot. There was a disturbance and the fine officers of our combined police forces made sure that nothing got out of control."

"Mr. Fletcher, it sounds to me like you have no idea what went on downtown. There were hundreds of people in the streets and the police came in and hit and kicked them as if they were dogs. I was there and I saw blood on the pavement. There was even a young man lying unconscious who was dragged off by the cops. This isn't the way our city ever was before. You are going to have to do a better job of looking after this town, mister."

She hung up before Dave had a chance to argue with her about her characterization of the night's events. For the first time in his radio career he was unable to think of a quick response and he went to a commercial. When the ad finished a caller came on with nearly the same story, and Dave came close to losing his temper in an argument over how well the police had handled the situation. He went to a back-to-back public service announcement and commercial and spoke to Deb through his 'phones.

"You've got to get us out of this. I need a calm caller who can talk about recipes. Run down to the graphics department and get one of the girls there to call in and say something bland."

The commercial ended and Dave came back on the air.

"We're back and we have another caller on the line

and this time I think it's someone with a recipe. I'm not sure about you folks, but I could use a break from all the seriousness."

"Hello, Cara, you're on the line. I understand you have a recipe for us."

"Yes, sir, I do have a recipe and it's a good one. I think you will really like this one, sir."

The line went dead for an extra beat.

"Cara, are you there? You said you had a recipe for us."

"I'm sorry, sir, I do have a recipe."

Another beat of dead air.

"Well, could you tell us your recipe?"

"Yes, sir. I don't know much about cooking, but my mother makes blueberry crumble and I'm pretty sure I know what's in it."

Dave glared at Deb through the control room glass.

"Cara, if you'd been listening, you would know that we've already had a recipe for blueberry crumble. Can you give us a recipe for something else?"

"I'm sorry, sir, I don't know any recipes. Ms. Collins came down to our office and told me I had to call in to you. I'm sorry, sir, I don't know anything about recipes."

"It sounds like the cat has Cara's tongue, so we'll just go to another commercial and I'll be back with you in just a moment."

"Deb! What in the hell was that?"

"You told me to get someone from graphics to phone in and I did. It's not my problem that the girl couldn't perform just the way you wanted her to."

"You are finished. When this show is over, you can

pack up your things and you don't have to come back in again."

"David Fletcher, I'm quite certain that you aren't running this station. Last I heard, it was the manager who did the hiring and firing in this place. And do you understand why your program works? You just sit out there and talk. The only reason everything runs smoothly at all is because there is someone behind the scenes making it all work. But you know what? They can't pay me enough to keep working with you. I'm done. Not at the end of this show, right now. Let's see how you finish up on your own."

There was a buzz of static in Dave's headphones and he could see Deb storming out of the control room. The commercial finished as she left the room.

"We're back, folks, and we've had a bit of a technical problem here, the phone lines are down so we won't be able to take any more calls today. I can see Johnny O just outside the studio, and we'll have to get him in a little early to spin a few tunes for you."

The disc jockey stepped into the studio and pointed at his watch as he shook his head. Dave wrinkled his nose and extended a middle finger in the man's direction.

"It seems Mr. O isn't ready for you just yet, so we'll carry on for a while."

Dave paused, pushed his mute button and took a long drink of coffee. It wasn't like him to go silent while on air, but he was struggling to find something to say.

"We have to remember, folks, how lucky we are to have missed the disease here in Newfoundland. We have to focus on keeping safe. I just heard a rumour this morning that there may have been a case of the virus up in Corner Brook. Now it's just a rumour, but what would happen to us if that was true? You know we'd all be dead in no time."

Dave rambled on for seven minutes that seemed more like an hour. When the clock showed his slot was finished he slammed his headphones on the table and made his way to the manager's office.

"Did you hear that mess on the radio? Deb walked out on me and that moron Johnny O didn't step up to help me out. I want the guy canned as soon as his show is over. Disc jockeys like him are a dime a dozen. You could find a kid from any high school in the city that could do what he does."

The manager opened a drawer in his desk and pulled out a bottle of rum and two coffee cups.

"I think you could use a drink right now. Just settle down for a minute and we will work this all out."

He poured two half cups of liquor that disappeared down their throats.

"Now, I'll talk to Johnny, and I'll make sure that he understands how things work around here. I'll give the guy one more chance, but if he pulls a stunt like that again he's gone. We've all got to stick up for each other. Will that work for you?"

"I can live with that, but if the bugger ever does anything like that again you won't have to fire him, because I'll kill him."

The manager shook his head just perceptibly as he responded.

"That's fine, Fletch, you kill him if you feel you have to, but we're all good now are we?"

"I suppose. You'll have to get someone to produce my show. I'm pretty sure Deb's not coming back."

"I'll look after that. I've got one question for you about today's show, Fletch. What was that about an outbreak in Corner Brook? You haven't heard anything, have you?"

"Naw, I just made that up. I was drowning out there and I needed something to grab on to. You know, maybe a scare like that is just what we need to straighten things out here."

Dave drove directly home and didn't go in to City Hall for the rest of the day. There were calls on his answering machine from four council members asking for an emergency meeting to revisit the question of a city curfew. He called each of the councilors back and told them that although he was too exhausted to come for the night's meeting, they should go ahead without him. Everyone knew what he thought about the curfew.

The meeting was held without public notification and the council voted unanimously to enforce a citywide curfew starting at sundown that night.

The police patrolled the downtown area with full riot gear and announced through bullhorns that anyone engaging in any suspicious activity would be summarily taken to prison. A few rocks were thrown in the direction of the officers, but there was no organized resistance, and no one was foolish or brave enough to confront the police directly.

Dave brought his public relations officer with him to the radio station the next morning and told the manager that she would be looking after the phones for his show. He explained this would be a double win for the station.

They had someone in the control room who they could count on and there was one less salary for the station to worry about. The manager didn't hesitate to accept the offer.

He started his program by bringing up his rumour about problems on the other side of the island.

"I mentioned yesterday on the show that I'd heard something about a case of the Ottawa virus in Corner Brook. Today let's talk a bit about this, it's important. I'd like to know if anyone else has heard these rumours and what you think we should do if there ever was an outbreak in another part of the island. Maybe the people out west aren't being as careful as us about keeping the disease out."

"And first up we have Mark calling from right here in St. John's"

"Yes, Fletch boy, I believe that I did hear something about the disease being on the go in Corner Brook, and even if I didn't hear it, it sure sounds like something those sleeveens would be up to."

"Well this is certainly worrying news, Mark. What do you think we should do about this problem?"

"Well, sir, the way I figure it, no one wanted to believe you when you told us something was up way back when the disease started. The government types and everyone else on the TV and radio said there was no problem. Where would we be now if we hadn't listened to you?"

"I appreciate your vote of confidence, Mark, and I have to agree with you that people should have learned a lesson about not getting complacent. We need to keep on our toes. What do you think we should do now?"

"If I was running things, Fletch, I wouldn't take any chances. There's a simple solution that I can see. We can cut them off down around Bellevue. The isthmus is pretty narrow there, and if we blocked off the road I think we could keep ourselves pretty safe down here."

"That's an interesting idea, Mark, and thanks for calling in this morning. I'd like to hear more of your thoughts on what may be going on in the province."

The show continued with more and more extravagant claims of stories that had come out of Corner Brook and suggestions for how to keep the disease away. Mark's original idea of blockading the Avalon Peninsula from the rest of the province proved particularly popular. A number of callers suggested that it would be a simple matter to build a wall and shoot anyone who came close to either side.

That night a group of men drinking in a shed in Whitbourne paused from their dart game to assess the province's situation.

"I don't know about you, boys, but I'm going to be fine this winter. I have a full moose in the freezer, and the missus has put away all kinds of vegetables. There are going to be fellas in town getting hungry, but I'll be fine."

"Me too, brother. Lots of grub in my freezer. I've filled my licence for moose, but there's no sign of wardens around, and I believe I'll get another one before the winter's out."

There was a general indication of approval and clinking of beer bottles.

"The only thing I'm worried about is that disease coming down here from out west."

"I haven't heard anything about no disease around here."

"Well, sir, I heard it on the radio this morning. Apparently there's been a big outbreak up in Corner Brook or maybe it was Gander. And you know when it comes down to our end of the province, we will be the first ones to get it."

The discussion went on with wilder and wilder stories of loss of life on the island. As the talk and drinking progressed, the six men in the shed decided that it was their civic duty to protect their end of the province. It was up to them to close off the highway from the disease.

Phone calls were made and eventually a platoon of six pickup trucks set out for the turnoff from the Trans Canada highway to Bellevue Beach.

The men parked three trucks across the road and gathered up enough wood to start a fire just north of their blockade. The first vehicle to come along, twisted around the fires and was starting to drive along the shoulder to get by the trucks when a defender set up in the overlooking Doe Hills fired his rifle in the direction of the car.

The driver wasn't interested in discussing the situation and immediately shifted into reverse. He didn't turn around until he was out of what he thought might be rifle range.

By the morning, dozens of vehicles had been turned back. Not one of the drivers got out to argue about being stopped or shot at.

CHAPTER 22
CHANGING PLANS

Mandy was up and outside by the time that John woke. He pulled himself out of bed and found her sitting on the veranda.

"So what are your plans now?"

"We can still get over to the island, but we're going to have to lay low here for a while. Those guys in the boats aren't going to forget about us soon."

"What's wrong with just staying here? I've spent my whole life in Labrador, and I'm really not in much hurry to move."

"The trouble, Mandy, is that there is no one here. Everyone seems to be dead. It's just you and me. If we can get to the island we can get back to some semblance of a normal existence with other people around us."

"Maybe we'd be better off here. What we have now is freedom. There is no need for fences or walls and there are no other people we have to worry about or even try to please. I have no trouble being alone with you. We could be sort of like a couple. I like you. We could set up a comfortable life here and maybe even have some kids some day."

John didn't know how to answer that one. Mandy certainly was cute, but he had no intention of spending the rest of his life with her.

"I like you too, Mandy, but there is a real world waiting for us over on the island. We just have to be patient and maybe find a different place to cross. There's no hurry. We have shelter and there's lots of food around here. The first thing we need to do is go back to our boat and get our camping stuff."

They had a quick breakfast and drove to within a half kilometre of the ferry terminal. In order to draw less attention, they decided to walk and carry their gear back to the car.

When they got back to the inn, they spent some time shifting everything from their vehicle into their room. This was going to be their residence for some time, and there was no need to be continually moving things around.

Mandy cooked up a meal for lunch and suggested that what she would like to do best was to get back in bed with John. Despite his worries about her suggestions of becoming a permanent couple, he couldn't resist her offer.

Their amorous adventures didn't progress much beyond what they had done before. Despite John's interest in moving along, Mandy insisted that this was only their second date, and she wasn't the kind of girl to give guys ideas. With little conviction John said he understood.

Their lives settled into a domestic pattern of exploration and waiting. They investigated all of the stores along the north shore and slowly built up a supply of non-perishable food in their room.

In an outdoor store, Mandy was excited to find fishing

rods and lures, and they soon added fresh trout to their diet. As the temperatures began to drop, John wondered to himself whether there was any chance that they would get to the island before the next spring.

Three weeks after they had moved in, they were still exploring shops around the area. They drove as far as Red Bay and decided to limit themselves to one new establishment a day.

John was looking at the cough medications in a small drug store when Mandy came up behind him.

"I was thinking that it could be time for us to get a few of these. You never know when we might need them."

John turned around to see her waving a package of condoms between her thumb and index finger. He still hadn't figured Mandy out well enough to know if this was a joke or an offer.

"You know, we should use these until we decide that we want to have kids."

"Hold on, Mandy, there's no rush to get into things like that."

As the words came out of his mouth he wondered what he meant by "things like that." He wasn't sure how he felt about Mandy or what he wanted from her. She was good company, fun, and helpful. They hadn't had a serious argument since they'd been together. A part of him wanted her in every way, but his heart saw her as no more than a friend.

"Are you worried that we need to get married or something before we have kids? If you're old fashioned like that, I don't mind if we break into a church and go through the motions. There's no priests around of course.

Maybe we could wait until the winter and get a snowman to do it."

John laughed. She was clever. He enjoyed being around her, and he always looked forward to their times together in bed.

The next morning was the first time that Mandy coughed. John didn't take it seriously. He joked that he should have picked up some of the medicine he'd seen in the drug store. They would have got more use out of it than the condoms that still sat in their package.

Mandy didn't laugh at his comment and continued to cough throughout the day. Her hacking got worse in the afternoon, and she was too sick to want supper that night. John put her to bed early and went for a walk by himself in the moonlight.

She coughed enough during the night that neither of them got much sleep. It was obvious that she was much sicker by the next morning. She had no appetite and asked John if he would go out for a drive and leave her alone for the morning.

He took the short trip to the hill above Blanc Sablon and checked the strait with his binoculars. There was no one stationed off from the ferry terminal, but he saw two fishing boats travel along the far shore. Their movements suggested to him that they were patrolling more than they were fishing.

When John came back into the main room he called out as he entered.

"How are you doing?"

"Stay out of the bedroom, don't come in here."

With some hesitation, John moved past her door and

into the bathroom to wash his face. As soon as he stepped inside he saw blood spattered around the toilet and sink. His heart fell as the reality of the situation sank in. Before that moment, he hadn't even considered the possibility that either of them could ever come down with the disease.

"Mandy, are you OK?"

There was no immediate answer, and he regretted his meaningless question.

"Mandy?"

"Go away, John, just get out of here. I've got it. It's happening just like it did with everyone else back home. I've got the disease and there's no need for you to get sick as well."

John opened the door to the bedroom and moved to the side of the bed. Mandy was curled up in the middle of the mattress and the sheets around her were wet and red.

"Please, John, leave me. I don't want to make you sick."

He crawled across the mattress and held her against his chest, not caring about the blood that was everywhere.

"You are the one always asking me to get in bed with you. I'm here now and we should just go to sleep. Don't worry about me, I've been as close to the virus as anyone and I've never got sick. A little hug with you isn't going to hurt me."

As he pulled her closer he could feel the muscles in her arms relax. His mind went blank as he fell asleep.

John had no idea how long he had been sleeping when he came to. The weather had taken a turn for the worse and he could hear the wind howling outside. Mandy's body was still beside him, but she was gone. He pulled himself from the bed and walked outside into freezing rain. He stood in the middle of the parking lot looking back at the door as the blood drained off of his clothing and ran down the slope of the pavement.

It was dark by the time he made his way back into their room. All he could do was sit in a chair in front of the television and watch the blank screen. His wet clothing soaked his seat and formed a puddle on the linoleum below him.

The next morning, John decided that he would continue to live. He had lost his companion or his friend or his lover or whatever she was, but he was still alive. The island still lay just across a short stretch of water and he tried to convince himself that nothing was any different than when he had left Ottawa.

His initial dilemma was what to do with Mandy. At first he wondered if he should break into the funeral home that he'd seen and get her a proper casket for burial. Then he thought it would make more sense to weigh her down with something and put her in the ocean. That gave way to the idea that he could soak her in gasoline and cremate her. He couldn't face the reality of doing any of these things and he decided that a simple burial would be most respectful.

John found a shovel at a hardware store and spent two days digging a deep hole in soft ground that he found just outside of Forteau. He washed off Mandy's body and dressed her in the jeans and sweater she had worn when he first found her. He wrapped her in an orange tarpaulin and covered her over.

When he had finished the burial, John spent two full days on the hill above Blanc Sablon looking out over the water. The Newfoundland fishing boats continued to move back and forth across the far shore. He considered getting into his boat and heading directly for the island. If the fishermen shot him, it would be no big loss. But he never moved from the hill. When the night came on, he would only walk down to his car and sleep until the sun returned.

It wasn't until the third morning that John was able to make any concrete plans for his future. The first decision he had to make was whether he still wanted to, or if he should, go to the island. His choice balanced on the reality of what had happened to Mandy.

There was no question that she had succumbed to the Ottawa virus. But how had she come down with it so long after everyone else around her had died? It was possible that this disease had such a variable incubation time that she had been infected and doomed since before he met her. He also wondered if she had somehow initially avoided contact with the virus and had picked it up from an animal or from something in one of the buildings they had explored. The final possibility was that he had infected her. While they hadn't had sex, they'd been in close enough proximity. Perhaps he was a carrier.

If he had given the disease to Mandy, there was a moral obligation for him to stay out of Newfoundland. If he moved to the island and infected one person, the whole society would be ruined.

John decided that he would stay for some time on the north shore of Labrador. He would make a few changes that would fit his new plans.

He settled on moving away from the Blanc Sablon end of the shore. People in Newfoundland knew that someone had been trying to get to the island from that area and they were undoubtedly watching for him.

He left all of his food and equipment at the inn and drove to Red Bay. Once in the town, he parked his vehicle and walked the streets checking every house that looked inviting. He wanted a well insulated home with a woodstove and no corpses inside. Two days of searching resulted in three houses that fit his requirements. He chose the place with the most comfortable furniture in the living room.

His next move was to replace the Mercedes. A diesel pickup truck would be a more functional vehicle for the life he was about to embark on. He remembered reading that any kind of fuel had a life span and that diesel would stay good a little longer than regular gasoline.

He spent a day filling the house with food from local shops. There was plenty of firewood stacked up around residences in the area, but John decided he would get the chainsaw from the shed behind his house and collect some of his own.

Walking around Red Bay, John came across the kayak strapped to the back of a pickup truck that he'd seen earlier. The truck doors were locked, but he could make out a paddle, life jacket, and spray skirt in the cab. It took some work to break through the truck's safety glass, but John soon had a full sea kayaking outfit.

He had paddled a few times with friends when he was younger, but John knew he was far from expert with a kayak. He resolved to get on the water each day and develop some skill. The kayak might some day be a way to make an unobserved trip to the island.

John kept busy enough with his wood collection and kayaking that he had little time to worry about his present situation or his future. As the days and weeks went by, he began hunting and started eating more complex meals.

By the time the snow began to accumulate, John was well settled into a comfortable if somewhat lonely life in Red Bay. He had access to a radio in his truck, but couldn't bring himself to listen to evidence of the possibility of a life with anyone else.

CHAPTER 23
SEPARATE US

When Dave came in to work, Captain Pickford was waiting outside his office.

"Morning, Mr. Mayor, have you heard about what happened last night?"

"More riots downtown? I hope you have a bunch of those rabble-rousers ready to go to Nova Scotia. We get a few of them sent away and things will settle down."

"No sir, it's something new. A bunch of men in pickup trucks have blockaded the highway up by Bellevue Beach. I got a call in from a patrol car this morning asking what he should do about it. He says he'll need reinforcements. The guys that have set up the barrier are armed, and they insist that they are protecting us from the disease."

"Let's just leave them alone for a while. We need something for the people to think about. Right now our big concern is food. We all know there are going to be people in the city without enough to eat this winter, but we have to distract them somehow. This idea that there is a risk from the rest of the island may be just what we need."

"But there isn't any disease on the island, is there?"

"Who knows? You never can tell where these stories

start. There just may be something to them. I think we would be best to either leave those guys alone or maybe even send some officers up to help them out."

"You may be right, sir. Things are getting hot in the city, and we could certainly use something to keep people off the streets."

That afternoon, Dave returned to the topic of the supposed disease outbreak in the western portion of the province. In his introduction, he let slip the information that a number of well meaning citizens had set up a roadblock to keep all traffic out of the southern portion of the province.

The first four callers were enthusiastic supporters of the blockade. Their only question was why it had taken private citizens to initiate these protective measures. Each of them insisted that government needed to put some sort of permanent barrier up between the Avalon Peninsula and the rest of the province.

The fifth caller was a doctor from the medical school at Memorial University.

"Good afternoon, Dr. Wells, it's great to have a medical person on our show today. You of all people will recognize how serious this virus is and how important it is for us to keep it out."

"Good afternoon, Mr. Fletcher. While I agree wholeheartedly with your characterization of the disease, I must take issue with your contention that there has been an outbreak in the western region of the province."

"But, doctor, surely we can't be too careful."

"Being careful is one thing and causing unnecessary panic in the populace is quite another. I am leading an ad hoc committee at the university studying the effects of the

Ottawa virus. As you suggest, the virus has had a devastating effect on every portion of the planet that we've been able to assess. However, we have also set up a monitoring system with hospitals and clinics around the province to help notify us of any suspicious cases. To this point we have had no worrisome reports from anywhere in the province. After hearing the rumours from your program two days ago, I made a point of directly asking medical personnel from Corner Brook about their situation and they assured me there have been no cases that have caused them alarm."

"Don't you think it's possible, doctor, that there has been a case that the medical people up there haven't heard about?"

"That is very unlikely, Mr. Fletcher, and your continued focus on baseless rumours and your support for this ill-conceived restriction of travel across the island concerns me greatly."

"Doctor, you probably can remember how everyone in the medical field felt that I was overreacting when the first reports came in about the disease in Ottawa. Where would we be if the people here had listened to the experts instead of me?"

"That's a completely different situation. You were right and there was a real threat from the mainland."

"And maybe I'm right again. Do you think the people of the province should be taking that chance? With that, I'll thank Dr. Wells for calling in and move along to the next person on the line."

None of the callers for the rest of the program sided with the doctor's opinion. Most simply ignored his concerns and went on to emphasize how important it was to get a wall across the isthmus. One man referred to the call from the University as typical over-educated nonsense. In his opinion, the university was always full of crackpot ideas and he didn't understand why government put any money into it.

After the program, Dave headed back to City Hall and called together Pickford, his public relations manager, and two councilors who tended to be sympathetic to his policies.

"I've asked you to come in today to talk about the disease situation in the province. As you've no doubt heard, there are rumours of an outbreak in Corner Brook. A few brave men have closed off the highway, but I think that something more permanent is called for."

One of the councillors was brave enough to raise a concern.

"But, sir, from what I hear, the university and the medical association have said that there is no problem. I was listening to the other radio station and they've been having doctors on all afternoon."

"First off, you shouldn't listen to the lies that come out of what you call the other radio station. Those guys know that their competitors represent city government, and they will say anything they can think of to make trouble. You can assume that everything you hear from them is fake."

"I see what you're saying, sir."

"What we need is a permanent barrier across the Trans-Canada highway. I want to know if I have the support of everyone in the room."

There were murmurs of affirmation and nods all around.

"Now, I know that some will argue that the city of St.

John's has no business building a wall that far out of the city. But the barrier needs to be built, and if we don't do it who will? The provincial government is a lost cause. They have no workers now and they have abandoned our part of the province. We need to move."

There was an awkward silence around the room until Pickford spoke up.

"If we are going to look at this we must consider some of the consequences. And then, if after careful consideration we decide to wall off the province, we must do it effectively."

"Please carry on, Captain. It's important that we consider your concerns."

"There are a few things that immediately come to mind. A high proportion of our agricultural land is in the western parts of the province. I think with care we can grow enough on the Avalon to feed ourselves, but it will be more difficult without the rest of the province. Secondly, essentially all of the electric power we have is generated outside of the Avalon. I don't think we can count on power still coming down to us if we try to cut them off.

"As well, one of the few resources that we are rich in is petroleum products. Oil is still coming in from Hibernia, and the refinery at Come by Chance is still producing gasoline, diesel fuel, and heating oil. We need all of these products to keep our society functioning comfortably. If we do decide to divide up the island, I think it's critical that we keep the refinery on our side of the wall."

"I'd have to agree with everything you have said, Captain. I think that we all know that one of the narrowest parts of the isthmus between us and the rest of the island is right at Come by Chance. That's where we need to put our wall. I propose that we put some kind of structure completely across so we can be sure that no one comes in."

Two nights later the city council met, and one of the councilors who had been at the mayor's meeting introduced a motion directing city workers to erect a barrier between the Avalon Peninsula and the rest of the province. When one councillor suggested that she wanted more details about the type of wall, she was shouted down by spectators in the gallery insisting that she was a coward.

The motion passed after just twenty minutes of discussion. Within two days, a municipal crew brought concrete barriers to just north of Come by Chance to shut down the highway. It took another week for them to install nearly five kilometres of wire fencing across the isthmus.

Dave continued to support the fence on his radio program and insisted that there would be no cost to taxpayers on the Avalon. His advisors convinced him that he couldn't tell his listeners that people on the other side of the wall would be paying for it; that would be ludicrous. He abandoned that strategy and announced that there would be no paid officers maintaining the site. Instead, any able bodied citizen who was concerned about the safety of the region was encouraged to bring a firearm and take a turn guarding the wall.

For the first two weeks there were more volunteers than could park within two hundred meters of the barricade. One of the men who had set up the first barrier took it upon himself to make up a schedule and assigned people to shifts either watching the highway or patrolling the fence out to the ocean on each side.

Memorial University senate and the student union

held a joint information session pointing out that the city council had far overstepped its authority. Speaker after speaker suggested that civil freedom was being eroded by a council that was out of control.

As time wore on, the crowds of strikers at Provincial Government buildings dwindled. The union ran out of funding for strike pay and soon there was no evidence of the provincial government or its workers on the Avalon Peninsula.

The government continued to meet in Corner Brook, but decided that there was no point in trying to maintain any presence south of the blockade. The premier spoke on the one local radio station in Corner Brook that was still operating and assured the public that order was still in place in the province north of the barricade. The one surprise in his statement was his suggestion that the actions of the council of St. John's indicated to him and his government that the Avalon Peninsula had chosen to no longer be a part of the province.

At the next session of government, the members from both parties who represented ridings in the south complained that the premier's statement had made it clear that he no longer represented all of the province. He had given up on most of the population. In response, the premier asked how those members intended to represent their ridings when they couldn't even travel to see their constituents.

Opposition members from south of the wall walked out of the new house and a vote to have politicians who were unable to travel to their ridings removed passed narrowly.

A number of the displaced members set up a protest

outside of the government building where meetings were being held. After a day of derision from locals, they realized that there was no sympathy for their position and they moved on.

News of the provincial government's abandonment of the most populated part of the province travelled quickly to the Avalon. Mayor Fletcher called an emergency meeting of the St. John's city council.

Dave opened the meeting by saying that everything had changed with the provincial government's move to isolate the Avalon Peninsula.

"The fine government members from our portion of the province have been removed from their posts in an unlawful coup and we have now effectively been abandoned by our government.

"Of course, we need leadership and direction or our whole society will collapse. All of the Avalon Peninsula outside of the city of St. John's currently has no order. As the sole remaining survivors of the terrible Ottawa virus disease, we must stand together and watch out for each other. To maintain order, I am proposing today that the leadership of the city of St. John's accepts the burden of governing the rest of our peninsula. As of today I suggest that we expand our area of jurisdiction to include the new city state of Avalon."

There was polite applause after the mayor's speech. There was no warning of Fletch's plan, but no one rose to argue that his suggestion was a bad idea. A vote to incorporate all of the Avalon into the city's jurisdiction passed unanimously by a group that included no one from outside the city.

CHAPTER 24
STILL COMFORTABLE

By the time the vegetables were harvested, Joan was well prepared for winter. There was enough food put away to look after the twenty relatives and friends who now lived in the enclave. Her biggest stress that fall had been the death of her father. Seventy-four seemed too young to die for a man who had been healthy and energetic for his whole life. Her only consolation was that he had gone doing what he loved. Dropping over dead on the seat of a tractor with no warning or pain didn't seem like a bad way to go.

The snow had just started to cover the ground when Joan had her first visit from a representative of the new Avalon government. The guards allowed a harmless looking man driving an old station wagon to pull up to the front of the house.

When Joan answered the door, he identified himself as a revenue agent and he wanted to talk with her about the new taxation system.

Joan immediately asked for identification and when the man indicated that he had nothing of the sort and had never been asked for this kind of thing before, she closed the door in his face.

He returned a week later with a photocopied letter on City of St. John's stationary signed by a member of the council. The letter indicated that the bearer, a Mr. Hayward Snow, was authorized to collect all appropriate taxes from citizens of the Avalon Peninsula.

Joan wasn't particularly impressed by the unofficial looking document or the man's unkempt appearance, but she decided to give him a hearing.

"Alright, Mr. Snow. I'm quite busy with the farm, but if you can be quick about it I'll hear whatever it is you have to say. I hope you don't mind if we just chat outside, I find a little cold weather tends to cut down the bullshit."

"Yes, Ms. Mercer. I am led to understand that you are the proprietor of this farming establishment."

"You have indeed been led in the right direction, now get on with it." She hated when semi-literate fools tried to dress their diction up with sloppy attempts to sound intelligent.

"Well, Ms. Mercer, as you may be aware, there is no longer any income tax or for that matter federal or provincial taxes of any kind being collected in this province."

"That makes sense, Mr. Snow, considering that there is no evidence of the provincial or federal government doing anything in this area."

"However, we have not fallen into complete anarchy. There still is a governing body for this region and the government needs some way to pay for its activities."

"I understand where you are going with this, but I just wonder what it is that this new government is going to do for us out around the bay. You are the first person who has anything to do with them who has even shown their face around here. I haven't had anyone from any kind of agriculture department visit, and no one seems to be paying any attention to the roads. We've had snow here already and there has been no sign of anyone from government doing anything about it."

"Ms. Mercer, there is far more to government than clearing snow. Our people have only assumed power this year, and it will be some time before a full range of services will be available throughout the region.

"All that we are asking for is a twenty-five percent tax on all sales in our area of jurisdiction. As a farmer you will have sales of meat and vegetables, and you must pay us twenty-five percent of the money you take in."

"And exactly what do you plan to do if I refuse to pay the tax? I'm happy to pay my share if there is some benefit to me or even to the people who live out here. I'm sure there are lots of things your government will be doing for St. John's residents, but there is nothing you are giving us, and frankly there is nothing that we need from you."

"I would be careful talking that way if I was you, Ms. Mercer. My bosses in town take this taxation business quite seriously. I can go back and tell them that you have refused to co-operate, but I don't think this will end very well for you. What you are talking about here, Ms. Mercer, is nothing short of seduction."

"Well, Mr. Snow, I have a lot more important things to do today than standing here in the cold arguing with you. You would be best getting back in your car and driving on to St. John's where you belong. We don't need your type out here.

"And by the way, the word you were looking for is sedition."

Hayward Snow didn't immediately drive back to St. John's. He was a persistent and practical man. There were small convenience store operations between Bay Roberts and St. John's that would be easier targets than this troublesome woman. He decided that reporting her stubbornness to his bosses in St. John's would only make his life more complicated. He didn't need to get caught up in arguments that would slow down getting his share from tax collection.

Joan didn't lose any sleep over Snow's visit. Her initial anger soon dissipated and she even forgot to tell the boys to keep a watch out for his car. She had a tractor that wasn't running smoothly that took her full attention for the rest of the day.

Her suggestion that no one was looking after the roads proved both right and wrong. No one from the new government involved with transportation was seen all winter in the Bay Roberts area. However, a man who had worked with the previous government at the local transportation depot took it upon himself to clean up after significant snowfalls.

The man had nothing to do after he had collected enough wood to burn for the winter and decided it would be interesting to see if the plows at the depot would still start. Once he got a plow going, he drove out to his residence and cleared the road. Next, he decided it would be a nice surprise for his wife if he cleaned up as far out as her mother's place.

He stopped a number of times on the drive to talk

with friends and a number of them offered him food if he would plow the roads in front of their houses. Eventually he set up a private business of snow clearing that provided enough food for his family to eat well until spring.

Bay Roberts had a largely uneventful winter. Local fishermen sold their catch to people in the immediate area and many residents filled their freezers with moose and caribou. Between the assistance of friends and relatives, people in the town who couldn't provide for themselves were looked after and survived.

CHAPTER 25
HARD TIMES

The first winter after the outbreak of the Ottawa virus was difficult for St. John's. There was a constant stream of people leaving the city to move in with parents and relatives in rural areas on the Avalon Peninsula and beyond.

When the first refugees approached the highway barricades at Come By Chance, the self-appointed guardians were unsure how to react. The barrier had been constructed to keep traffic from coming into the Avalon, and no one had considered that more people were actually attempting to move in the opposite direction.

At a hastily arranged meeting in Whitborne, there were two opposing opinions. The hard liners insisted that a wall was a wall and by allowing anyone to cross, they were not doing their jobs. More reasonable men suggested that it was in everyone's interest to let people leave the Avalon. If they didn't like it here, good riddance. Hadn't their leader Fletch said something about Avalon, love it or leave it?

The invocation of the leader's name and opinion swayed the conversation and soon everyone agreed that the wall should be a one way affair. Only movement into the Avalon would be curtailed.

Fletch was furious that it took a full week for news of the new arrangement to reach him. He felt the wall would look foolish and even redundant if people could easily cross it. It worried him that eventually no one would take the barrier seriously.

He called Pickford and Mac in for an emergency meeting.

"Captain, have you heard what is going on at the wall?"

"Do you mean about people getting through to go north?"

"Yeah. So you've already heard?"

"Some of the boys were up on a patrol earlier in the week and talked with the guys on the barricade. They mentioned it to me about five days ago."

"And you didn't think to tell me about this?"

"First off, I thought you would have known from your radio show. Those folks tell you everything, don't they? As well, I didn't think this was a big deal. The purpose of the wall was to keep this Corner Brook outbreak you are so excited about from getting on the Avalon. People moving the other way aren't any kind of a threat to us. As a matter of fact, we would be a lot better off if a few more folks from the city would move out."

Fletch fumed, but he could see that he had no room to maneuver. Pickford had taken liberties with his position. The government and Fletch himself had to be seen to be in control of what went on in the Avalon. He had to make sure that his grip on power stayed firm. As well, he knew that any attempt to remove Pickford from his position would be futile and perhaps even risk a coup.

"Of course you are right, Captain. I just don't like the way that this has been handled. Understand that I need to know about everything that is going on. If I get on the radio and don't know what's happening, we will all be in big trouble. I have to count on you, Captain, to keep me up to date. Do you think that will be a problem?"

"No, sir, I completely understand your concern, and I will make an effort to more completely inform you of the situation on the ground."

"Thank you, Captain. I knew I could depend on you. Now, we need to decide where we go from here. Should we stop this movement through the wall or is there some way we can make it look like it's all our idea?"

Mac had been silent to this point, and he uncharacteristically raised his hand like a shy student in a classroom.

"If I might, sir, I have a suggestion for this."

"Go ahead, Mac."

"Isn't it possible for us to make this a paying proposition? We could announce that we have decided that anyone who wants to can move out of the Avalon. We have said something like that from the beginning concerning boats. We have never objected to anyone leaving the island. But, what we need to do is set up an emigration office out in Whitborne. Have it something like our tax system. Let the guys who are watching the wall make some money. We charge for an exit permit and let the boys out there run a little office and take a percentage of the fee."

Fletch and Pickford immediately conceded that this was a fine solution to their problem. They also agreed that there was no need to run a technicality like this through the council. It was a simple matter of sending a patrol car up to the barrier and explaining the concept to the guys at the wall. There was no concern that the men would have any problem with making a little money for what they were already doing.

Fletch was on the radio the next day explaining the new government policy. There wasn't much response from his listeners. No one seemed too concerned.

The main effect of the announcement was an increase in the traffic leaving the Avalon. More and more people in the city were suffering from the food shortages and the fact that so many were heading north suggested that there might be a better life elsewhere.

Despite Fletch's attempt to stoke the worries about the threat of disease from the rest of the island, interest and concern around the issue decreased. He tried to get the subject into people's minds again on his show.

"Welcome again to the wonderful world of radio. It's your buddy Fletch here on this snowy afternoon, and today I'd like to talk a bit about what I see as our growing complacency around the big disease. We all know now that this virus from the mainland has killed just about everybody it came in contact with. I'm the one who warned you all about how dangerous this was, and, because of my warnings, we are still all alive. But we can't forget what a precarious position we are in. All it would take is one slip and we would be in the same shape as the rest of the world. I think we need to talk more about this and keep awake. And we've got Vern on the line. How are you today, Vern?"

"Not just the best, Fletch. I've always been a listener

of your show, and I appreciate what you have done for us. But it's getting desperate out here. I haven't had any bread for a month now, and I'm just getting by on the bit of fish and vegetables that I'm getting from the food bank. I'm in my seventies, Fletch, and my kids are, or maybe I should say were, on the mainland. I can't go out and find food myself. I just wish someone would drive me out west. Lots of people are going, so things must be better out that way."

"But, Vern, aren't you worried about the virus out there beyond the wall?"

"I'm starting to wonder if there really is any virus in the rest of the province. I haven't heard a thing from anyone who knows about people who have actually died out there. I'm beginning to think this northern virus threat was a big hoax."

"Vern, I didn't steer you wrong when this disease started. Don't you think you should trust my instincts again?"

"I'm sorry, Fletch, but this whole thing doesn't make sense to me. You fellas have opened up the wall to people who want to head north. I understand why you would do that, people have to be free to see family and maybe move on to a better life, but I can't understand how you could let those people go if you really believed that there was disease beyond the wall. I know you're a good man, Fletch, and it would take a monster to send all those people off to certain death."

Fletch was stuck for an answer. He let a full three seconds of dead air pass before he admitted that Vern had brought up some valid points. The words weren't out of his mouth before he regretted them. He thanked Vern for calling and went to a commercial.

His public relations assistant, who was behind the glass, knew better than to comment. Fletch had backed himself into a corner and nothing could save him.

He pushed the button that put him through to the control booth.

"Mary, put on a piece of music. I want you to thoroughly vet the next call that comes in, and make damn sure that whoever I talk to thinks the wall is the best thing since sliced bread. Take your time getting me a good caller, but if this fools up you can find yourself a new job."

Mary was careful, and the next caller on the line was a true believer.

"Fletch boy, I don't know what's up with people that won't listen to you about the dangers from the north. You've never steered us wrong, and if you say there's disease up there I believe it."

"Well thank you, Rod. It's good to hear that there are people out there with some sense."

"Yes, boy, the way I sees it, it doesn't really matter whether there is a disease or not. Those folks up there are just bad people. The wife's brother is from Gander, and, my son, you couldn't trust a word out of that man's mouth. I tell you they are bad people."

"You've got a good point there, Rod. Those living off the Avalon have always had it easy. The cost of looking after this province has been carried by the city of St. John's. We were always the ones paying the bulk of taxes. Those people out there never appreciated how much we put into their highways and ferries. They have had a free ride for far too long."

"You're right on with all of that, Fletch. They've always been a burden to us here in town. If I had my way, I'd get that navy boat in the harbour to sail up off Gander and fire a couple of missiles into the place to let them know what we think of them."

"Well, I'm not sure if I completely agree with using missiles, but I think you have a pretty fair understanding of the situation, and I thank you for calling in this afternoon."

The phone lines lit up and everyone wanted to discuss the possibility of using missiles or of starting some kind of ground based invasion of the rest of the province. One caller suggested that this kind of thinking was dangerous and if there was any virus in the rest of the province we certainly didn't want any of our citizens sent up into that kind of risk. The next caller said that anyone with such cowardly ideas must be from the university. It was clear to him that thinking of that kind could only come from the school.

For the next week, discussion in the city shifted from the lack of food to the evilness of the people of the rest of the province. Grafitti appeared coining the term "westers". The westers were blamed for everything from the disease to the lack of food.

Callers on Fletch's show concentrated their anger on the people beyond the wall. A common refrain was that there were all kinds of moose and caribou in the western forests, and it was obvious that those people weren't suffering the same way people in the city were. Questions were raised about why these people hadn't been sharing the great bounties of food they had.

The city seemed divided between those who felt the westers were the embodiment of evil and those who believed that there was food and comfort beyond the wall. The exodus of people out of the city and the Avalon Peninsula increased.

Once they left the Avalon, refugees from St. John's spread stories of hatred and xenophobia. Anger soon built up in residents of towns north of the wall.

A group of young men from Clarenville decided they had enough of the disrespect that they had heard from the south. A half-dozen of them drove down within five kilometres of the wall and began attacking electrical towers with grinders powered by a generator. It took them no time to bring down two of the structures and interrupt the flow of electricity.

The north half of the Avalon immediately lost all of its power and there were blackouts in St. John's.

Fletch contacted the director of Newfoundland Hydro to see what had happened to cause the outages. The man explained that it was apparent that the problems had been caused by an interruption of power somewhere off the Avalon.

A helicopter was sent out to inspect the power lines and came back with news of the downed towers.

Fletch and Pickford met with Hydro officials and decided that it was critical to restore power flow across the isthmus. The hydro managers said that they were still in contact with staff off the Avalon, but had been told that no one was willing to attempt to replace or repair the downed towers. Those who weren't sympathetic to the terrorist actions were afraid that they would be attacked if they even inspected the towers.

Pickford suggested sending out a heavily armed group of men to protect the workers sent up for repairs. Two armoured vehicles and a group of thirty soldiers crossed the line with four hydro repair crews, their vehicles, and a large boom crane truck. It took eight days to put the towers back up and reinforce the structures.

Before returning to the city, the soldiers planted explosives around the towers, fenced the area and left signs indicating the area that was mined.

Full power returned to the Avalon, and it looked like the problem had been solved until a sixteen year old boy wandered into the mined perimeter of one of the towers. The boy survived the explosion because his friends had the presence of mind to torniquet the stump of his blown off leg.

The next day four towers north of the ones that had been repaired came down.

By this time, Fletch had stopped even pretending that council had any say in decisions made by the government of Avalon. He picked a group of trusted advisors who, besides Pickford, were the only ones involved in any questions of government actions.

The group met to discuss how to respond to this latest threat from beyond the peninsula. Pickford was the first to speak.

"Gentlemen," (and it was gentlemen he spoke to, there was not one woman in Fletch's new inner circle), "we have here the greatest threat to our survival since the disease itself. We must act decisively and let the terrorists know that this kind of action will not go without reprisal."

The Hydro official spoke next.

"I'm not sure how we can beat this. We can go back in and put those towers up and they'll just take down the next ones along."

"That's why we need to be decisive. These people need to see that we are serious. The HMCS *St. John's* is equipped with both Harpoon and Sea Sparrow missiles. I believe that just one of these weapons deployed outside of the town of Clarenville would convince those people that they should leave our electrical supply alone."

There was a moment of shocked silence around the table. The Hydro man spoke again.

"You can't be serious, Captain. That would mean war. Electricity is important, but you are talking about firing a missile into an area that could be populated with innocent people. Can you imagine how angry the parents of killed children will be? They won't stop taking down towers, they'll start blowing up buildings in St. John's."

The table went quiet again. Fletch stood, walked around behind Pickford and placed his hands on his shoulders.

"You've both brought up excellent points. We need to act here, but we don't want to throw ourselves into a needless war. How about if we try a compromise? I suggest that we go up again, repair the towers that are down, and, when we finish, the armed group continues into Clarenville and meets with the mayor. You could head this up, Captain – speak with their leaders and tell them about your missiles. Let them know that we have no desire to attack them, but if they keep interrupting our power supply we will have no alternative."

There was muttering around the table and the Hydro

official closed his eyes and shook his head. The meeting ended quickly with a decision to go ahead with Fletch's suggestion.

It snowed hard the week after the meeting and the roads on most of the Avalon were impassable.

Fletch and Pickford arranged for a plow to open a path so that the Hydro crews and its military support could make their way up to the fallen towers. The structures were restored faster than the first time, and Pickford and his heavily armed contingent followed the plow into Clarenville.

The mayor and council of the town met with Pickford. The captain presented his case that, while he had no interest in causing any harm to the good people of Clarenville, it was imperative that the power interruptions cease. The residents of the Avalon needed electricity to survive the winter and any further attacks would unquestionably be responded to seriously. Before leaving the meeting, almost as an afterthought, he reminded his listeners that the HMCS *St. John's* was equipped with missiles, and that he had been pressured to use them to prevent further terrorism.

Pickford returned to St. John's unimpeded, and the mayor of Clarenville held public meetings explaining the threats from beyond the wall. Whatever the mayor's intentions were, the meeting intensified anti-Avalon feelings.

For the next three days, there were marches in Clarenville with people carrying signs saying that they wouldn't be bullied. On the fourth day, the refinery in Come by Chance was demolished by the detonation of fertilizer and fuel packed in the back of a pickup truck.

CHAPTER 26
ALMOST SETTLED

John had a comfortable if somewhat lonely winter in Red Bay. He stopped shaving and grew a respectable beard. Every day was busy with trips into the bush to fish, hunt, or gather wood. For the first month after the snow started falling, he was so tired when he got home each night he would immediately go to bed.

With improving fitness, his free time increased and he started missing the books that he had collected in Ottawa. His new house had a collection of paperbacks, but there was nothing that stimulated his imagination. The situation inspired a new quest to inspect all the houses in the area for books. By this time, he wasn't bothered by corpses in houses; they were frozen solid, and there wasn't much bad odour left behind.

He hit the jackpot in a small house that had been lived in by an elderly lady. He knew this because her remains were still in a rocking chair in the living room. Her library contained most of the books he'd picked out in Ottawa and plenty more classics.

War and Peace was a great escape from the realities of his situation and on nights he couldn't sleep he would slog through Proust. He was surprised to realize he was finally starting to understand *Ulysses*. Something about the story resonated deeply. Reading became a major joy in his life and he found himself returning earlier to the house each evening. Between the canned food he found in the neighbourhood and his fresh meat and fish, he had no trouble finding enough to eat.

When spring came, John found a roto-tiller and expanded the area of the largest garden in Red Bay. He was surprised to find seeds in the hardware store in L'Anse-au-Clair and soon had a garden planted.

As the weather got warmer, life became easier. There was no shoveling to do, and he had so much food put away that his trouting expeditions were more for pleasure than any real need.

By late May, the snow was completely gone and John decided to take a holiday. He packed his truck with survival gear and set off in the direction he had originally driven in from. Goose Bay was a city compared to Red Bay, and he planned to explore the stores and residences more carefully for interesting and useful material. It also crossed his mind that he should make a careful search to see if there were any more survivors. Surely Mandy wasn't the only one in Labrador who had come through the disease.

The road back to Goose Bay wasn't in the same condition as when he had driven down. The snow and months without maintenance had resulted in rough sections and potholes. He wondered how long it would be before the route would be impassable.

Goose Bay didn't disappoint. His memories of Mandy

kept him from staying in any of the hotels, but he found a spacious home for his visit. The perishable food around town was mostly ruined, but he did find some potatoes and turnip that were edible if somewhat shriveled. His biggest delight was a large store that carried camping gear and army surplus equipment in its basement. He filled the bed of his truck with every manner of fishing and hunting gear. While the mess kits and sleeping bags there weren't modern lightweight models, he delighted in their seeming indestructibility.

On his third night in Goose Bay, he was driving through a residential section when he saw a light in a shed behind a house. When he stopped his truck, he could hear music coming from inside. Someone else was alive! His first worry was that the person in the shed might shoot him if he surprised them. He needed to let them know of his presence from a safe distance.

John got out of his vehicle and stood behind it.

"Hello! Is there anybody in there? I was driving by and saw your light."

There was no answer, so John called out again. His second call got no response, and he wondered if the person inside could hear over the music. There was no way he would chance walking up to the door, so he got back in the truck and leaned on the horn.

After nearly thirty seconds, the shed door opened and a grey bearded man wearing a woman's fur coat looked out into the dark.

"What do you want? If you're selling something, there's nothing I need that you could possibly have."

"Hello, sir. I'm not selling anything. I was just visiting

Goose Bay and I saw your light on. I thought it would be nice to have a talk."

"Why didn't you say so in the first place? Come in and have a beer. There's no shortage of booze here. The town's full of it and I'm the only one drinking."

John tentatively moved towards the shed, and when he could see the man wasn't armed he stepped inside. The two lights in the ceiling revealed that the shed was lined with walls of car batteries. In the confined space, the music coming from an expensive looking stereo system was overwhelming. He recognized a Talking Heads tune from one of their later albums.

When the man saw him looking at the turntable he went over and lifted the needle from the record.

"You'll have to excuse my manners. I don't get many visitors here."

"How many people have you seen since the disease came through?"

"Let me see. Well, actually you are the first."

"Do you know if there is anyone else around in Goose Bay?"

"Don't think so. When things first got bad I drove around looking for others, but I pretty well gave that up when winter came on."

"Did you know there are people living on the island of Newfoundland? I'm from the Rock originally, but I was in Ontario when the disease started. I've been trying to get back, but they are watching the coast pretty carefully."

"People alive in Newfoundland, are there? Well, good for them. Glad to see someone's doing alright."

"I'm so glad to have found you, maybe you and I can

do something. Perhaps the two of us can figure out a way to get to the island."

"Listen, son, I'm an old man. I just turned sixty-five, and I have no intention of moving from here. I'm not sure how many years I've got left, and from what I can make out the world is falling apart."

"How can you say you're an old man, you're only sixty-five. You could have decades ahead of you. If the two of us worked together…"

"Just hold on. I'm not going nowhere. I can understand your excitement about moving on to the island, and, believe me, I wish you the best of luck with your efforts."

"But, couldn't you even help me? I'm alone and I need someone to be with."

"Couldn't agree with you more there. You do need someone to be with, but you don't need an old fart like me. You need to get to Newfoundland and find yourself a woman. I've just been listening to that old philosopher David Byrne this evening. He says that the world moves on a woman's hips. David was right you know. From a man's point of view the world is all about women. It's all about a woman.

"I was married for thirty-five years to a wonderful girl before this disease came along. We had two boys, they both had successful businesses here in town, and now they are all gone.

"The purpose in life is to find a woman and pass on your genes. I had my chance and it didn't quite work out the way I had hoped. I know that the future isn't going to change the significance of my life. I'm happy to just sit here in the shed and listen to music from the past until

I'm gone.

"I grew up in St. John's, you know. Went to university and met Lucy there. She was from up here, and I just followed her after we finished school. The draw of a woman is something to be reckoned with. The first art man ever did was of those little fertility goddesses. Clay women with big hips. That's what makes us move, and that's why you need to get to the island. Go and get yourself a woman, have some kids, leave something for the future. Find yourself a city to live in."

"I'm not just sure that I can do this by myself. When I came from Ontario, I did find a woman. She followed me from Lab City down to the north shore and then the disease got her. She died and I don't know why. It might have been me who killed her. I'm worried that if I go to the island, I may bring the disease to all of those people."

"I'm sorry to hear about your woman, but your case is completely different than mine. I'm all about the past. I sit here and listen to The Beatles and Elvis Costello and Talking Heads. It's all music from years ago, and that's where I want to live. The music is like everything else in this world, there hasn't been anything worth listening to since I was young. I've done what I can in this world, and now I'm just waiting out my time.

"But you're special. You've been in contact with the virus, but somehow you haven't got the disease. It's young folks like you who are the future of this planet. Those people on the island think that they can stop the disease from coming. They're just dreaming. Just look at how fast and completely this problem has spread. If it can get to places like Goose Bay and just about wipe out the population, what do you think ten kilometres of water is going to do to protect them?

"We don't know anything about this disease. What if it's passed by birds, or even something like a fox? It's just a matter of time before someone or something brings the virus to the island.

"And when the disease hits, people like you need to find a woman who is immune like you and you need to have kids. That's the only way that people are going to survive. Morally, I don't think you have any choice; you have to get to the island. I think you are more special than you realize."

John stayed and talked late into the night, but when his host didn't offer him a place to stay, he eventually said goodnight and drove back to his adopted house. In the morning he realized that he hadn't heard the man's name. After breakfast, he headed back to the shed to continue their talk. He still hoped that he might convince the man to join forces with him.

The streets of Goose Bay were a little confusing, and it took some circling around before he found the place he had been to the night before. The shed door was closed, but there was no answer when he knocked. John let himself in and found no one home. The batteries, lights, and stereo were all still in place, but his companion from the night before wasn't in.

The house beside the shed was just as empty, and there was no evidence that anyone had slept or eaten there recently. John started checking all of the houses within a hundred meters of the shed. Not one of them showed signs of any human presence for months.

John wondered if the previous night had been some

kind of hallucination. He went back to check the shed more carefully. In the daylight, he could make out solar panels along the roof and a sophisticated connection between the panels and the batteries. The lights and stereo still worked. A stack of vinyl records was piled next to the rocking chair. Nothing there was more recent than the 1980's.

The situation unnerved John. He wondered if his time alone had made him so desperate for company that he had invented the previous night's conversation. It was obvious that no one slept or ate in the shed, and he couldn't see any other place the man could have been staying. Surely someone who had lived so completely alone would want to prolong the contact that they had shared the previous night.

There was no doubt in his mind that he had listened to music in the shed. The same Talking Heads record was on the turntable. On reflection, he wondered why he hadn't heard the music through the silence of the nights he spent in Goose Bay before he found the shed. Perhaps he had come in and listened to the music by himself and it was the words from the record that had spoken to him. If there really had been someone with him last night, he obviously didn't want to continue their relationship.

Either way, John decided that it was time for him to get back to Red Bay. His trip had only provided him with more uncertainty. He had no idea whether he should stay in Labrador or move on to the island.

Back in Red Bay, John was excited to see that his garden was starting to show signs of life. The area he had cleared was a big as his house. The plants took his attention away from his worries, and he spent most days on his knees pulling out individual weeds and removing insects one at a time.

When the first radishes came, he relished the sharp taste and the snap in his mouth as he bit into them. Summer passed quickly into fall and John's mind was filled with plans to put away vegetables in the root cellar he found and to harvest enough seeds to ensure that he would be able to plant a garden the following year.

Between the apples he found on trees scattered throughout the local communities and the raspberries, blueberries, and bakeapples he found growing wild, John developed a diet that was healthy and delicious.

It wasn't long after he returned from his trip to Goose Bay that he found his truck would no longer start. He tried a number of different vehicles using either diesel or gasoline but nothing would move. Outboard motors and his rototiller all suffered the same fate.

The things that John wished for most were a cow or two and a horse. Cows could have provided him with milk and butter, but he couldn't find evidence that anyone close to where he lived had kept cows. There was one horse barn, but the two horses inside had been tied on securely and died of starvation when their keepers hadn't continued to bring feed.

He found a bicycle and fashioned a small platform over his back wheel, but this new system of transportation severely limited the amount of material that he could bring back from any communities outside of Red Bay. There was still some canned food left in the convenience stores and residences in the village, but it was fast becoming apparent that this was a finite resource.

It occurred to John that his problems with non-functioning fuel would likely be plaguing the island as well. To satisfy his curiosity he took a bicycle trip down the shore to Blanc Sablon and spent two full days and nights watching the water off the ferry terminal. He saw no boats and assumed that the islanders would know that gasoline powered refugees were no longer a risk to them.

Gathering food to eat and store kept John busy enough that he had been spending little time in his kayak. The realization that there were likely no guards along the strait inspired him to start paddling again.

At night in bed, he often dreamed of Mandy, and when he woke he wondered if it would be possible for him to find another partner. The idea from either the man in Goose Bay or his music, that the world moved on a woman's hips, kept coming back to him.

During his time in Red Bay, John had seen a number of dogs. Most of them had been desiccated carcasses that he found trapped inside the homes that he entered. It amazed him how many of the animals were curled up next to their owners. They could have lived at least a while longer if they had chosen to take nutrition from the bodies of the humans.

There was a small pack of dogs that he occasionally saw running through the community. He recognized two as German shepherds and one looked like it might have come from a poodle and beagle. The animal that fascinated him most was a gold coloured lab. In his experience, animals of this type were usually exceptionally friendly.

It took a long time before John tried to make contact with the pack. The shepherds had shown their teeth a few times, and he was frankly worried about being attacked. He started by leaving moose bones outside of his house.

The bones always disappeared overnight, but the dogs initially wouldn't come close during daylight hours.

John changed his strategy to putting bones out during the day and watching from his window. The first daylight raids were undertaken by just one of the shepherds. The rest of the pack would stand back while the dominant dog rushed in to pull the bones away from the house.

His next tactic was to leave so many bones outside his door that they couldn't all be removed at once. The alpha shepherd again came and removed the choicest morsels from the pile. Less than a minute after he ran off, the second shepherd moved in and took its share. The pattern continued until only the lab was left warily watching the remaining bones.

John came outside when he was satisfied that all of the other dogs had gone. He went back into the house and brought out a small piece of dried meat. He sat on his porch and softly called out and whistled to the lab. The dog tipped its head to the side and whined as if remembering some long lost association with a human.

John continued to speak quietly to the lab and placed the meat on the deck of the porch beside him. The dog slowly advanced. As it licked its lips, saliva in long strings dripped down from its mouth.

When the animal came up to the porch, there was a moment when it seemed she would bolt. Every nerve was on end as she sniffed at the meat and finally took it into her mouth.

From closer up, John could see that this was a young female. Her coat was a Rastafarian mess, and she was obviously undernourished. He continued with quiet reassuring comments and gradually reached out and touched the dog's back. The lab relaxed, moved over closer and licked John's hand.

A rough low growl was the first sign that the dominant German shepherd was approaching. Its ears were pinned back and its ferocious teeth were on full display. As John looked, the animal started moving in faster. He jumped up and bolted in through his door. He could only watch in horror as the shepherd jumped on the lab and started biting into her belly and legs. The lab wasn't killed, but her back left leg dragged as she slunk away whimpering.

John stopped putting out feed for the dogs and the only times that he saw the pack was when he would surprise them on his bicycle. He never was able to make out the lab in the group.

John's experience with the dogs drove home the fact that he was truly alone. Mandy was gone, the man from Goose Bay at the very best didn't want anything to do with him, and now he had been robbed of the opportunity of having even a canine companion.

As he pondered his situation more and more, he thought he should move to the island the next spring. There was no future for him in Labrador. Staying here would do nothing for him or for anyone else.

It had now been well over a year since he had first contacted the virus in Ottawa. He searched his memory for lectures from his foggy past for information on how long a virus could last. He could remember stories of fungi and bacteria that remained virulent for decades or even centuries, but it seemed unlikely to him that he could possibly still be a carrier of the disease. As well, if the virus did last that long, an island like Newfoundland was doomed anyway.

CHAPTER 27
A DIFFERENT WORLD

After the bombing at Come by Chance, the uncomfortable reality that the supply of gasoline in Newfoundland was finite started to sink in. The refinery was in ruin and there was no other facility in the province to produce petroleum products. Experts suggested that without offshore material, it would be impossible to put the facility back into production. Gas prices were such that only the richest were able to drive. As spring came on there was less and less traffic on the roads. As well as its high cost, much of the gasoline was starting to go bad.

Horses that had been kept as pets were suddenly valuable commodities. Two different businesses in the St. John's area began manufacturing horse drawn carts and wagons. A horse powered taxi service started up in the city.

Fletch and his advisors met after the bombing and debated how they should respond. In his anger, the mayor was starting to look more sympathetically at the notion of firing missiles either around or directly into the town of Clarenville. He was surprised when the captain voiced his reservations.

"Sir, when I went up and met with the mayor and council of Clarenville it was evident that those people are genuinely committed to controlling any further attacks that would cause us difficulties. But the problem is that they aren't in control of their own people. This bombing was just a bunch of yahoos out for a thrill. It seems to me now that anything we do in retaliation is only going to make things worse. I think they've beat us on this one. Unless we are willing to invade the rest of the island, we're just going to have to let this go. Short of a full scale invasion, I don't see any way that we can safeguard the flow of electricity from the rest of the province."

"Do you realize how much of our power comes across the isthmus? I've been speaking with people from the power company and they tell me that there is no real chance of reliable power generation here on the peninsula. The Holyrood station was mothballed years ago, and even if we did have oil to burn it would take years to get it up and running. But we have to do something. Our people will see us as weak if we don't respond."

"We are in a tough situation, Fletch. My engineers on the *St. John's* are telling me that our fuel can't be relied on for much longer. They are worried that even now we'd be risking a breakdown if we tried sailing out too far. Can you imagine what would happen if we got stranded somewhere off the coast of Clarenville? We have to be smart about this and think through our response."

Mac coughed delicately and started quietly.

"I think the captain is right, sir. We are in a tough spot and we have to be strategic. You need to get on the radio and tell everyone that unlike the people beyond the wall we are a peace loving society. Talk about the innocent workers killed in the explosion and how this has shown the true nature of those outside of Avalon.

"I agree that we need to do something. Why don't we close off the wall completely, make it higher, and dynamite trenches on either side. Everyone who wanted to cross has already gone. We know that none of this will accomplish anything, but at least it will look like we are taking action."

The group agreed with Mac's suggestion, and the next day Fletch broadcast his response to the bombing.

For the first time since he had started his radio career, Fletch genuinely felt like he was the voice of reason. Caller after caller insisted that blood had been shed and revenge was needed. He left the station exhausted and discouraged.

The Ellen Marie was an offshore supply vessel that hadn't had work since the disease started. Her owners had unsuccessfully tried to find ways to use her and with the deteriorating situation in St. John's, saw an opportunity to finally to make a profit. They started visiting drinking establishments in the city and asking the clientele if there was any interest in leaving the island. It had been a long time since the disease had struck and they suggested that people might be better off taking their chances on the mainland.

Within three days they had over a hundred applications for a four hundred dollar trip to Nova Scotia. When the Ellen Marie left with a full passenger compliment, four other vessels offered the same service and were filled just as quickly.

About five hundred St. John's residents left on boats for Nova Scotia. None of the boats returned to the island

and no one was sure whether they had found a safe new home, had perished from the disease, or had been unable to make the return trip.

Fletch's car was one of the last to stay running. He was one of the few with access to the navy controlled gas that had been carefully maintained with the best fuel stabilizers.

By the late fall there were no fossil fuel operated vehicles running. Cars, trucks, and busses disappeared from the roads, motor driven boats were no longer seen on the ocean, and the air was free of planes and helicopters.

The offshore oil drilling platforms were abandoned when it became apparent that there was real danger of the workers being stranded at sea.

Within a month of the last repair to the electrical towers on the isthmus, there was a complete loss of electricity on the Avalon. A military team made an incursion across the wall and reported that all four lines were down as a result of at least a dozen flattened towers. The mayor and his advisors met to discuss the situation, but it was apparent that there was nothing practical that could be done to restore power.

Without electricity or fuel to run generators, radio stations were unable to continue broadcasting.

Fletch's car stopped running before the radio station did. Without reliable transportation he decided that it was futile for him to try to continue with his program. His shows in the time running up to his immobility had been getting more and more out of his control. He moved out of his house and set up residence in City Hall where he still held meetings and kept a staff of workers who dealt with finances and logistics.

The HMCS *St. John's* became a floating barracks. More and more of the sailors moved out until there were only twenty-five on board. They had enough food for perhaps a few more months, but it was becoming obvious to everyone that the ship no longer was a symbol of power.

The second winter after the disease broke out, there was actually more food for the people of St. John's. The population had continually decreased and there had been a massive increase in vegetable production. A number of thriving farmers' markets developed in the city.

If food was the main problem for St. John's first post viral winter, heat was the problem the second year. No one seemed prepared for the loss of electricity and fuel oil, and many residences in the city had no source of heat. There were hundreds of deaths from hypothermia, especially amongst the elderly.

Money was still useful in the first year after the disease, but more and more people insisted on goods rather than cash in their transactions. The government's twenty-five percent tax discouraged anyone from taking money and stores that sold anything beyond absolute necessities went out of business.

The tax system completely failed in areas outside of the city. Although tax collectors were active throughout the Avalon, they found increasing numbers of people refusing to pay. The government effectively stopped providing any service outside of the city and eventually gave up on attempting to collect any rural taxes.

The protests in the city dried up mainly from weariness and a lack of interest. With no vehicles running, the police began laying off staff of every sort. Law enforcement in the city became more primitive. People caught stealing were usually beaten by locals and the police were not called.

Len Pickford was the first to leave Fletch's inner circle. He came into City Hall and met the mayor in his office.

"Morning, boss. I won't beat around the bush, I've decided to give it all up."

"What do you mean? Are you thinking of moving off the *St. John's*?"

"That and a lot more. I've done my time in military. Spent thirty years in the Navy and now time here in the city. I've just had enough."

"I wish you wouldn't go, but I know you're a determined man."

"What are we doing here anyway, Fletch? This is a new world and we need a new model for how things run. There's no electricity and no cars. All the things that government used to be useful for are gone. Even the police have become redundant. I saw stocks set up out in front of a bar downtown. A city this size isn't viable any more, even more people are going to have to move out into the country. I'm tired of all of this and I just want to go somewhere and set up a farm. Maybe I can find a woman to share the rest of my life with."

Pickford left without shaking Fletch's hand. Fletch sat quietly at his desk and wondered what had happened to all of his dreams. He'd come to this island for a simple job in a radio station and had never really felt that he'd accomplished anything. His first aspiration had been to move on to television, but that had somehow been lost in the fog of his program.

His government was fast becoming redundant. Maybe Pickford had the right idea.

CHAPTER 28
THIS IS WATER

Spring came slowly and brutally to the north shore of Labrador. The snow lingered until John wondered if the ground would ever be green again. Every day the wind roared along the straits and through his community. Herds of shingles blew through the streets, and every day more homes had balding roofs.

The drawn out loneliness of the winter convinced him to leave for the island as soon as the winds died down.

This trip would be different from his escape from Ottawa in that he wouldn't have the luxury of carrying an extensive supply of food and equipment. Once he reached the island he would have to find a new means of transportation. If the gas on the other side had gone bad like his had, he couldn't imagine any way to get quickly to his family home on the Avalon Peninsula.

As John pondered what he should pack in the limited space of his kayak, it occurred to him that there was one commodity that he had completely forgotten in his solitary existence. Money was meaningless to him in his present situation, but when he moved into populated areas, it might become useful again.

He began a systematic search of houses and businesses for cash. He began in Red Bay and eventually moved further down the shore. There was money everywhere. His first thrill at stuffing piles of bills into the bag strapped to his bicycle gave way to a sardonic realization of what money really was. Unless someone agreed that this paper was of value, it was worth nothing. He had no idea what the fifty thousand dollars he collected would mean on the island. Still he spent hours bundling his cash and tying it into stacks of a thousand or a hundred dollars.

It was the middle of June before the weather was good enough that John decided it was time to leave. If his truck had still been running, he would have driven the kayak to the narrowest portion of the strait. As it was, the crossing from Red Bay was over ten kilometres, but he was confident of his paddling ability.

He spent many nights staring at maps and plotting his move to the island. Communities near the ferry crossing like Flowers Cove would be the most watchful for people coming across the straits. He reasoned that if he headed for the small village of Cook's Harbour, he could pass himself off as an adventurer from further south on the island.

John packed a one-man tent and sleeping bag, his copy of *Ulysses*, a map, a small assortment of food, and his pack full of money into the kayak. The water was smooth as he set out from the shore near his house.

The trip across the strait went without incident. He stopped a number of times to watch the birds and appreciate the silence of the world. Everything would change once he came in contact with the Newfoundlanders.

It wasn't hard to find Cook's Harbour, and he was

surprised that the place was even more desolate than Red Bay. There were beaches suitable for landing, but the place was dominated by rock. The difference was that there were people in Cook's Harbour.

John tried to hide his excitement when two young boys came up to his kayak as he landed.

He dragged his boat up the beach and explained to the boys that he was from Gander and had paddled up from Baie Verte for an adventure. He had picked Gander for his cover as he hoped it was big enough that no one would feel they knew everyone from the town.

He pulled his pack of money from the kayak and offered the kids a twenty dollar bill if they would watch his boat. The boys found it odd that anyone would think a vessel should be watched but were happy to take his money.

As soon as he reached the main road, John could hear a woman singing. He followed the sound to a small restaurant in the centre of the village. As soon as he stepped inside, John noticed that the place had power. Steam rose from a coffee warmer just behind the counter and the second hand on the wall clock moved in an appropriate manner.

He ordered a plate of fish and chips and started into conversation with the young woman who served him.

"I heard you singing when I came into town. You have a lovely voice."

The girl laughed and said her songs were the only thing that she had left to bring in sailors. She verified that there were no vehicles running in the area, but that locals had gone back to fishing and were now getting to their nets with oars. One local fisherman was working on a sailboat that he hoped to have ready by the end of the summer.

She told John that he was the first outsider to come into the village since the previous fall. There would be people stopping in once the fishing really got going, but it had been a lonely winter. People in Cook's Harbour didn't miss much from the outside world, her greatest disappointment was that they didn't have radio to listen to any more.

When she introduced herself as Sandy, John swallowed hard. As she reached up to take some sugar down from a high shelf, he stared openly at her delightful curves.

"Why don't you take a picture? It'll last longer."

"I'm sorry, I didn't mean to be rude. I guess I've been on the water too long."

They continued with small talk and John mentioned that he intended to stay a few days to enjoy her fine cooking. When he asked about the best place to put a tent, she insisted that he could stay with her.

John walked the short distance around the village and talked with locals for the rest of the afternoon. He returned to the restaurant for a late supper of moose stew and walked with Sandy to her house after she closed up.

Mandy and Sandy may have had similar names, but they were completely different women. Sandy soon made it clear how lonely she had been for the winter and insisted the John spend the night in her bed. She tore his clothes off as soon as he was in the bedroom, and the night was filled with energetic sex of every imaginable variety.

They shared breakfast before Sandy set off for work.

John spent the morning lounging around the house. He was exhausted from the previous day's paddle and the night's exertions. He couldn't decide whether to feel fulfilled or guilty. The previous evening had been fun, but there was no way he could remember it as lovemaking. He looked through his maps and considered how he could get back to his home at the south end of the island. Even if he could find some means of transportation, it was a long trip just down the northern peninsula.

He spent the next three days planning and unsuccessfully looking for a horse. His nights were filled with action.

When he came to the restaurant for lunch the fourth day, Sandy casually mentioned that he would have to move out for a night or two. A fishing boat with jury-rigged sails had come in from St. Anthony that morning, and one of the fishermen was a good friend of hers.

After a quick lunch, he returned to Sandy's house to move his meager possessions back to the kayak. It was time to move along. He understood Sandy a little more and realized that his trip south would have to start from somewhere other than Cook's Harbour.

The wind was down, and he paddled straight for Schooner Island and then into five kilometres of open ocean. The waves were a little more active than when he had crossed from Labrador, but there was nothing bad enough to frighten him. Once he reached land, he continued on, hugging the coast. He knew he could save time if he would cut across the heads of bays, but he wasn't confident enough to risk being blown out to sea.

The winds picked up in the late afternoon just as he

spotted an open grassy plain. He landed and was surprised to see the he had come upon the L'anse aux Meadows historic site. This was a place the Vikings had lived in centuries ago and was now an interpretive centre. There were primitive shelters and signs, but no people. The water continued to get rougher, and he decided to stay the night in a sod covered Viking home.

The next morning the sea was calm again, and he headed out along the coast. His only stop was at the village of Quirpon where he spoke with a fisherman and verified that he was within a day's paddle of St. Anthony. After turning down the coast he set a straight course for his destination.

St. Anthony surprised him with its size and sophistication. The town obviously had thousands of inhabitants and looked prosperous. There was a large container ship at the wharf and houses and businesses ringed the harbour. There was no noise from motors of any kind, but there were people walking on the streets.

He pulled up near what seemed to be the centre of town and walked up to the road. A man and woman stopped him and asked where he had come from. It was obvious that a stranger would still stick out even in town of this size. He answered vaguely that he was on a kayaking adventure and had paddled up from the south.

The couple invited him to the nearby Tim Horton's establishment and treated him to a hot drink that they called tea. It had an unusual taste and he suspected that it was made of recycled tea grounds and some kind of local bark. When they asked how life was on the more southern parts of the province, he again said he was from Gander and gave vague answers that things were much like here in St. Anthony.

When they finished chatting, John asked if there was a hotel in the area. They answered that there wasn't really any tourism left to speak of, but that the Grenfel Heritage Hotel was still open and serving meals. Although their food was nothing different than what locals had, people still liked going out for special occasions.

John got back in his kayak and paddled the short distance out the bay to the hotel. When he entered the establishment there was no one at the front desk. He rang the bell on the counter and a young man in an apron came out.

"Good evening, do you have any rooms available?"

"Skipper, all of the rooms are available. We haven't had anyone stay overnight for over a year now."

He stopped abruptly and looked around the room.

"Now, there's no need for you to tell the boss I said that."

John agreed and paid cash for four nights accommodation. Once he had his room key, he took all the gear from his kayak and moved it up to the hotel. Before he lay back on his bed he wondered if his pack full of cash felt a little lighter. At first he assumed that he was being paranoid, but when he counted, there was nearly five thousand dollars missing. He was certain that Sandy was bragging to her fisherman friend about her amazing scam. It didn't bother him at all. Good riddance to the girl and the cash. He realized that payment for her attentions was only appropriate.

He spent his days walking the roads of St. Anthony.

The hospital was impressive and he found someone to tour him through the local museum. The guide said it was unfortunate that the Lance aux Meadows site wasn't operating, he was sure that John would enjoy it.

After two days he stopped asking about the availability of horses. There were none in the town. In the winter, people had set up two dog teams, but once the snow was gone everyone was satisfied to walk to anywhere on land they needed to go.

Other than one lunch he ate at a small fish and chips joint, John took his meals at the hotel. He was friendly but reserved with the waitress and left good tips. On his third evening, she spoke to him as she delivered his desert of partridgeberry preserve.

"I think you are good luck for the hotel. We've had no business at all and now there are two of you staying here."

She pointed towards an older man in a worn tweed jacket sitting at the other end of the room. When he finished his meal, John walked over to the other man's table.

"Do you mind if I sit down with you for a minute?"

"Certainly, I'd love the company."

"I heard you are a visitor here. How did you come to St. Anthony?"

"I'm here on a sailboat. I've come from St. John's. I was a cardiac surgeon, but there's not much call for my expertise any more, so I decided to take the sailing trip I've always dreamed of. My plan is to circumnavigate the island."

"How's your trip going?"

"To be honest, it's a bit of a disappointment. I'm by myself, and at times the boat's a bit much for me to handle. I'm wondering if I just might turn back."

John saw his opportunity to get to the Avalon.

"I understand how you feel. I'm here on a kayaking trip and I'm just worn out. What would you think of taking on a mate for a trip back south? What I'd really like to do is to get back to my home in Bay Roberts."

The man extended his arm across the table.

"The name's Johnson, Whitford Johnson, and I'm am your new shipmate. Give me a couple more days just to explore this place and we'll be off for Bay Roberts.

Two mornings after meeting Johnson, John was sitting in the hotel restaurant with a cup of Labrador tea when he saw a familiar fishing boat with a homemade sail come into the harbour. The vessel pulled up nearby and two men supporting a weak and coughing colleague stumbled up the road towards the hospital.

Johnson came into the restaurant shortly after and sat with John.

"Morning, Whitford. We've been here a couple of days now and I'm itching to get going. Any idea when we will be leaving?"

"Just give me another day. I met one of the local doctors at the pub last night and he's offered to give me a tour of the hospital before we leave. I'm curious to see if they are doing any better than we are in the south. I'm sure they're out of drugs like us, but at least they have electricity. Once I have my tour, I'm satisfied to head out. How about if we leave tomorrow morning?"

CHAPTER 29
HOMECOMING

Spring came on and again there had been enough food to comfortably feed everyone in Joan's compound. Over the winter there had been occasional raids, but since the gas powered vehicles had stopped running, there had been no groups from St. John's.

The weather was beautiful, and she decided to walk out to the blacksmith's shop that had set up near the harbour. All of the preparation of the ground for the year's planting would have to be done under horse power this year. She had enough sturdy horses to do the work, but there were still pieces of equipment that had to be made up.

She spoke with the blacksmith about the harrows he had nearly finished and walked on to the wharf to watch the fishermen rowing out to their grounds. As she chatted with an elderly man about how things had returned to the way of his grandfather, they spotted a vessel coming into the harbour under sail. There were about a dozen sailboats from the area that occasionally would come into Bay Roberts to trade or visit relatives, but she soon realized that this wasn't one of them. She turned to the man beside her.

"Do you have a rifle nearby?"

"Sure, it's just in my house across the road there."

"I think you better run and get it. I don't recognize that boat, could be anyone from anywhere."

The man turned and, a little slowly for Joan's satisfaction, shuffled across the street. She walked to the wharf and stood watching with her hands on her hips as the sailboat threw out an anchor and launched a small Zodiac. She called out as they approached the wharf.

"OK, fellows, how about you just stop right there until we figure out why you are coming to Bay Roberts."

The thin bearded young man in the back of the Zodiac stood.

"Joan?"

"Yeah, I'm Joan. Who are you?"

"You don't recognize your own brother?"

"John?"

"Joan, I'm home."

Joan's concerns evaporated as she ran to the edge of the wharf. John scuttled up over the metal ladder and embraced his sister.

"I thought you were dead. How did you survive? How did you get here? Who's this guy?"

John explained that there was a long story to tell and that Dr. Whitford Johnson from St. John's had been good enough to bring him home from St. Anthony.

Joan stepped forward to shake Johnson's hand.

"I guess there are still some decent people in St. John's."

"Well, ma'am, the ones that are left in the city have

seen pretty desperate times. You'd have to have been there to know how bad things got. Still, it's my home and I'm close enough that I can smell it. I'm best heading off now. Thanks for your help on the trip, John."

John walked back to Johnson and embraced him.

"You have no idea what you've done for me. Thank you so much."

Joan and John walked back to the farm with their arms around each other's waists. It occurred to both of them that this was the most interaction they had ever had.

As they approached the house, Joan took his hands and looked into his eyes.

"I'm glad you came home. You are all I have for family now. Dad died from a heart attack working out in the field last fall. He was too young to die, but he went doing what he loved. When people get sick here now, they usually don't survive. There are still doctors around, but there isn't much in the way of drugs left. The world is a different place."

John had seen so much death that the loss of his father left him oddly unmoved. He didn't comment, but asked his sister if she could show him around.

Joan toured John through the complex and explained the changes in the Avalon and the whole island since the Ottawa virus had started. They sat in with the farm hands for a hearty lunch of beef, vegetables, and potatoes. It seemed to John that he hadn't had such a satisfying meal in years.

After lunch, Joan got around to asking John how he had ended up home in Bay Roberts. It had been nearly two years since the outbreak, and the island had been sealed shut.

John hesitated before starting his story. Could he trust Joan with the truth of his odyssey? She knew that he was on the mainland when the disease began, but she was family. If there was anyone in the world he could tell his story to, it was his sister.

He started with the disease outbreak in Ottawa and disclosed almost everything. He described his trip across the mainland and the few survivors he had met. He told of his heartbreak at the loss of Mandy and his difficult decision to cross over from Labrador. The story took an hour to tell and the only significant event he left out was his relationship with Sandy. The thought of his behaviour brought him shame. This wasn't the kind of thing a sister needed to know.

"The thing that amazes me the most John is how you survived the disease in the first place. You were there right from the start. Obviously you were exposed to the virus."

"You know I've considered that and the only thing I can think of is that I have a special immune system. It must be genetic. I can't remember ever being sick for my whole life, and Dad was the same."

"You could be right. It's probably a family trait. Mom wasn't especially healthy, but you and Dad and I never got sick. I don't think I missed a day from my whole school career."

When John admitted that he worried about carrying the virus to the island, Joan dismissed his concerns.

"You know, we have been so careful about trying to keep things out and it never works. Those idiots in St.

John's even built a wall to separate the Avalon from the rest of the island. Everyone around here knows that there have been boats crossing Trinity Bay. Neither diseases nor people can be stopped with a wall. Whatever is coming is coming. We just need to keep our heads down and make sure that there is a future. If we look after the land and do what we can, our society will go on. There are sometimes difficult decisions to make, but we can only try to do the right thing."

John moved into the same house as his sister and stayed in his father's room. The family was reunited and they lived an idyllic life for nearly a year.

CHAPTER 30
TIME'S UP

No one other than Mac noticed when Fletch moved out of City Hall. The growing irrelevance of his government was impossible to miss, and when Mary stopped coming in he simply gave up.

He took the bottle of rum he'd saved for some long forgotten future and three rifles from the already ransacked City Hall armory and walked to his original house. The key still fit and he was pleased to see that no one had bothered to break in. There were even a few cans of vegetables still in shelves under his counter.

For four days he stayed in the house and wondered about putting one of the rifle barrels in his mouth. His career in radio and in government were over, and he had no skills that would help him survive. He drank and worried, but couldn't find the courage to finish his story.

When the bottle was empty, he took up one of his rifles and walked to the gate of one of the fortified Mount Pearl farms.

The guard on duty was more restrained than many of his colleagues and spoke to Fletch before he shot.

"What are you looking for, son?"

Fletch disregarded the reality that this kid was probably fifteen years younger than him.

"I have a proposition for you. If you can find me something to do that will feed me, I'll give you this rifle and another one I have at home."

"Well, sir, this is your lucky day. The guy that guards this very farm overnight cut his leg and the infection just isn't getting better. The boss asked me this very morning if I could come up with another guard. For two rifles, the job is yours."

Fletch started working nights at the farm and spent his days walking through the remains of St. John's. Much of the downtown area was deserted. The windows were broken out of most of the stores and the HMCS *St. John's* was the only large vessel left in the harbour. The frigate had been an attraction for the curious for the first month after it had been abandoned, but now it was neglected.

He talked with people he met, and no one recognized him as the former mayor. He developed an interest in how the people of the city and the rest of the province were faring, but no one seemed interested in anything beyond how they would continue to feed themselves. Gardening techniques and seed varieties were favoured topics of conversation.

On a dreary Saturday, he sat watching the harbour after his shift at the farm. A small sailboat drifted in through the Narrows and approached the open space behind the HMCS *St. John's*. Always eager for news from beyond the city, Fletch walked up to the vessel.

The boat banged against the wooden structures of the apron and gently settled astern of the frigate. He watched for a full ten minutes, waiting for the captain to climb up from the cabin. When he saw no one emerge, he called out. There was no answer, so he climbed onto the deck and rapped on the cabin door before going below.

Inside was a man in a worn tweed jacket completely covered in blood. The man looked up and coughed violently when Fletch asked him what was wrong.

epilogue

i have been the storyteller of my clan since i lost my sight after my three children were born and every year when the snows recede my seeing guide and i take all of the children who have reached mating age from our village and walk for two days to the hills above the forbidden city where they all look down on the city and i tell them the tales of our people and it is easy for them to see that the place is filled with decay and destruction because there is no life there and every structure is twisted or broken and i warn the children to never venture into this valley of death even though it is a truth they are not told until they are older that this city is also the place of our birth and i relate how the old ones tell how Jon travelled across the water on the great vessel Jon which can still be partly seen in the waters of the city and how after many great adventures he returned to his sister in the city named for him and so our people began and i tell them that the vessel and the city and the twins were all called Jon because Jon and Jon the brother and sister twins were the mother and father of all of us and how in the olden days there were many people in our land and many lived in the forbidden city but the people did not pay attention to the laws of Jon and Jon and most of them were destroyed by a great plague and since that time we understand how important it is to abide by the laws and the laws are simple and there are only three laws saying that we must stay out of the forbidden city and brothers and sisters must not mate and all must prove their worthiness by having offspring and those who do not have children are removed from the clan and only those who are strong and healthy are allowed to live with us and this season there were many children who followed me to the hill but we still have many weak children who die when they are young and many more who live but cannot have offspring and everyone knows that this has been the way of our clan since the stories were first told and there are those who say that some day all that are born will be healthy and i can see that even in my lifetime more and more of the children are worthy and this has been a special trip to the hill even though i told the stories that i always tell them and i showed the deadness of the city but just as we were preparing to leave the children told me that they saw three vessels with tall poles and sheets come in to the waters of the forbidden city and there have always been stories of how people in the past went out onto the waters but i had never thought they were true so now when i return home i will tell the elders of what the children have seen and they will decide how the clan will respond and even though we are told not to go into the city a part of me burns to know who is in the vessels and i wonder if they are people from another land beyond the waters or are they gods or are they Jon and Jon come back to lead us and i suppose that the elders will debate these things and perhaps our ways will change

Footnotes

[1] Recipe for Blueberry Crumble

4 cups fresh blueberries
2 tablespoons lemon juice
1 cup brown sugar
3/4 cup oatmeal
1/2 cup all-purpose flour
dash of salt
1/3 cup butter*

Mix blueberries, lemon juice and ½ cup of brown sugar in an ungreased baking pan.

Mix oats, flour, remaining brown sugar and salt together

Add butter and work together to make a crumbly topping.

Sprinkle this over blueberries.

Bake uncovered in 350° oven until topping is light brown (about 40 minutes).

If oven is unavailable, assemble in a frying pan covered with foil and cook over low heat until blueberries bubble.

in the case of societal breakdown, margarine may be substituted for butter

[2] Ibid.

Author's Note

Viral was written shortly before the COVID-19 pandemic. My time working with monkeys in a lab animal facility in Ottawa was a major inspiration for the story. This experience and my study of epidemiology in veterinary school made me acutely aware of the very real possibility of a pandemic.

The fictional virus that causes the disease in Viral is much deadlier than the coronavirus disrupting the world in 2020. While working on the book, I spent time wondering what it would be like if the worst of all possible viral mutations occurred. What would happen if a virus developed that was easily transmitted and killed almost everyone it contacted? These thoughts made me realize how lucky we have been with COVID-19.

I owe a debt of gratitude to many people who have helped me with the writing of this book. The members of the Freshwater Writers' Circle – Dorothy McIntosh Harvey, Pat Collins, Marylynne Middelkoop and Jesse Bown – have been wonderful encouragement in my writing life. Dermott Kelley introduced me to the joys of Ulysses and The Odyssey. Every writer should be so lucky to have such inspiring friends.

My running partner, Jesse Bown, was a captive audience for most of the concepts that made up this book well before they were put on paper. Running is a wonderful way to work out ideas and I was fortunate to have a thoughtful friend to listen and comment.

David Moriarty MWO (CD) (retired) was kind enough to check the book for the accuracy of the depictions of naval life. I was privileged to have this 38-year veteran of all three branches of the Canadian Armed Forces read through sections dealing with areas I knew little about.

Matthew LeDrew of Engen Books was an early supporter and made it possible for the book to be released during the trying times of COVID-19. Brad Dunne provided sensitive and accurate editing and my favourite photographer, Kaleigh Middelkoop provided the beautiful cover.

My family – Liam, Adrian, Astrid, Amanda, Jordan and Stuart - were enthusiastic early readers and I appreciate their support and interest.

As always, my first reader and most trusted advisor has been Ingrid. Thank you for everything.

COMING SOON FROM ENGEN BOOKS

BIFOCAL: CURIOUS TALES & THEIR REFLECTIONS

Engen Books is proud and honored to announce our first 2021 reveal: 'Bifocal: Curious Tales & Their Reflections' by Andrew Peacock, with art by the astonishing Kaleigh Middelkoop.

Kaleigh Middelkoop is an amazing artist and photographer who primarily uses self portraiture as a means to tell stories and express ideas with the aid of costumes and props she makes by hand. Heavily influenced by fairy tales and the slightly strange, her work has surreal and magical elements woven throughout. Kaleigh is a featured artist at Bellazo in downtown Wabash, IN as well as Ocean View Art Gallery in Carbonear, NL.

'Bifocal: Curious Tales & Their Reflections' is a collection of short fiction by Peacock, with accompanying images by Middelkoop. It examines the human condition and imagination, and is a must have for any collection.

"I'm thrilled to be working with Kaleigh Middelkoop and Engen Books on the illustrated short story collection "Bifocal". Kaleigh and I have been working for a number of years on this project and we can't wait for everyone to see our pictures about stories and stories about pictures." -- Andrew Peacock

DARK STORIES FROM ENGEN BOOKS

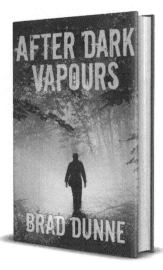

THE HOWL BECONS
Growing up without his father, Tyler had no way of knowing the horrible secret that has plagued his family for generations. To free himself and find the cure, he will have to look beyond himself and into his dark history.

"A very ambitious novel... the horrors of everyday life can be worse than anything in fiction. The idea of using werewolves as a metaphor – to me this pushes the book a bit above much of what is out there... Brad [Dunne] is a very good writer and obviously has a deep background."
— Andrew Peacock

WESTON'S WAR
Something evil grows in the heart of Colorado. Bill Weston was a man of the West. He knew it – its land, its people, its stories. It was where he plied his trade, hunting men for money. His life wasn't easy, but it was predictable. That all changed when he captured Faraway Sue and he was led on a trip through the Colorado forests

"Take a little Zane Grey. Add a little Penny Dreadful. Read with Sam Elliot's voice. Discover Jon Dobbin's masterful The Starving."
— Darrell Power,
Great Big Sea

NEWFOUNDLAND FANTASY FROM ENGEN

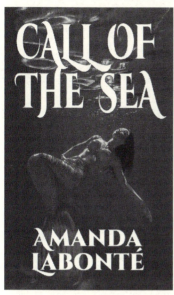

HEED THE CALL

After a heated fight at sea between twins Ben and Alex, Ben vanishes from their boat without a sound or even a ripple in the water. Unwavering in his dedication to find his brother, Alex begins the adventure of a lifetime armed only with the help of a local girl named Meg and his own mysterious musical abilities… the key to which, and to the mysteries that surround him, may be tied to the alluring song of the dangerous girl he finds among the ocean's frothing waves.

"A mysterious figure in the ocean, a suspicious loss in the waves, a riveting treasure hunt, and surprise after surprise, how could anyone not want to read this novel?"

~Alice Kuipers
author of Life on the Refrigerator Door

"Loved this book and can't wait for the next one."

~Helen Escott
bestselling author of Operation: Wormwood

"It's been a while since I've read an entire book in one day, but…Whenever I tried to put it down, it would call out to me, luring me back like a siren's song."

~Ali House
author of The Six Elemental & The Fifth Queen

"Call of the Sea seamlessly weaves together the hardships and humour of rural Newfoundland life with a fantastical storyline that will leave you wanting more. This book will not disappoint."

~Lauralana Dunne
author of Ashes

ABOUT THE AUTHOR

Andrew Peacock was born in Toronto and raised in the town of Kapuskasing in northern Ontario. He practised veterinary medicine in rural Newfoundland from 1982 until 2010.

His book *Creatures of the Rock* was long-listed for the 2015 Leacock medal for humour and won the Newfoundland and Labrador Book Award non-fiction.

In 2019 his children's book *One Brave Boy and His Cat* was published by Flanker Press. He currently lives in Freshwater with his wife, Ingrid, and dog, Charlotte.

Manufactured by Amazon.ca
Bolton, ON